The Other Me

Suzanne van Rooyen

Harmony Ink

Published by
Harmony Ink Press
5032 Capital Circle SW
Suite 2, PMB# 279
Tallahassee, FL 32305-7886
USA
publisher@harmonyinkpress.com
http://harmonyinkpress.com

This is a work of fiction. Names, characters, places, and incidents either are the product of author imagination or are used fictitiously, and any resemblance to actual persons, living or dead, business establishments, events, or locales is entirely coincidental.

The Other Me
© 2013 Suzanne van Rooyen.

Cover Art
© 2013 Anne Cain.
annecain.art@gmail.com
Cover content is for illustrative purposes only and any person depicted on the cover is a model.

ISBN: 978-1-62798-643-4
Library ISBN: 978-1-62798-645-8
Digital ISBN: 978-1-62798-644-1

Printed in the United States of America
First Edition
December 2013

Library Edition
March 2014

To Mrs. J, my high school music teacher, who nurtured my passion for all things musical and who continues to inspire.

And to Mark, with love always.

ACKNOWLEDGMENTS

The Other Me is a deeply personal work drawing on a myriad of experiences. I wish I could thank each and every person who touched my life and thus made this book possible, but that would be a novel unto itself.

There are a few extra special people I'd like to thank: Elizabeth, Anne, Paul, and the rest of the team at Harmony Ink Press for giving this story a home. Jordy Albert, my agent, for all her encouragement, enthusiasm, and continuous support. Wiz Green for reading an early draft and convincing me this story should be shared with the world. Gail Jacobs for being the best music teacher, for inspiring me to become a music teacher myself, and for being a good friend, even if we can't quite agree on the virtues of jazz. Mark Kourie for being by my side along the rocky path of self-discovery and for always being my best friend despite the distance between us. Mandy, my sister, whose compassion, kindness, and courage have been an inspiration. My parents for all their love and support even when I painted my nails black and dyed my hair purple, especially Mom who spent many hours listening to Marilyn Manson, Linkin Park, and Diary of Dreams with me. My pooch, Lego, for being an excellent listener when I needed to read passages out loud, for providing puppy kisses when I was down or frustrated, and for accompanying me on extra long walks when I had writer's block. And finally, my husband Mark, for his unconditional love and support, without whom I would not be who I am today, and this book would certainly not exist.

GLOSSARY

atchar: South Asian pickle, usually a spicy, fruit-based condiment eaten with bread

bakkie: pick-up truck

bankie: small bag of marijuana

beerboep: rotund belly associated with excessive consumption of beer

biltong: jerky

bliksem: lightning, used as an expletive to express shock. Can also be used as a synonym for 'jerk' or 'asshole.' To 'bliksem' someone is to hit someone.

bobotie: traditional minced meat dish with raisins and egg-based topping

boerewors: traditional South African sausage

boet: Afrikaans word for brother, can be used casually to mean 'friend'

Bovril: Beef-based spread for bread

braai: barbecue or grill

brollie: umbrella

bru: slang for brother or friend

cozzy: short for swimming costume or swimsuit

dagga: marijuana

deurmekaar: confused, dazed, bewildered

diabolus in musica: The 'devil in music' or tritone, the interval of an augmented fourth or diminished fifth in music

donner: thunder, meaning to hit someone

dop: an alcoholic drink, usually a small amount such as a tot

dronkverdriet: depression or misery brought on by drunkenness

dwaal: state of befuddlement, 'away with the fairies'

eish: expression of exasperation or disbelief

gatvol: fed up, had enough, extreme exasperation

hadedahs: colloquial name for ibis family of birds

haw wena: Zulu expression of surprise or disbelief

highveld: geographical region where Johannesburg is located

hoopoe: small, colorful bird

hou jou bek: Afrikaans for 'shut your mouth' where 'bek' refers to an animal's mouth, similar to 'shut your trap' or 'shut your gob'

howzit: contraction of 'how is it' meaning 'how are you?'

hubbly: hookah or waterpipe

ja: Afrikaans for 'yes' used by all South Africans

jislaaik: expression of positive or negative surprise

Jo'burg: colloquial name for Johannesburg

kak: shit, also meaning rubbish or nonsense like 'don't talk kak'— don't talk nonsense

Karoo: a semi-desert region in South Africa covering parts of the Free State, Northern, Western, and Eastern Cape

kif: cool or neat

klap: smack, slap or similar open-handed strike

Klipdrift: type of brandy typically used in mixed drinks such as Klippies and Coke

Koki: a particular brand of fiber-tip marker pen, used colloquially in reference to all colored markers, particularly popular among schoolchildren

koppie: rocky outcropping or hill

larny: slang for posh or snobbish

lekker: nice

lightie: a young or inexperienced person

lilo: inflatable air mattress for swimming pools

lourie: type of bird

mampoer: strong home-distilled version of peach schnapps

Maties: people who attend Stellenbosch University

matric: final year of high school, also standard ten or grade twelve

mieliepap: corn-based porridge

milktart: traditional milk-based pie-like dessert

moffie: slang for queer or gay

NG Kerk: Nederduitse Gereformeerde Kerk or Dutch Reformed Church, typical Afrikaans Christian denomination

oke: guy, man

ouma: grandmother

pasop: beware, be careful, watch it!

polony: ground beef/pork sausage similar to Bologna

Prestik: South African brand of adhesive

robot: traffic light

rooibos: traditional type of tea now found internationally

samoosa: spicy, Indian style pastry—also samosa

sif: gross, disgusting, filthy

skiff: to give the stink-eye or a dirty look

skinder: gossip

snot 'n trane: snot and tears, melodrama, excessive emotional displays

sosaties: skewered cubes of meat and fruit typically made for the braai

stoep: porch, patio, veranda

stompie: cigarette butt

sutari: nonsense word made up by Treasa for her fan fiction

syringa: type of tree popular with louries

takkies/tekkies: sneakers

tuck shop: kiosk or similar small cafe on school property where students can purchase snacks and some hot food such as toasted sandwiches

technikon: technical universities, now known as universities of technology

vetkoek: traditional fried dough ball; can be eaten with savory or sweet toppings

voertsek: get lost, go away, eff off

wussie: weak, afraid, similar to scaredy-cat

GABRIEL

I'D HOPED Y2K would bring about the apocalypse, but here we are limping into the twenty-first century. I thought the new millennium would at least feel different. It's been two months since the nines became zeroes, and nothing has changed. At least, not for me. Not even turning eighteen made a scrap of difference.

"…and in sports news, with two matches drawn and two in the bag, the Proteas are looking good for a test series victory when South Africa plays England at…." The radio drones on, but I tune out. We're coming up to my corner, and my palms are sweating. It's the same every school morning as my father makes this turn, a moment where I think *If I open the door and hurl myself out onto the road, maybe the days won't bleed into that ineluctable gray sameness.* Every day I clutch the door handle, pop open the lock, and wait for that perfect moment when the inertia of the bakkie will send me hurtling across the tarmac. I imagine the pain of shredding skin and snapping bones. I imagine waking up in the hospital surrounded by concerned faces: Mom alive and at my bedside, my brother bringing me a get-well card the way he's never bothered with a birthday card, and my father…. I imagine him apologizing. For everything.

He focuses on cricket scores and dodging potholes, not even aware of me. He changes gear, and the bakkie splutters up the hill—my moment lost. I lock the door, fiddle with my tie, and resign myself to the fact that I lack the courage to change my life.

"Please, God," I whisper. "Please let today be different."

TREASA

AS IF the fact that I love brussels sprouts isn't evidence enough of my being an alien, there's also the fact that no circuit board in the physics classroom works in my presence.

"Could just be the batteries," Jordan says. She scribbles a few lines on her exam pad, finishing the circuit diagram.

"All ten of them?"

Jordan cocks her head to the right and chews on the end of her braid. "Point. Maybe there's a problem with the crocodile clips."

Or I'm an alien, and my intergalactic force field is messing up the current. Is there another explanation for why living in this body makes me feel so claustrophobic? My gaze strays from the struggling lightbulb on our desk to the clock on the wall. Another forty-two seconds, and the bell will ring.

"Well, it's not rocket science, right? Connect the cells, connect the wires, and ta-dah, the bulb lights up." Jordan finishes the diagram, writes our names across the top, and passes it forward to the teacher's desk.

I dismantle the umpteenth circuit board that plain refuses to work if I'm within three meters of a component. The bell shrills, and we join the stampede headed for lockers in our homeroom. It takes seven minutes to pack away textbooks, sweep homework into our bags, and navigate the clogged corridor past the statue of the Virgin Mary before we escape the confines of the building. Freedom and a blast of summer heat. We've got twenty-three minutes to kill before choir practice, so we colonize a patch of playground shade beneath the twisted branches of a syringa tree, far away from the vicious tongues and judgmental eyes of our classmates.

"If a lourie craps on me, we're swapping shirts." Jordan squints in disgust at the noisy chorus in the branches and collapses in a pretzel of limbs on the grass anyway.

"That's the tenth time we've had a circuit board fail."

"Clearly, you're an alien or a poltergeist," she says in a conspiratorial tone.

"I think I'm a little too corporeal to be a poltergeist."

She shrugs and stares off into the near distance in contemplation.

The day is sweltering. While the best thing about my school uniform is definitely the maroon tie, after 2:00 p.m. in the heat of late January, it feels more like a noose than an accessory. I loosen it up a little and break a rule by undoing the top button of my blouse. A breeze stirs through the grass, air-conditioning the backs of my knees. I hate having to wear a skirt, though it does make the fact that I wear boy's boxers a little less conspicuous.

"Let's make a list," Jordan says. "Ten Reasons Why Treasa's an Alien." She scrawls across a clean page in her exam pad.

"I'm adopted with no record of my birth parents." Which means no record of who I really am, where I'm really from. It's so messed up that I could have siblings or cousins, that I could pass them in a shopping mall and not even know we're related.

"You think those files getting lost in an office move was a conspiracy to cover up your extraterrestrial origins?" Jordan waggles thin brows at me.

"I'm serious, you know."

"Okay, so, the adoption. Reason number two?" Jordan humors me.

"Those circuit boards never work when I'm around."

"Faulty components."

"Or I'm an alien." Which is the real reason I battle to relate to my peers. Telling the guidance counselor I think I'm an alien would only add to my problems.

"Yes, that's the more obvious and logical conclusion," Jordan says.

"What about what happened last year?"

"I'm pretty sure that nurse didn't mean anything by it." She sighs.

"She said thirty-seven degrees was normal for a human being. She must've been implying something."

"Ree, you had meningitis. I don't think your brain was working properly."

"Maybe, but I do like brussels sprouts."

"And I like asparagus." Jordan rummages through her backpack and fishes out a can of deodorant. She douses both of us in Citrus Bliss before she jumps to her feet and brushes the grass off her skirt, which is two centimeters too short to pass inspection. It's a long, hot trek past the tennis courts to the music block.

"So maybe we're both aliens," I say.

Jordan spins on her heel, irritation flashing across her face. "Enough with the alien stuff, okay? So we don't fit in, but would you really want to fit in with this lot?" She waves a hand above her head.

"I guess not." It's not a lie, exactly. It's not that I want to fit in with the "in crowd" so much as I want to be comfortable in my own skin.

"Then suffice it to say we're different. Don't have to be from Mars for that."

And with that, the conversation is over as Jordan changes the topic to her latest crush, Bryce Oberholzer of our fellow Catholic single-sex school, Cosmas College. I listen, smile, and nod when appropriate. Mostly I've tuned out, my thoughts on *Project Blue Book*. There's another clue to my deep space origins. It's got to be more than just coincidence that the main character of the TV show, who happens to be a very good-looking alien from the planet Kazar, has the same name as me. So it's mostly just my family who calls me Resa, but still, I think the universe is trying to tell me something. I'll ignore the fact that Resa the alien happens to be a boy.

"Did you watch last night's episode?" I ask when Jordan runs out of ways to describe Bryce's hotness. She's the only other person I know who watches the series, and probably does only because of me.

"I reckon they need to give Liam St. Clare more time with his shirt off. He's damn fine. Almost as good-looking as Bryce."

"I've got new pictures to put up." As if my room wasn't already chockablock with pictures of Liam, aka Resa from the planet Kazar.

"You're obsessed."

"Totally." There's nothing I don't love about Liam St. Clare, except the fact that he lives in California and is about as attainable as an A in physics, so not at all. He's got brown hair that just reaches his eyes, a lightning-bright smile, emerald eyes, and a body so ripped—

"Urgh, just look at her." Jordan interrupts my daydream by sticking a finger in her mouth, pretending to make herself sick. I follow her gaze to a gaggle of fellow grade tens loitering near the tuck shop. The "her" is Candyce. Not the ordinary Can-diss. No, she goes by Can-dees and woe betide anyone who dares diminish her Venus-like status by calling her Candy. She and her posse have their socks folded down past their ankles so as not to impair the tan on their freshly waxed legs stretched out beside their Wilson and Dunlop tennis rackets. Dad said he'd get me a Wilson racket if I made the team. Guess I'll forever be the laughingstock at trials with my no-name-brand knockoff, since even the D team is reserved for those who know better than to try to catch the ball with their hands.

"Hey, Candle Sticks," Jordan starts. "Looking good. Guess you must've puked up that samoosa I saw you eating at lunch."

"Jordan, don't," I say under my breath. Why she has to antagonize the cool group, I don't know. Candyce responds with her middle finger and a flick of her thick blond ponytail. Jordan and Candyce are sworn enemies, for reasons unfathomable. Apparently it has something to do with a certain boy at a grade seven social. All that happened before I joined the maroon-and-white-clad ranks at St. Bridget's.

"Give anyone herpes today, Banana Split?" Hannah, one of Candyce's groupies, shoots back at Jordan.

"Not yet." Jordan smirks and saunters past them with me in tow. She never lets it show, but that everyone thinks she's a slut does hurt her.

"They might stop calling you that if you didn't wear black G-strings to school anymore."

"I should be able to wear whatever the hell I want to. One time, Ree. The first and only time I slept with a boy, and now the whole school thinks I'm a walking STD." She stomps along the pathway.

"I don't."

"That's why I love you." She loops her arm around my shoulders as we enter the choir room. We both reek of sweat and lemon deodorant. On a day when the mercury slips past thirty degrees Celsius, everyone's going to stink by second break. The whirring ceiling fans and warm breeze wafting through the open windows do nothing to stem the flood free-flowing from every pore. When I grow up, I'm moving to Antarctica.

Jordan gives me a final squeeze before joining Sibo and the altos while I sit next to Lethi with the sopranos. Mrs. McArthur blows in with the force of a tie-dye hurricane, leaving a trail of sheet music in her wake. Grade eights scramble to catch the papers as our choir mistress takes roll call. I take the moment to ogle my choir file, plastered with magazine cutouts of Liam St. Clare, mostly as Resa, also from fashion shoots and roles in other films. The wait between episodes is physically painful. Maybe if I wrote a letter to M-Net, they'd consider airing *Project Blue Book* every night.

Mrs. McArthur secures her copious curls in a bun with two pencils and fans herself with music by Karl Jenkins.

"He's late," she says, as if we know what that means. He? The only he at St. Bridget's is our doddery physics teacher, who is as baffled by my inability to understand vectors as I am by the effect I have on circuit boards.

Mrs. McArthur rearranges the multicolored tiers of taffeta draping her body and clucks in disapproval as the minute hand ticks past 2:30 p.m.

"Well, we'll just have to start without him. A capella warm-ups are good for pitch control."

She directs us through an ascending scale of "oohs" and "aahs." As the notes spiral ever higher, the perpetual tension drains from my shoulders. When I'm singing, I'm not Treasa, I'm not a girl with braces or a freckle infestation, I'm not too short or too strange, I don't feel trapped. I'm just a controlled diaphragm and vibrating vocal chords. And now I'm choking on the vowel sounds as Liam St. Clare walks into the music room. My heart stutters and sweat slicks my palms. Time slows down as my brain battles to process the sensory input from my eyes. I blink, but the vision remains as his long fingers brush his soft hair off a pimple-free face.

"Sorry I'm late," he says in a voice richer and deeper than the SoCal celebrity. Still, same floppy brown hair tumbling into his eyes, same electric smile and piercing gaze. Only this boy's wearing the charcoal pants and blue-striped tie of Stormhof High up the road. His blazer—hooked casually by one finger over his shoulder—bears the blue ribbing of academic colors, so he must be in Matric.

"Mr. du Preez, you are late." Mrs. McArthur glares at him over her neon-pink spectacle frames.

"Sorry, ma'am. Won't happen again," he says with a glint in his eye.

"It surely won't." She gestures for him to take his seat at the piano.

"What happened to Mrs. Griswold?" Jordan asks.

"She's not feeling very well, so while she convalesces, Gabriel du Preez has agreed to be our accompanist."

"Why?" Jordan directs her question at Gabriel. "You trying to get out of detention?" The choir erupts in giggles.

"Actually, I'm hoping to do a teacher's licentiate and thought this couldn't hurt," he says. Teacher's licentiate—that's bloody impressive for a guy in Matric, especially since Stormhof doesn't even have its own music department. The giggles turn to flustered conversation, and Jordan catches my eye. She bites her bottom lip and twitches her head in Gabriel's direction.

"Settle down, girls. He's just a boy, you've seen them before, and we've got new repertoire to learn, so restrain yourselves, ladies." Mrs. McArthur raps the music stand with another pencil, pulled from the stash she must keep somewhere in the folds of her skirts. Gabriel rolls up his shirtsleeves, pumps the pedal a few times, and skims the keys with a scale.

We continue with several warm-up exercises before moving on to repertoire. I can't concentrate, can't focus on anything but Gabriel's fingers and the way they stroke the keys, the way the muscles in his forearms tense and shift beneath his skin, the way his shoulders bunch when he plays heavy chords.

"Treasa, less gawking at the accompanist, please," Mrs. McArthur yells above the chorus. Lethi jabs me with her elbow, Gabriel grins, and I am mortified. There's a conflagration of shame in both cheeks, spreading down my throat and up into my ears. The girls around me titter and stare as I try to disappear, willing a vortex of dark matter to swallow me whole.

AT 3:30, I make like a Kenyan and sprint out of the music room, hoping Mom won't be late. I scan the parking lot for the familiar beige Toyota and see only Mercedes-Benzes and BMWs.

"You should try out for the athletics team." Jordan strolls up behind me, tie hanging loose and shirt untucked. If a prefect sees her leaving the property like that, she'll get detention. Again.

"I just needed some air."

"I'm sure you did." She grins. "Piano Boy is hot."

"I didn't notice."

"Come on, Ree. You've got to be blind not to notice, and even a blind girl would feel the waves of hotness rolling off him."

"You're despicable."

"At least I'm not in denial." Jordan gives me a one-armed hug before traipsing toward the red convertible pulling up at the gate. "See you tomorrow." She waves and disappears into the leather interior. Her mom gives me a brief smile before pulling off with a V8 roar.

"Treasa, right?"

Oh. My. God. He's standing right behind me. Maybe I can pretend I didn't hear him, pretend I'm not here. I'm such a freak.

"Treasa?" Now he's facing me, and pretending I don't see him would be weirder than anything else I'm likely to do. I keep my gaze on his tie. The stitching along the edge is loose, and the tie looks worn.

"Hi," I manage to croak, praying I don't have remnants of lunch trapped in my braces.

"Mrs. McArthur asked me to give you this." Gabriel hands me my choir file. "You dropped it on your way out."

With my face burning once again, I take the file and jam it into my satchel. I wonder if there's a world in which he didn't notice all the pictures of the celebrity who could be his twin glued onto my file.

"It's not a bad series."

"What?" I'm nothing if not eloquent as my gaze inches up his tie, lingering on the breadth of his shoulders.

"*Project Blue Book*. I noticed you're a fan." He holds my gaze, and the intensity of his stare is unnerving. I search his face for signs of mockery and find nothing but a sly smile and bright green eyes.

"Yeah." I can barely breathe, let alone hold a conversation with this guy.

"See you next week, Treasa." He slips on his blazer and saunters into the parking lot to an ancient Beetle. Another guy sits in the driver's seat, also dressed in Stormhof charcoal. Gabriel gets in, and they drive away while I'm left gawking, mortified, and wishing my alien powers were more like Resa's. Then I'd be able to rewind time and have that conversation over, have an actual conversation and not act like I'd swallowed my tongue. Gabriel watches *Project Blue Book*—we could've talked about half a dozen things to do with the show, and I blew it, mushroom-cloud nuclear fallout blew it.

And now I've got an entire week to wallow in my misery, thinking about all the things I could've said. The French call it *l'esprit d'escalier*. It should be illegal to have such a beautiful name for something that makes me feel like such an idiot.

GABRIEL

THAT WASN'T nearly as bad as I thought it would be. So what if doing this involves forcing a smile on my face and losing an hour's worth of practice time? At least I'm getting paid to play piano. My first real step toward financial independence, albeit twenty bucks a week.

"Told you." Dirk grins as he starts the spluttering engine. "This gig'll get you laid, man."

"All you ever think about is sex."

"Like you don't."

"I'm not doing this for sex."

"Not just for sex." He smirks. "But don't tell me you didn't check that redhead."

Treasa. She looks like a Celtic princess, like one of the girls on the cover of Dirk's mom's romance novels, with her mass of red hair and a splatter of freckles.

"You'll bonk anything in a skirt," I shoot back at Dirk and turn up the volume, letting Norwegian black metal drown out any further mention of potential screws. Despite how fierce Treasa's fiery hair made her look, I caught a glimpse of something else in her eyes. They're blue and brittle, and there's sadness in them like she's drowning in unshed tears. Hell if I'm going to tell Dirk that and spend the next year being called gay for noticing her eyes at all. It's not like I didn't notice her boobs.

"Find the ones with daddy issues," Dirk shouts over the screeching guitar.

"Why?"

"They're the ones that'll blow you, no problem. They all end up being strippers anyway."

"You're a dick."

He laughs and lights a cigarette before handing me the box. I light up, and the smoke blazes a caustic trail down my throat and back out through my nose. I don't want to be with a girl who has issues with her father when I've got enough of my own to worry about. I don't want to be with some high-maintenance prissy bitch, period.

"To the dojo?" Dirk asks.

"Always." Hitting something will help take my mind off the fact that Treasa actually got my attention. She doesn't seem like one of the cool kids who wear their skirts too short or bleach their hair. Pity about the skirt, though, because she has nice legs, what I saw of them. I've also never met anyone else who watches *Project Blue Book*, and that, not her cup size, makes me curious. I wonder if she's into aliens and ufology, or just into the actor she's got plastered all over her choir file.

Girls ruin guys. They gobble up their money, their time, and their ability to concentrate on anything happening above the waist. That's the last thing I need right now, between academics, piano, karate, bloody rugby, and trying to get the hell out of the house.

"Be back at seven," I tell Dirk when he pulls into the parking lot outside the dojo.

"Might be late—you know how band practice can get."

"Just don't get drunk."

He crosses his heart, which means he'll at least try not to, and lights another cigarette as I haul my karate gear out of the backseat.

SOMETIMES I let myself get hit. This lightie brown belt circles around me and prepares to strike, his right foot destined for my ribs. I could deflect it, but I don't; I absorb it. And the next one and the next, until I can barely breathe.

"Come on, man, you're not even trying," he taunts me.

I lose count of the strikes, my body aching and the studio swimming into a haze before I lose my footing and tumble onto the mats. The fight stops there, and the kid offers me a hand.

"I don't get you, bru. You're way better than me."

"Next time," I promise and hobble off to shower and change. My sensei gives me a knowing look. He's never questioned my "off" days, not that that means he understands. It's not that I like pain or anything weird like that. Pain brings clarity, and getting beat like this is nothing more than I deserve.

Twenty minutes later, I'm standing outside in the cool of the evening, a welcome respite from the day's heat.

"Having an off day?" Sensei Nathan joins me, squinting at the stars through the gloam of pollution blanketing the city.

"I guess."

"Since you enjoy your time on the mat so much, I was wondering if you'd be interested in helping me out with something."

"Sure." I check my watch. Dirk's only ten minutes late.

"There's this self-defense course I'm giving at Riverstone Country Club. I need an assistant." He stretches his bulky arms to the sky, popping his shoulders.

"So you need someone to demonstrate the moves on?"

"I'll pay you. Twennie rand an hour, every Saturday morning."

Another hour out of my schedule, another potential hour of practice or study time lost, even if it is money.

"Thirty," I say as Dirk pulls into the parking lot.

"Twennie-five. Meet me here eight thirty Saturday." Nathan claps me on the back. "This way you get paid to take the hits." He winks at me and walks back into the dojo as Dirk's Beetle judders to a halt centimeters short of my shins.

Maybe God's listening after all. Today was certainly different.

AM I AN ALIEN, TREASA TEST #01

HYPOTHESIS: Extraterrestrials may look like humans, but differentiate from human beings on a cellular level.

GOAL: To prove that my cells are different from a normal human being's.

METHOD:
Swab the inside of my cheek with an ear bud.
Swab inside of Dad's cheek with ear bud.
Cut and place samples onto slides.
Dye cells with gentian violet for easier identification.
Place cells under microscope* for comparative analysis.

RESULTS: Dad's cells appear uniform and rectangular. My cells appear slightly less uniform and more oblong.

CONCLUSION: While some structural differences are apparent, this could be due to a number of causes (Dad had just eaten biltong; I'd just brushed my teeth), and therefore results are inconclusive. More extensive, and accurate, tests are required.

*from children's home biology kit—not the best quality. May affect results.

TREASA

WE'RE UNDER beetle assault. The glossy flying peanuts crash into walls and dive-bomb lamps. It's too hot to close my window, even though I'm inviting the whole of six-legged Africa into my bedroom, not to mention the eight-legged hunters lurking in the corners. For the third time in the past hour, the stench of roasted Christmas beetle permeates the room from the standing lamp. The stupid bugs are too entranced by the light to notice they're getting cooked alive.

Riker stalks into my room and hops onto my bed, observing me with mismatched eyes: one amber, the other wintry blue. His tail twitches back and forth as he watches my hands.

Trying not to inhale roasted beetle fumes, I smooth the contact plastic over the latest Liam St. Clare collage made by painstakingly cutting and gluing magazine pictures onto cardboard. The sticky plastic is a pain to work with. Get it wrong, and you screw the whole thing up. Get it right, and it transforms a magazine picture into a laminated work of art. I smooth out a crinkle over the image of Liam as Resa, all bruised and bloodied after his run-in with the FBI. Having placed perfect balls of Prestik on each corner, I add the new images to my bedroom wall. Seeing Liam in profile is seeing Gabriel. Would it make me a terrible person to hope Mrs. Griswold stays ill for good so that Gabriel becomes our resident accompanist?

Reluctantly, I turn away from Liam and back to math homework while Riker proceeds to groom himself all over my pillow.

"More pictures?" Mom stands in the doorway, studying my wall.

"Not a bad view, right?"

"No, but your father's already having a fit about the paint."

"If I ever get tired of looking at Liam, I'll repaint the whole house. Deal?"

Mom chuckles and sits down on my bed, shifting the cat off my pillow and onto the duvet. I run a mental replay of dinner, wondering if anything was said that might warrant a lecture or pep talk. My tummy tightens in anticipation.

"Any mention of the Charity Ball yet?" Mom asks, probably already imagining me in some hideous pavlova concoction of frills and ruffles. She strokes Riker, and a deep rumble emanates from his belly.

"Not yet." We've only been back at school for like a week.

"You got a date?"

I roll my eyes and slide the math textbook onto my lap, hoping Mom will take the hint.

"I'm concerned about you."

"Why?" My internal organs turn to rocks.

"I found this." Mom hands me a crumpled sheet of exam pad that looks as if it's been through the wash. It's a letter from Jordan passed during French last week, asking me if I'll go with her to get Gillette Minora blades.

"It's for an art project."

"Really?" Mom's skepticism is palpable.

"Yeah, what do you think she's doing, cutting cocaine?"

"Don't be belligerent, Resa."

"Just because of what happened with her mom, doesn't make Jordan a bad person." Back in grade eight, her mom showed up drunk at a PTA meeting and propositioned the chairman. It made for salacious parking-lot gossip. No one ever considered the backlash on Jordan. Her mom also used to be a stripper, way before she had Jordan. Apparently, Jordan's dad was one of her regulars. That all came out during the divorce, after the chairman incident.

"No, it doesn't, but it makes her...." Mom trails off in search of the appropriate euphemism.

"Troubled?" Jordan's smart and beautiful too, in that naturally athletic kind of way that makes me want to puke, but she dyes her hair black and reads too much Edgar Allan Poe to sit with the in crowd.

"Yes, and I don't want my daughter getting roped into anything she can't handle."

"How about you make a list of all the girls you think I should be friends with, and we can pick some out for me?"

"Honestly, Treasa." Mom throws her hands up. "I'm not telling you not to be friends with this girl. I'm just saying to keep your distance, is all. Ever since you've been in high school—"

I pick up my headphones and snap them in place before making a show of turning up the volume on my hi-fi. Mom glares at me, shakes her head sadly, and stalks out of my bedroom while Creed screams about what ifs into my ears.

I know what Mom's going to say—that ever since I started high school, I've been different, distant, quiet, introverted, strange. That was two years ago. I don't know what changed, what turned me from a vivacious overachiever—Dad's words—into a girl who skulks through corridors hoping nobody will notice my C-cups or Coke-bottle legs. It's like I hit the teens and turned into someone else. My body betrayed me, literally turning pear shaped where before I'd been skateboard straight. Maybe puberty activated my alien genes; maybe that's what's made me go weird.

I tried broaching the subject with Mom once, fishing for info about my biological parents and suggesting that maybe I was "foreign"— complete with finger-made air quotations. Mom thought I meant Irish when I meant Martian. All delving into my biological background ended abruptly when they sheepishly admitted they'd "misplaced" my records. Apparently, they hadn't put all the records onto the computer before the move. Convenient. It's almost like I don't really exist, since all I have is the new birth certificate with my adoptive parents' names on it. At least they didn't change my birth name. I'm still Treasa Rae.

The song changes and with a sigh, I return to homework. Trigonometry defies comprehension. I slam shut my workbook, not caring for the moment that unfinished exercises will get me a demerit tomorrow. I've got three to earn before a detention, so screw trig. I fire up my PC instead and open up the Word document titled "Tristan." It's the only way I can alleviate the agony of a week-long wait between episodes of *Project Blue Book*, and it doubles as my creative writing homework.

In my story, Resa hangs out with my character, Tristan—another alien and Resa's bodyguard on Earth—and, while waiting to return to Kazar, together they fight the government that wants to eradicate all evidence of extraterrestrial life. Personally, I think the producers should've asked for my help here, because having Tristan in the picture makes the story way more entertaining.

Writing from a boy's point of view should be hard, according to my English teacher. I wouldn't know, since I've never written anything from a girl's perspective. Never wanted to.

The cursor blinks, waiting for my words....

TRISTAN EXAMINED his reflection in the cracked and grimy bathroom mirror, not satisfied with the color of his tie.

"It would look better blue." Resa zipped up and sauntered toward the sink.

"Which shade?" Tristan waved a hand over his tie, rearranging the molecules into turquoise, then aquamarine, then indigo.

"Try periwinkle." Resa grinned and ran his wet fingers through his hair.

"Is that even a color?"

"It should be."

Tristan settled on cerulean so the tie matched his eyes. "Why are we doing this?"

"To blend in." Resa smoothed down the lapels of his tux.

"And going to senior prom without dates is how we blend in?"

"We've got each other." Resa winked and tucked an unruly wave of blond hair behind Tristan's ear. Tristan sighed, not really looking forward to hanging around alone all night while Resa flirted with other guys' dates.

He felt the music vibrating along the corridor a minute before he heard the nasal whine of some pop princess straining over growling bass.

"Just stay away from the punch. Overheard the quarterback saying he was going to spike it with gin," Resa said as he pushed open the gym hall doors. A cloud of perfume and aftershave assailed Tristan's nostrils before he could dull his too-sensitive senses.

"Do you think they have proms on Kazar?"

"I hope we've evolved beyond this primitive mating ritual." Resa grinned. "But I try to see the good in every situation." He swaggered into the gym-turned-ballroom, approaching a group of cheerleaders-turned-Barbie dolls.

Tristan ambled past the snacks, speared an olive with a toothpick, and picked up a custard pastry. He crammed both of them into his mouth, savoring the sweet-salty explosion, and leaned against the wall in a dark corner, contemplating turning himself off-white so he'd blend into the wall.

He watched the humans, laughing and interacting so effortlessly. He watched Resa lead a pretty brunette wearing a crimson gown onto the dance floor as the pop song faded into a rock ballad. Resa pulled her close, his hand on the small of her back, his lips brushing her ear as he entranced her with his mellifluous voice. The girl's date showed up, a scowl on his acned face when he saw his date leaning into Resa. Tristan's gut tightened, anticipating the worst as the football player marched across the dance floor and tapped Resa on the shoulder. Tristan's sensitive ears tuned into the conversation as the jock grabbed Resa's jacket and shoved him away from the girl blushing the same shade as her dress.

The jock, Mitch, pulled back his fist, aiming for Resa's nose. That's when it happened. Tristan couldn't control the impulse hard-coded into his triple helix. He was Resa's bodyguard. His whole reason for being was to protect the exiled emperor of Kazar. He flung out his hand, condensing the atoms around Resa to form a protective, if invisible, barrier. Mitch's fist met the barrier, and he screamed as the bones shattered in his hand. Resa spun around to face Tristan, anger etched into his expression before making a run for the door. Tristan released the atoms and followed Resa into the corridor.

Resa whirled on him, shoving him into a row of lockers. "What the hell was that?"

"He was going to hit you."

"And?" Resa's green eyes swirled through various shades, indicating severe rage.

"And I'm meant to protect you. I have to."

"Maybe I'm tired of you protecting me. Maybe I'm tired of being this and want to be that." He jerked his head toward the gym. "Even if it means getting a black eye once in a while."

That was impossible. Resa's cells regenerated in nanoseconds.

"Well, maybe I'm tired of that, and want to be this." Tristan acted before really thinking about it as he wound his fingers through Resa's hair and pulled him close. Their lips brushed together, and every light in the corridor exploded in a shower of sparks.

GABRIEL

"NO SON of mine—" My father tears up the application form, leaving my dream in tattered strips on the kitchen table.

"It's my life."

"It's my money." His face is ruddy from one too many beers. This is the worst possible time to pick a fight with him, but I can't stop myself. I hate him, hate him so much I want to put my fist right through his face, to break him and leave him a soggy mess on the floor.

"Just because your dreams turned to shit, doesn't mean you get to bugger up mine."

He stares at me as it takes his beer-soaked brain a moment to process what I said. His face distorts, a grotesque mask of rage. How did Mom ever love this man? I could block his hand; of course, I don't. If hitting me makes my father feel better, then so be it. I probably deserve it. Mom would've put atchar on my tongue; my father slaps me and storms out of the kitchen as much as a man with a limp can storm. Just another breakfast in the du Preez household.

I salvage the pieces of my application form. No bachelor of music for me, then. Forging his signature wouldn't help much either, not when the deposit needs paying as well. Why my father even cares what I do when he's got Jean-Pierre to be proud of escapes me. My father tore his ACL twenty-five years ago on the rugby field, the injury ruining his chances of Springbok glory. I can understand him wanting to live vicariously through my prop-forward brother, so why can't he just leave me alone?

The front door bangs shut, and a moment later, the bakkie growls as my father revs the engine. He won't wait more than a minute for me to grab my school bag and blazer. Tires churn on the gravel driveway and the electric gates grind open. He didn't even give me a minute. I'll have to call Dirk for a lift again. Either that or a bloody long walk and detention for being late.

I pause at the piano and run my fingers along the keys. My father reckons playing music makes me a *moffie* because all male piano players are obviously gay, despite my repeatedly telling him I'm straight. Things would be different if Mom were here, and it's my fault she's not. There aren't even pictures of her on the walls anymore. My father made sure of that, tearing down every framed image of us as a happy family days after we put Mom in the ground. He doesn't know I kept some, that I've got them hidden in a box under my bed.

I dial Dirk, and he answers on the third ring.

"Need a lift?" he asks.

TREASA

WITHOUT JORDAN beside me, I feel vulnerable, as if I've got this giant bull's-eye on my back.

Walking down the corridor between classes is like running a gauntlet, only I'd take the threat of physical damage over the lash of tongues any day.

"Oh look, it's Beam Me Up Scotty!" Gillian—one of Candyce's posse—thinks she's hilarious, giving me a Vulcan salute. She can't even do it right, her ring finger struggling to maintain the separation from her middle finger. Correcting her would only make matters worse.

"Howzit, Brace-Face, seen any flying saucers today?" Hannah cackles as the girls shove past me.

Maybe I invite their ridicule, considering my space case is covered in National Geographic cutouts of nebulae and crop circles. Having pictures of *Star Trek* and *Project Blue Book* plastered on my books probably doesn't help much either. If only Jordan were here, she'd have already silenced Hannah with some brilliant riposte, but I'm eternally cursed with stair wit.

Face burning and stomach feeling like a washing machine on the spin cycle, I keep my head down, hoping to avoid any more verbal abuse. Jordan, my savior, appears at the end of the corridor, and I scurry toward her, dodging a cluster of grade eights.

"Wait for me," I shout above the tumult of the changing classes. She leans against the wall and studies her nails; her hands are spattered with black paint. Hannah and Gillian skiff her and she ignores them.

"How's the art project going?" I ask as we file into the classroom.

"Good, I guess. This term's theme is great. Pick any lyrics and create something." We take our seats near the window.

"Which lyrics are you doing?" I dig around in my bag for the unfinished math homework.

"'Catholic School Girls Rule' by the Red Hot Chili Peppers." She grins.

"Jordan." There's an edge of admonishment in my voice that makes me sound an awful lot like my mother. I know that song, and it's only going to get Jordan into even more trouble than usual.

"What?" She grabs my math book and a pen. I protest as she elbows me out of the way and finishes off the problems in a blur of cos and sin. Jordan does my math homework, I do her French homework. We've got the perfect symbiotic relationship.

"They're not going to like those lyrics," I say.

"Wait til you see the artwork I have planned." She nibbles on the end of her pen.

Our math teacher walks in, and Jordan slides my now complete homework across the desk.

Another arduous hour begins. Jordan dozes with her head on the desk and still manages to get every answer right when she's called upon. I'm not so lucky. My turn at the whiteboard yields a chorus of snickers from Hannah and crew as my inability to solve for x becomes public knowledge.

What would Resa do? He'd probably solve the equation in two seconds and swagger back to his chair, prop his feet up on his desk, and wink at the teacher. What would my Tristan do? He'd do something passive-aggressive like turn Hannah's blond hair gray with a twitch of his fingers. With my cheeks burning, I glare at Hannah and Candyce, willing their hair to turn white. The teacher orders me back to my seat before the molecular manipulation can be completed. Or I just don't have superpowers because I'm not from Kazar, which doesn't really exist, according to the space atlas I found in the World Book. Granted, they've probably discovered a lot more planets since 1985, when the books were published.

Defeated, I crumple into my chair, wishing I could disappear. Why is math even compulsory? If I could drop it, I would, and stick to languages and history—the stuff I'm good at.

Jordan sidles closer to me and whispers, "Screw them."

AT THE end of the torturous hour, we're redirected to our homerooms for a briefing on the Charity Ball. Bliss—Gillian and Hannah aren't in our class. Unfortunately, Candyce is.

"Since I did your homework for you, you kinda owe me," Jordan says as we find our seats at the back of the class.

"I'm sure I did your French homework on Monday."

"True, but there were more math problems than French verbs."

"Fine." Last time I owed Jordan, we tried to get into a sex shop because, apparently, sex shops sell the coolest clothes. I'm not convinced.

"There's a self-defense training course starting this weekend at Riverstone Country Club."

"How much?"

"My treat." Jordan winks. "Be at my house nine o'clock Saturday morning."

"I'll have to ask my mom."

"It'll be fun, I promise." Jordan puts her arm around me like I imagine a protective big sister might.

"Get a room," Candyce shoots over her shoulder.

Jordan just squeezes me tighter and ignores the rest of the mumbled insults. Moments later, our teacher walks in carrying a basket full of envelopes. Some of the girls squeal with excitement as the invitations are handed out. I peel open the envelope and remove the card with wary fingers. The front image is a chessboard with a fancy serif font scrawled across it declaring Grade 10 Charity Ball 2000.

I've got til the end of the holidays to find a partner. More than two months. That's manageable. The theme is black and white: girls in white dresses, boys in black suits.

"Damn, Bryce would've looked good in white." Jordan shoves the envelope into her bag.

"Wearing a white dress is just going to make me look like a corpse."

"Get some fake tan," Sibo teases.

"You'll look stunning in white," I say.

"You think so?" She cocks her head to the side, her henna-dyed ponytail falling over her shoulder.

"You know so."

Jordan beams. "You'll look good in white, Ree. You must have Irish genes."

Looking Irish is just a polite way of telling me I have too many freckles, that I'm pale, and that my hair is that weird reddish color no one knows what to call so it ends up being dubbed anything from strawberry blonde to ginger. My mom calls it auburn. I think it looks more carrot.

"Who are you going to take, Ree-Ree?" Sibo rocks back in her chair to be part of the conversation.

"No idea."

"We can help." Lethi smiles. "Our cousin. Mm-hm. That boy is fine."

While I appreciate the twins' offer to help out the dateless mutant in the back row, I'm not sure I even want to go to the ball.

"I don't think I'm going," I say as the break bell rings.

"What? *Haw wena*, of course you're going," Lethi says as she and Sibo sweep up their invitations.

"You could take Gabriel," Jordan says.

"Gabriel? Like choir Gabriel?" Sibo frowns.

"No."

"Yes." Jordan nods vigorously. "He's perfect."

"He's in Matric," Lethi says, as if I need reminding.

"And he'd never agree if I asked him."

"We'll see." Jordan winks, and my insides turn to knots as we file outside in search of shade.

"He is good-looking for a white boy," Sibo says before heading for the tuck shop with her sister.

Jordan and I find a patch of dappled grass and settle with our lunch boxes.

"Please don't make a big deal out of this."

"Me? Never." Jordan feigns innocence as she pops open a bag of Jelly Tots.

"I'm serious."

"Cross my heart, promise." She offers me a sugared candy, which I eat with a cheese cracker.

"You must be an alien," Jordan says. "Or pregnant."

"I am so not pregnant." Gross. If I could get sterilized right now, I would.

"Stef eats the weirdest things. You ever tried milk tart with tomato sauce?"

"Maybe your sister's an alien too," I say.

"She is the size of a planet. But I think you're the only extraterrestrial among us."

Jordan acknowledging my weirdness usually makes me feel good, feel better about being such a freak, but right now, despite the heat sucking the moisture out of everything, I shiver with a prickle of cold. I don't want to go to the Charity Ball, I don't want to fight with my mom about wearing a dress, I don't want to have to find a partner and end up asking some distant relative for a favor. Right now, I don't want to be me.

GABRIEL

I CAN'T sleep. Thunder rumbles somewhere to the south, too far away to be soothing. There's something consoling about the violence of a highveld thunderstorm. The more vicious the lightning, window shaking the thunder, and torrential the rain, the less angry I feel. For those brief minutes when the heavens wreak havoc on the earth, I feel a kind of peace. Mom loved storms, said they were nature's way of reestablishing equilibrium. Too bad it can't rain inside my head and wash away all the shit clogging up the works.

The night is a symphony of crickets, with the wind rattling percussion in the tree branches outside my windows. I'd love to be able to practice right now, wouldn't even need to turn on the lights—just let my fingers feel their way through the music. Doubt my father would be too impressed if I woke him up at 1:00 a.m. with Beethoven. Mom used to play late at night. I remember waking up as a kid in the early hours of the morning to the pianissimo strains of Chopin or Clementi.

I've got the matinée coming up. Not that my father knows or even cares. If Mom were still around, I bet she'd come to my concerts and she'd be proud of me.

Using a torch under the duvet, I start writing another letter. I'm not sure why I do this; it's not like I have anywhere to send them, and it's not like Mom will ever read them. Sometimes just writing these helps as much as getting hit at the dojo does.

Dear Mom,

Do you think I'll make a good chemical engineer? That's what Dad says he'll pay for. They even offered me a scholarship, but I don't want to do a BSc. I want to study music, like you.

I know he hates me, almost as much as I hate him. We blame each other for what happened, but I think he's right. It's my fault and I'm sorry. Wherever you are, I hope you know how sorry I am.

For the first time in five years, tears prick the back of my eyes. Pain is good for creativity.

Artists should suffer. The greatest pieces weren't ever composed in a moment of elation. Tragedy is what spawns the most profound creations. Thinking about Mom might be good for my composition.

I've been working on this sonata since Christmas, and it's going to be the centerpiece of my Matric portfolio, but it's lacking inspiration. The music seems pedestrian, too normal, too derivative.

The harmonies are uninspired, the melody boring, the structure predictable. When did Chopin first hear the melody for his Nocturne in B-flat minor? How did Beethoven feel as he sat down to compose the Moonlight Sonata? Maybe being sad just isn't enough.

AM I AN ALIEN, TREASA TEST #02

HYPOTHESIS: Extraterrestrials possess superhuman abilities such as telekinesis.

GOAL: To prove I can move objects with the power of my mind alone.

METHOD:

Place five objects of varying weights and densities on a regular surface (my desk).

Concentrate on individual objects for exactly three minutes.

Attempt to move objects at least five centimeters along surface of desk.

RESULTS: The only objects that appeared to move were the leaf and ball of cotton wool. However this may have been a result of the breeze through the window and not telekinesis. The ball of Prestik did not move, which may indicate that alien powers do not work on polymers. The bottle of nail varnish and pen showed no movement.

CONCLUSION: Results are inconclusive. I may not have fully developed my alien powers yet, or my powers may be more limited than previously thought. That the leaf moved in the direction I wanted it to indicates possible partial telekinesis on organic compounds.

Treasa

Nine o'clock Saturday morning, Dad drives me to Jordan's. Despite my complaints, Dad tunes into the cricket and I'm forced to listen to descriptions of batting and fastballs and innings and wickets.

"Are we winning?" I ask when Lance Klusener hits a six.

"Oh, Resa, I give up with you." My dad shakes his head, and we pull into Jordan's driveway.

"So we aren't winning?" I grin.

He gives me a you-know-better look and turns down the commentary. "You sure about this?"

"Sure about hanging out with Jordan, or taking a martial arts class?"

Dad frowns, his eyebrows gathered in a thicket of lines above his nose. "You've got your cell phone. Call me if you're uncomfortable, okay?"

"Thanks, Daddy." I kiss him on the cheek and hop out as Jordan's mom sashays onto the *stoep* in a flimsy sundress.

"Howzit, Dave."

"Hi, Sheryl." Dad waves, his smile tight and forced, before driving away.

"Come in, Ree." Sheryl whisks me inside. I like Jordan's house, an open-plan sprawl of glass and feng shui thanks to her father's child-support checks. Jordan bounds down the stairs in skimpy yoga shorts and a black halter top. I feel overdressed in the board shorts I got from the boy's department and a T-shirt. At least the new sports bra is working, flattening the bulbous protrusions on my chest.

"Ready?" She pauses in the hallway mirror to sweep her long hair into a haphazard ponytail that somehow looks designer messy.

"I guess."

"Class starts at ten. We should go. Ma!"

"Coming." Sheryl lights a cigarette and picks up her keys.

Minutes later, we cruise into the country club, the wind making ragged sails of my hair despite all the hairpins trying to hold it in place.

Riverstone Estate is an oasis sandwiched between office blocks and shopping centers. The houses here are palatial; some even have Grecian pillars and porticoes. In the center of this Utopia lies the country club and ultramodern sports center replete with twenty-four-hour gym. The annual club membership fees are probably more than my school fees. Sheryl parks and says to meet her at the pool when we're done. Jordan saunters into the sports center as if she owns the place.

"I've never been here before."

"Don't worry, Ree. These uppity bitches won't bite. They're too busy worrying about their cellulite and wrinkles to notice us."

"You fit in here."

"Gee, thanks," Jordan snaps.

"I mean, you're one of them, one of the beautiful people with a big house and a convertible."

Jordan stops in the middle of the reception area and turns to face me, left hand on her hip. "I'd be happy with a fifteen-year-old Toyota and townhouse if it meant I had two parents at home working regular nine-to-fives."

"Sorry." I don't know what else to say.

"It's okay." She releases the breath she's been holding. "But money is hardly what matters in this life."

I can't argue with that. Jordan keeps walking, and I follow her into the change rooms where we lock up our bags and fill water bottles before heading into Hall C. There's a poster on the door advertising the self-defense class being run by the Cedarbranch Karate Academy. The guy demonstrating a superhero kick looks a little familiar. The image isn't high quality, so it's hard to be sure.

There are a dozen other teenagers, mostly girls, gathered in groups around the edges of the mats. Thankfully, I don't recognize anyone from St. Bridget's. Jordan and I stand in the corner, watching and waiting.

"Oh look, Ree, it's Gabriel." Jordan nudges me with her elbow as Gabriel and a middle-aged man walk in.

Gabriel turns and scans the hall, his gaze resting on us. He waves in greeting with a smile plastered across his face. I can't breathe.

"This'll be fun." Jordan grins as we're instructed to take our places on the mats.

"You knew?" I manage through clenched teeth.

"Of course, why do you think we're here?"

"You're mean."

"I'm devious." She smirks. "And doesn't Mr. du Preez look mighty fine in his *karate gi* and black belt? See, black and white. He's already nailed the look."

The sensei claps his hands, calling for silence before introducing himself as Sensei Nathan and Sempai Gabriel. Then we start with some basic warm-up drills, and it takes all my concentration not to look like a flailing walrus while doing star jumps. Jordan glows with a sheen of perspiration, while I'm soaking in sweat and left wishing I'd worn less when we start the hand-to-hand maneuvers.

Jordan and I pair up for a simple takedown. Someone grabs you from the front, you grab his wrist, bend over, and take him down with a knee to the shoulder. Gabriel and his sensei demonstrate the step, and it looks like a dance move, fluid and easy. I grab Jordan first, and we do the move in slow motion a few times before trying it for real. Of course, Jordan pins me to the floor in seconds.

We swap and she grabs me. She resists, and not wanting to hurt her, I relent. Jordan swivels around fast and knocks me to the floor.

"Sorry, Ree, but you're gonna have to try harder to take me down." Jordan helps me up as Gabriel comes over.

"Hi. Treasa, right?"

Oh God, he remembers my name. I manage a nod.

"And?" He gives us a smile showing too much teeth. It's the first time I've noticed his smile doesn't really touch his eyes.

"Jordan." She holds out her hand and they shake.

"Do you mind?" Gabriel asks, stepping between us to partner with me. *Please let him think my face is just red from exertion.*

"Go for it." Jordan steps back, giving me an encouraging thumbs-up.

"You need to use your full body weight," he says. "Don't be afraid of taking the other person down."

Is that a veiled way of saying he thinks I'm fat?

"Try it." He grabs my shirt. I stare at his hand a few centimeters above my breast before blinking back into the now.

"You won't hurt me, promise." He grins, and this time there's a flicker of amusement in his emerald eyes. Tentatively, I wrap my fingers around his wrist. His pulse throbs beneath my fingertips.

"Now use your other arm and bend at the waist, rolling me down and away."

"Come on, Ree." Jordan yells encouragement.

"Like this?" I ask, pushing my arm across his biceps as I bend. Gabriel offers no resistance and falls to the floor with my knee pressed against his muscular shoulder.

"Like that, only mean it this time."

He grabs me more aggressively, and I go through the motion again. This time he manages to squirm away from me before I can pin him on the mat.

"Again," he says, grabbing me and tugging me closer. "You're short, but that doesn't have to be a disadvantage."

I close my eyes and pretend it's not Gabriel. Candyce's face flashes through my mind as I grab the wrist holding my shirt. There's a moment of resistance before I pin the guy down hard.

"Okay, okay." He pats my knee, and I let him up. Jordan stares at me, wide-eyed.

"What?"

"That was really good." Gabriel rubs his shoulder.

"Did I hurt you?" I raise my hands as if to, what? Soothe him, warp the molecules of his bruised shoulder and heal him like Resa would a friend? I drop my hands.

"Hardly." He gives me a measured look and jogs back to the sensei, ready to teach us a new move.

"That was awesome." Jordan stands beside me as we observe the next block.

"Really?"

"It was like poetry. You just closed your eyes, and the next second, the dude was down. You're a natural at this."

This time the flush of warmth beneath my skin has nothing to do with shame. "My alien side kicking in."

"Whatever it is, I like it." She grabs me with two hands as we start the next formation.

AFTER CLASS, we bow and mumble thanks in putrid Japanese before hitting the showers. Refreshed and feeling better than I have in forever, we join Sheryl at the pool.

"That better not be a Bloody Mary." Jordan's expression darkens even though her mom's been sober for almost a year now.

"Virgin. I promise." Sheryl offers the glass of tomato juice to Jordan, who takes a sip and nods. "Learn anything useful?" Sheryl asks.

"Ree is a machine, Ma. You shoulda seen this chick all kick-ass."

"Good for you." Sheryl waves over a waiter and orders us lemonade.

"And the instructor is super cute." Jordan slips off her slops and dangles a toe in the swimming pool.

"Is he?"

"*Ja*, and he happens to play piano for our choir."

"That a coincidence?" Sheryl gives Jordan a knowing look over the tops of her sunglasses.

"How did you know, anyway?" I sit cross-legged on a pool chair as the waiter hands me a tall glass full of ice.

"There's this thing called the Internet." Jordan slurps and then waves to someone behind me. Gabriel ambles over, his wet hair plastered in unruly strands across his forehead. He's got an earring I never noticed before.

"Ladies," he says. I wish I could see his eyes, currently hidden behind aviator Ray-Bans.

"This is my mom, Sheryl. Mom, this is Sempai Gabriel."

"Nice to meet you, ma'am." Afrikaans boys are nothing if not politeness personified.

"And you." Sheryl shares a look with Jordan before removing her intimidating parental aura from the vicinity.

"So how does getting your butt kicked by a girl feel?" Jordan asks.

Gabriel laughs, the sound deep and rich, spawning not butterflies but colossal fire-breathing, blood-warming dragons in my belly.

"Keeps me on my toes." He grins at me. "You should think about coming to the dojo and doing karate."

"Why?" I squeak.

"Because you're really good. You take lessons before?" he asks.

"Never."

"Impressive." Gabriel smiles, and I wish I could see his eyes to see if it's genuine.

"So, same time same place next week?" Jordan sips her drink.

"For sure. But I'll see you girls at choir practice, right?"

"Wouldn't miss it." Jordan pinches my leg, waking me from the dragon-storm stupor.

"Yeah, choir. Thursday. See you." I am such a spaz.

"Cheers." He waves and heads for the parking lot.

I watch him walk away, watch the way his shirt falls over his broad shoulders and billows around his waist in the breeze, how his feet turn out a little with every step in his Nike takkies.

"You should ask him to the ball." Jordan nudges me.

"On what planet would a girl like me get a guy like that?"

Jordan finishes her drink and gathers up her stuff before answering. "I know you think you're from Kazar or Andromeda or something, but on Earth all it would take is a simple question."

And what if he says no?

GABRIEL

I WALK away feeling their eyes on my back.

"Friends of yours?" Nathan asks as we throw our kit into the car.

"Not really." The last person I expected to see at the class was Treasa.

"That redhead's not half-bad. She done karate before?" He tosses me a bottle of water before reversing out of the lot.

"Apparently not."

"She should come to class. We need more women at the dojo. Work on it." He nudges me as he changes gears.

"If I'm going to be recruiting for you as well, then I think my fees just went up."

"Here, take the cash." Nathan hands me his wallet as we pull up to a red robot. Even in broad daylight in the northern suburbs, my palms start sweating, and I shove the wallet under my leg as I search the faces of the guys handing out fliers and offering to wash the windscreen, as if I can spot criminal intent. The lights change and we pull off without incident.

I take my twenty-five rand and shove the wallet into the cubbyhole. Nathan says nothing about my paranoia, and I turn up the radio, letting the Billboard Top 100 drown out any chance of conversation. Fifteen minutes later, Nathan drops me off at Dirk's.

"YOU RECKON it was just coincidence?" Dirk asks as he slides Vienna sausages into a pot of water for hotdogs.

"No idea."

"I told you, Catholic chicks. You should take full advantage of your situation." He licks his fingers, nails painted black for the weekend. His folks don't seem to care about their son wearing nail varnish and eyeliner or that he wants to study bass and be a rock star. They actually encourage him. A pang of jealousy skewers my chest.

"She's not half-bad," I say.

"The black-haired one?"

"The redhead."

Dirk nods and hands me a knife so I can butter bread rolls. "That black-haired chick is hot."

"Her name's Jordan."

"Like I ever remember their names." Dirk gives me a goofy grin. For all Dirk's talk about nailing chicks, I know for a fact he's full of shit. He falls in love, treats his girlfriends like princesses, and inevitably gets his heart broken, which he pours into the lyrics of his band. If that's what it takes to compose beautiful music, I'm not sure it's worth it, but I'll let Dirk keep pretending he isn't a supersensitive romantic sap if it makes him feel better.

"You think she's a virgin?" Dirk asks.

"Jordan? Does it even matter if?"

"Of course." His eyes widen in shock. "I don't want some oke's sloppy seconds."

I shrug, although I can't help imagining if Treasa's a virgin. Hell, it's not like I am. I lost that when I was fifteen to Janine in a tent on a camping trip. It wasn't romantic, not at all like in the movies. Just messy. Not that I didn't like it; it just wasn't all rose petals and candles. Then there was Karla last year. That girl is hot, and she knows her way around the bedroom. I learned a lot from her, and to be honest, I'd rather that than a girl who's never even seen a penis, let alone touched one. Virgins expect fireworks and life-changing orgasms. It's not like that. At least, it wasn't for me. Who knows, maybe I missed out. The pressure to make the world spin for some first-time princess is just too much to live up to.

"Invite her to the party."

"What party?" Dirk's mom walks in.

"The party I was going to ask if I could have that weekend you're away." Dirk fishes sausages out of the pot and drops them into the rolls.

"What's the occasion?" She hands him the tomato sauce and mustard from the fridge, and I catch a whiff of her perfume. Chanel. The same one Mom used to wear. It's only a fragrance, and it feels like a steak knife slicing through my ribs.

"Nothing special. Just some buddies hanging out."

"While I'm away with my drama girls?"

"Perfect timing." Dirk gives her an Oscar-winning smile.

"No booze, no drugs, and you get your father to manage the *braai*. Deal?"

"So strippers are fine, then?"

She slaps his shoulder and picks up Dirk's plate.

"Thanks for the hotdog, dear," she says over her shoulder as she leaves the kitchen.

"You're welcome, Ma." Dirk starts smearing tomato sauce onto another roll. "So bring her to the party?"

"I'll think about it."

"Ask Jordan too."

"You want her so badly, you ask her."

"Maybe I will." He sucks tomato sauce off his thumb.

We take our hotdogs up to his bedroom. We're supposed to be working on his biology essay; we settle in front of the PlayStation instead.

"Bloody Marlize." He throws the sparkle pony game across the room and goes in search of something with fast cars or guns instead.

"Where's your sister?"

"At the movies with her tween friends. If only she was, like, five years older, man. We'd have access to a whole herd of hot chicks."

"And some guy would be thinking about Marlize the way you're thinking about Jordan."

His smile becomes a scowl as the game starts up with a volley of gunfire. "Good thing I'm practicing now." He shoots an alien in the head. "And you better save up for bail."

"Why?"

"Because I'm going to kill the first guy who touches her."

We leave all discussion of genetic mutation in plants and focus on saving our starship from marauding aliens. At some point, Dirk's mom brings us Cokes and she tousles our hair, her hand lingering on my shoulder. I appreciate her treating me like one of her kids, I do, but sometimes being around a mother so much like my own is just too painful. Sometimes I wish Dirk's mom wouldn't hug me good-bye or make me birthday cake or buy me new socks. She means well, and I don't deserve any of it.

TREASA

RESA PULLED away, his emerald eyes widening in surprise.

"I'm sorry," Tristan mumbled, his face on fire.

"Don't be." Resa cupped Tristan's face with his long fingers and smiled. "Just wasn't expecting that."

"What the hell is going on here?" Coach Daniels crunched over shattered lightbulbs as he surveyed the corridor.

"Let's get out of here." Resa grabbed Tristan's hand and dragged him out of the school into the crisp air of the spring night. "Up here." Resa jogged to the fire escape, gesturing for Tristan to scale the frost-slicked steel. Coach Daniels burst out of the doors, shouting for those responsible to own up, or else. Resa and Tristan hauled themselves onto the roof and lay back, gasping, stifling giggles as the coach continued to berate nothing but shadows.

Resa led Tristan up the slope of the roof to the apex. He straddled the join and flicked his hair off his face before casting his gaze upward. "Beautiful, isn't it?"

If not for the lights of the town and the smog of the city a few miles away, they'd have seen the Milky Way spill across the black sky. Despite the pollution, stars defied the grime, glimmering in their constellations.

"Which one's Kazar?" Tristan asked. He'd been made for Earth, birthed from a pod en route to the blue planet as a bodyguard for the young emperor in exile while war ravaged their home.

"You can't see Kazar, but you can see our sun." Resa inched closer to Tristan until their knees touched. He raised his index finger and leaned forward as he pointed out a star only visible because of their enhanced vision.

"It's got a red tinge."

"That's the one." Resa smiled. "That's our home system."

"Do you remember any of it?"

"Not really. Part of the genetic manipulation required to let me survive on Earth resulted in a memory wipe."

"You were just a child."

"A sutari," Resa corrected. "I remember some words. That's all."

"You think we'll ever make it back?"

Resa shrugged. "Do you want to?"

"I'm programmed to want it." Tristan's DNA was hard-coded to protect Resa and to one day enable the emperor's safe return to Kazar.

"How can you want something you've never had?" Resa stared into Tristan's eyes.

"Sometimes the heart just knows what's right." The tension was palpable. Tristan leaned forward too, waiting for Resa to kiss him again, but the kiss never came.

"I think my human DNA is overriding my Kazari genes." Resa shuffled back, breaking the moment.

"You want to be human?"

"No, but I'm not sure I want to return to an arid planet to rule some sand-rat society."

"That's treason."

Resa smirked. "Treason against who? Me? I'm the emperor, remember?"

Tristan didn't answer; he just kept staring at the red pinprick sun burning however-many trillions of miles away. "I'd like to see it, just once, just to know what part of me came from."

"Maybe you should learn to be happy with what you have and not yearn for the unattainable," Resa said.

WITH A sigh, I save the file and contemplate Resa's words. My words, really. Would wanting Gabriel to be my date for the ball qualify as yearning for the unattainable? Of course it would. My fingers stray to my ear lobes, stroking the unperforated skin. Mom said I can get my ears pierced when I turn eighteen, which is just ridiculous, considering most of the girls I know got theirs done as little kids.

"You're up early. Want some coffee?" Mom pokes her head into my bedroom.

"Thanks. I'll come to the kitchen." I shuck my Snoopy pajamas in favor of a spaghetti-strap top and shorts. Not even 10:00 a.m. and it's already hot.

Dad's out in the garden with his shirt off, planting and weeding. Our entire property could fit into Jordan's atrium. I wish we had a swimming pool; I'd be in it 24/7.

Mom hands me my coffee and gets the ice out of the freezer, dropping three cubes into the mug before adding just as many spoonfuls of sugar.

"We got our invites to the Charity Ball," I say.

"Tell me about it." Mom picks up her sunglasses and walks out onto the patio. I follow, sitting in the umbrella-provided shade while Mom tans her legs. Riker's stretched out in the sun, tail twitching as he watches the lizards race up and down the brickwork.

"The theme is black and white, and tickets are fifty rand."

"That's reasonable, considering it's for a good cause." Mom waves away a fly buzzing around her coffee mug. "Have you got a date?"

"Not really."

"If you'd go to the youth group meetings like I suggested, you'd meet some more boys."

I can think of nothing more mind-numbing than spending Saturday evenings sitting at church discussing the Bible with a bunch of Catholic nerds.

"I did meet someone."

"Where?"

"At the class yesterday."

Mom turns her head. I can't see her eyes through the tinted lenses, so I'm not sure if she's looking at me. "Hmm."

It's amazing how she's able to convey such intense disapproval with a single syllable that isn't even a word.

"Didn't say I'd ask him, just that I met him."

"Does he have a name?"

"Gabriel."

"Where does he go to school?"

Bugger, Mom's not going to like this answer. She reckons government schools are a cesspit from which no teenager can emerge unscathed, destined for a life of crime and corruption. That's why she and Dad took out a second loan on the house to send me to a private high school, despite my objections.

"Stormhof," I say quietly.

"Hmm."

"I just said I met him. Not about to elope or anything."

"That's reassuring." Mom presses her lips together, clearly unimpressed. Time to change the topic.

"Mom, you know you said I could only get my ears pierced when I was eighteen. I was kind of wondering if I could get them done for the ball."

Dad grunts with exertion as he struggles with a wheelbarrow full of dead tree limbs. We watch him strain, his back already turning lobster in the sun.

"You need more sunscreen," Mom yells.

"In a minute," Dad shouts back.

"About my ears, I was—"

"You can wear clip-ons for the dance."

"Clip-ons? The theme isn't the eighties." I slurp my cooled coffee. It's still too bitter and catches at the back of my throat.

"Cute, Resa, but you don't need to irrevocably alter your body just for a dance."

"It's not irrevocable."

"It's certainly unnecessary."

"But I want earrings."

"Does Jordan have pierced ears?"

"That's got nothing to do with this."

Mom slides her sunglasses down her nose, all the better to glare at me. "Does she?"

"Yes." Three holes in one ear and five in the other, but I don't get into details. She's also got a belly ring and a tiny butterfly tattoo on her hip, which Mom definitely doesn't need to know about.

"That girl...." Mom sighs. "No piercings until you're eighteen. End of discussion."

"Because I can't alter my body?"

"Because you're too young to make that kind of decision."

"It's an ear piercing, not a facial tattoo." I slam my coffee mug onto the patio table. Riker yowls and disappears into the house in a blur of gray.

"Treasa Rae." Mom's tone is deadly. "You asked, and I said no. End of discussion."

I slump back into the chair, arms folded across my chest.

"When you're done being a sulky Sue, let me know and we can start talking about a dress." Mom gets up and grabs the bottle of sunscreen from the table before trotting after Dad, brandishing the SPF 35.

Never mind irrevocably changing my body, I'd like to irrevocably change my whole freaking life!

SUNDAY AFTERNOON, Dad drops me at Jordan's for a swim. Sheryl's tanning topless, and Jordan's drifting around the swimming pool on a *lilo* reading our English set work. We had an essay due two weeks ago, so I guess I'll be writing this one for Jordan too—I still owe her for some physics homework. She paddles to the edge when she sees me and steps daintily off the lilo onto the bricks.

"Why aren't you in your cozzy?"

"There's something I want you to help me with first."

Jordan raises an eyebrow. "Might this have something to do with one Gabriel du Preez?"

"Not really."

"Then what?" She fiddles with the strings of her bikini bottoms. They're barely there, just a scrap of striped fabric held together with string and beads, straining across her hipbones.

"Will you pierce my ears for me?"

"Why?" Jordan leads me into the air-conditioned interior and grabs two Creme Sodas from the fridge.

"Because my mom said no, and piercing places need parental consent because I'm under eighteen."

"That sucks."

"Yeah."

"My mom could take you, say she's your mom."

"It costs money." Like an entire week's worth of pocket money, which could be better used on magazines featuring Liam St. Clare.

"I could sponsor you."

"Thanks, but no. I'd like to try this DIY."

"Your mom's going to freak."

"My body." I shrug, feigning more nonchalance than I feel. Mom is going to kill me.

"Good for you, Ree."

Jordan heads upstairs, where she has a bedroom en suite entirely to herself. The room used to be her older brother's. When he moved down to Cape Town to study at UCT, Jordan recolonized, starting with turning the walls from boring beige to a psychedelic splatter of neon. Mom and Dad barely let me put up posters, never mind paint and draw on my walls. The wall opposite her bed is the mural wall where Jordan works out her artistic frustrations in acrylic and pen.

"Is that the Virgin Mary?" I study the latest addition.

"Yeah, working on a concept for art."

"For the Chili Peppers?"

"Nope, thinking of changing my song."

"To what?" I unpack the sewing kit I scrounged from Mom's cupboard and the various first aid items pilfered from Dad's bathroom cabinet.

"Ever heard of Bauhaus?"

"The German school?"

"The band, dork." Jordan strolls across her immense bedroom and plucks an album from the wall unit crammed to overflowing with books and CDs. "Craig must've left this behind when he went to Cape Town.

Never knew he was into this stuff." She hits play and turns up the volume. "Listen to the lyrics."

"Sounds like they're having an epileptic fit."

"I know. Isn't it rad?"

The guy starts singing—well, he's not singing so much as being strangled over psychotic guitar riffs. The chorus is a little better, where he actually manages to crow out a tune.

"Can we pierce my ears now?" Considering my ears are already bleeding.

"Sure." Jordan nods toward the bathroom. "Want some vodka for the pain?"

"Is it that bad?" My hands start shaking.

"Feels like a bee sting. You'll be fine." Jordan picks up the leather needle, the biggest in the kit, and runs it under the hot tap.

"What about ice?"

"Don't be such a wussie."

"Have you done this before?" I take a seat on the plush purple toilet cover.

"No, but how hard can it be? You got the ring?"

"Oh crap." The most obvious item, and I've completely forgotten. I'll need to put something through the holes once they're made.

"No worries. Disinfect that." Jordan hands me the needle, and I douse it with surgical spirits while she rummages through her drawers.

"Okay, let's do this." She takes back the needle and drops two matching silver studs into my hand. "Close your eyes, Ree."

I do and take a deep breath as Jordan drives the needle through my ear lobe. It stings, and there's a moment where I'm pretty sure she's going to tear my entire ear off, but then the needle's through. Jordan tugs it out the other end and pushes the stud into place before swabbing surgical spirits over the wound. Involuntary tears trickle down my cheeks.

"You crying?"

"No." I swat the tears away.

"I cried the first time I got my ears pierced." Jordan stands in front of me, her gaze shifting from one ear to the other. At least she's taking this seriously and trying to do a good job of it.

"You did?"

"Yeah, I was two, though."

I pull my tongue at her.

"But I did pass out when I got my belly button pierced last year."

"Did that hurt?"

"Don't know. I was unconscious. Okay, close your eyes again."

I do, and Jordan stabs the needle through my flesh. This one doesn't go as well, and she has to tug really hard to get the needle through. I'm sobbing by the time she's got the second stud in.

With a wad of toilet paper stemming the flood from my nose, I admire myself in the bathroom mirror.

"Happy?" Jordan asks.

She did a good job. They're evenly positioned and the studs are visible without being too obvious. Mom might not even notice.

"Thank you." I let my hair down so that only one earring is visible. I like that better. Pity two earrings are the norm on girls.

"How soon til I can change jewelry?"

"A couple of weeks. You'll need to clean them every night until the swelling goes down." Jordan tosses bloody cotton swabs into the bin and reseals the surgical spirits.

"Did you see Gabriel's?"

"Ja, of course." Jordan smiles.

"I want earrings like that."

"That's nothing special, just an ordinary ring and ball."

"That's what I want."

"We'll go shopping once your ears are healed." She stuffs everything back into the first aid bag. "Can we go swimming now, Little Miss Rebel?"

Minutes later, I'm floating on my back in the pool, feeling like a mermaid with my hair fanned out around me. My ears sting every time they make contact with the chlorinated water, but I don't care. It's my body, and whether I want to irrevocably change it or not is my decision. Mom's just going to have to deal with it.

GABRIEL

EVERY SUNDAY, my father goes to church, leaving me home alone with my piano for two fleeting hours. This Sunday is no different. I wonder if he even remembers the date. I try not to think about it too much, concentrating on piano. The Beethoven is almost flawless now, although Bach and Schumann are still presenting problems for my fingers, no matter how many hours I dedicate to Hanon exercises. It's better having a challenge, though. If the pieces are too easy, then what's the point? I want to have to work hard to get it right. I want to sweat at the piano, to struggle with runs and trills, to bruise my fingers playing the most bombastic fortissimo.

It's only when I'm playing piano that I can forget. The music is all consuming, leaving no room for memory or grief, anger or hatred. Especially Beethoven. I should be practicing Bach, should be memorizing Schumann, but playing Beethoven is liberating. Home alone, I don't have to worry about my father bitching that I'm playing too loud. He doesn't appreciate the value of a bone-rattling crescendo. There's no chance of me breaking a string, anyway, as much as that idea appeals to me. Not to damage the piano, just to be that passionate, that aggressively relentless with your playing that the instrument breaks, surrendering to the music.

Rachmaninoff broke strings, and I'm pretty sure Horowitz and Ashkenazy did too. It seems like a rite of passage: you're not a real pianist until you've snapped a string. Maybe when I tackle Rach's third piano concerto next term, it'll happen, preferably not on my piano at home. That'll be hell trying to explain to my father.

I'm just getting to grips with the Bach when Dirk arrives and holds down the gate buzzer. I let him in, and his Beetle churns up the gravel on our driveway.

"Look what I got." He holds out the *bankie* of weed for my approval as he follows me into the lounge.

"How's this?" I remove a bottle of Klipdrift from my father's booze cabinet.

"Nice. You think your Pa will miss it?"

"Doubt it."

We leave Dirk's Beetle in the driveway and amble down the street to the park. There's a family playing Frisbee with their border collie; besides them, and a few vagrants passed out in the shade, we're alone. We head for the *koppie* at the back of the park and climb all the way to the top of the rocks. From here we can see the whole suburb spread out below us: brick houses like Lego blocks, with patches of green lawn dotted with ink-splash swimming pools. Dirk rolls a joint, and I pop open the brandy. We sit in silence for a while, trading marijuana and alcohol back and forth.

"Did your Pa remember?" Dirk asks.

"Don't think so."

"JP?"

"I haven't spoken to my brother since Christmas."

Dirk takes a deep drag from the joint and passes it back to me. I breathe in, holding the acrid smoke in my lungs for as long as possible. I'm getting numb from the combined effects of drugs and alcohol. My limbs feel heavy, like my whole system is slowing down. Maybe even time itself is shutting down. This is how the world will end, not with bombs and earthquakes—just a *ritardando* toward death.

"To your Mom." Dirk raises the bottle, and I nod. Five years ago today, my mom died, and it seems I'm the only one in the family who remembers. Even after all this time, I feel her absence, the ache physical, kind of how I imagine an amputee must feel after losing a leg. You think the missing bit is still a part of you, and it comes as a shock every time you realize it's gone. Only I lost an internal part of me no one can see is even missing. Only I feel the loss, feel that huge gaping wound that might suck me right down into the abyss, if I let it. Mom probably wouldn't want me chucking myself out of the car or getting stoned with Dirk or shagging a girl like Karla. She'd like a girl like Treasa, though. Mom was a singer too.

"You know, she's been dead for years, and I still half expect her to waltz into my bedroom in the mornings with a cup of condensed milk coffee." I watch the family with the dog and the Frisbee, watch the mother pick the little kid up when he bails into the grass.

"Man, that was the best coffee ever," Dirk says.

Last time I had condensed milk coffee was the morning before Mom died. If only I'd known it was the last cup she'd ever make me, I would've savored it and not left half behind, too busy playing piano to pay proper attention.

Damn Klippies, now I'm getting all *dronkverdriet*. I backhand unwanted moisture from my eyes, and the snatch of a melody spins loose from my imagination. It's simple yet beautiful, music in a minor. If only I had my notebook with me. I'll probably forget the tune by the time I get home, even though I try to catch it, humming the notes under my breath in the hopes of remembering. This'll be the first theme of my sonata. Finally, I have something to work with. Maybe this is how all those great composers did it; maybe I should do this more often: get wasted, get morbid, rip the scabs off old wounds, and let myself bleed all over the staves.

TREASA

THE FIGHT ends with me slamming my bedroom door and wishing I had a key to the lock.

"Treasa Rae Prescott!" my mother yells from the passage. She could storm into my room, but there's some invisible barrier, and once my door's closed Mom respects the boundary. I collapse on my bed and clutch a pillow to my chest. Burying my face in lavender scent, I let the tears flow uninhibited, choking on the sobs as they well up from the black hole inside of me.

Why the hell is getting my ears pierced such a big deal, anyway? Mom had an apoplexy when she saw them, and then she tore Dad a new one for failing to notice when he picked me up. Of course, it's all Jordan's fault, and Mom threatened to speak to the school about it, at which point Dad wanted to know exactly what Jordan was guilty of and what the school should do about my dire rebellion. Then Mom and Dad started fighting with each other about me. That's when I ran.

They're still arguing in the kitchen. Mom's way of coping is to bake, which she does with the force of an F5 tornado, slamming cups onto counters and beating the eggs senseless. At least there'll be chocolate cake later. There's a pathetic mewling from just outside my door. I let Riker in and shut the door again, the barricade still in position. I catch a glimpse of myself in the full-length mirror on my cupboard. The earrings are hardly noticeable. The studs are tiny, silver, and inconspicuous. I don't know why they're so offensive. I study my face, turn to see the profile, and smile, trying to dimple my left cheek like Liam St. Clare's. I look like I've just had a stroke.

In the right lighting, and if I had short dark hair, I think I'd almost look like Resa. He's got a feminine face, and I've got a boyish square jaw. That's about all that's boyish about me. I shed my clothes until I'm standing naked and stare at the girl in the glass. It can't be me. When did I get so round and soft? My boobs look like udders, all swollen and veiny. Wonder how Mom would feel about me having a breast reduction. My hips have widened and my skinny legs have thickened. Oh my God, is that cellulite? I squeeze the skin of my thighs and gasp when the flesh dimples into a hateful orange peel. I hate the girl in the mirror. I hate her body, her face, her stupid freckles, her frizzy hair. When did I become her? In my head I'm still svelte and flat and boyish and cute. Not this. I don't want to be this. I don't want to be her.

There's a soft knock on the door, and I tug my clothes back on in a hurry. "Just a minute."

"Can I come in?" Dad asks.

"Yeah." I perch on the edge of the bed, teasing Riker and not minding when his claws draw blood.

Dad squats in front of me and lifts my chin. He brushes the hair off my face and turns my head left, then right, to look at my ears.

"I think they look very pretty and that your mother overreacted."

"You think?"

"Let's drop the attitude, okay?" Dad sits beside me and puts an arm around my shoulder.

"Sorry."

"You didn't have to go behind our backs with this. We could have discussed it."

"I tried to. Mom said end of discussion, twice."

Dad sighs. He smells like cut grass and newspaper and Old Spice. I lean into him and he kisses my hair.

"Growing up isn't easy, Resa. Not for you, and believe it or not, not for us either."

"I don't understand." I wipe away fresh tears threatening my cheeks.

"You're our little girl. All we've ever wanted was to protect you, love you, make sure you have everything. You're precious to us, and now it feels like we're losing you."

"I'm right here, Daddy."

He smiles, although his eyes are sad. "I know, but you won't always be, and it's the little things like getting your ears pierced that remind us you're growing up."

"I'll be sixteen in four months."

"But you're still my little girl. You always will be, and we'll always be overprotective of you."

"Because I'm adopted?"

Dad takes a moment to consider his answer. "We wouldn't love you any differently if you were our biological child. We couldn't possibly love you any more than we do." He hugs me again, and my tears soak his shirt.

"I just wanted to pierce my ears."

"I know, sweetheart," Mom says from where she's hovering at my bedroom door. "I'm sorry." She walks across the room and does the same thing Dad did, scrutinizing my ears. "Did it hurt?"

"A little."

"Did you clean them? Whose needle did you use?"

"Mom." There's no hiding the exasperation in my voice.

"All right." She steps away, hands up in surrender. "But next time, come to us and not Jordan." I bite my tongue. Mom seems to have conveniently forgotten that I did come to her with this, and she didn't even want to discuss it. So maybe that's how I should do things in future. Ask for permission and then do whatever I want anyway when Mom says no, because afterward she'll realize she overreacted and just deal with it.

"Cake'll be ready in half an hour. Want to help me make the icing?"

I nod and give my dad one last squeeze before following Mom to the kitchen.

GABRIEL

I GOT there too late to stop the scrum from giving Dirk a thrashing. They're so tough, it takes all five of them to beat up my scrawny-assed friend. I haul Kelvin off Dirk and shove him into the wall. The others glare at me as they back off. Piet van der Merwe even lunges toward me, a bluff, and I don't even blink. He might weigh ninety kilograms and have fists like anvils, but I'm fast, and he'll be down on the ground crying like a little girl in two seconds. They mutter a string of expletives before cruising out of the bathroom. If Piet was just a big dumb bully, I think I'd forgive him, but he's valedictorian and should know better—not that being clever ever made a person kind.

I offer Dirk my hand and pull him up off the floor where he's cowering between the urinals. Sometimes school feels like a warzone.

"Fuck." Dirk shoves toilet paper up his nose and blinks back involuntary tears. "That's another shirt full of bloodstains." He dabs at the blood splatter on his chest.

"You don't want to report it?"

"And get them coming after me with cricket bats next time? No, thanks." He splashes water on his face and gingerly prods the swollen flesh of his left eye.

"What happened?"

"The usual." He shrugs.

"I don't know why you provoke them."

"Hey, if they tune me about not being built like a rhino, then I'll tune them right back. They have small dicks. I was only being honest. Besides…." He peels back his bottom lip, inspecting the damage. "Rumor has it that you can kill an oke by touching some pressure point with your pinkie."

"That's rubbish."

"No harm in keeping up your reputation. Even Piet won't mess with you." He grins despite his split lip. We traipse out of the bathroom and head toward his car. Dirk never thanks me for these rescues. I know he appreciates them, because he's let himself cry in front of me more than once while we're patching up his face in the bathroom. That's the other thing I envy about Dirk. When he hurts, he cries. I don't care how much of a moffie that makes him, I respect the guy.

When Belinda broke his heart in grade ten, Dirk spent two days crying over her in my bedroom. When his fifteen-year-old Rottweiler died last year, he spent a week sobbing about it. Even his dad got teary-eyed when Buster pegged. The last time I cried was at Mom's funeral, until my father told me real men don't cry, or did I want everyone to think I was a baby. I was only thirteen.

I HAVE to give points to my father for learning how to cook. My aunt lived with us for a while after Mom died, and she taught us all how to make toast and do laundry. Guess my father got extra lessons because he doesn't make half-bad macaroni and cheese, although Mom's was better. Mom's food tasted good because she loved to make it; she loved to feed her boys. My father cooks because we have to eat to survive, and you can taste the difference.

Tonight we eat in silence. The tension at dinner is usually alleviated by the TV, except there's no *Project Blue Book*. They could've scheduled that pointless awards ceremony any other night and preempted a multitude of crappy shows, but no. So now we're eating at the table, each of us trying to ignore the other's existence. At least he doesn't pretend anymore, doesn't even ask me how my day was or what's happening in my life. My father glances at the two empty seats—his gaze lingering longer at the space Mom used to occupy. We still use the place mats she made in one of her craft classes, and like everything else since her death, they've faded from canary yellow to washed-out cat vomit.

I catch my father staring at me while I'm doing the dishes. "What?" I scrape dregs into the bin.

"You need a haircut." He grabs a beer from the fridge and heads for the patio. That's about the limit of his parenting. I finish the dishes and retreat to my bedroom. Marilyn Manson leers at me from a poster on the wall as I hit play on the hi-fi. Angry metal pours out of the speakers and I jump around, whipping my too-long hair back and forth in time to the drums. Dizzy and with a headache clawing its way up my neck, I collapse on my bed with a clean sheet of paper.

Dear Mom,

I wish it had been Dad in the car that night. I know it's my fault, and that it makes me a terrible person for even thinking it, but I don't care. I wish it were him who died. Or maybe even me. Anyone but you, Mom.

AM I AN ALIEN, TREASA TEST #03

HYPOTHESIS: Extraterrestrials possess superhuman abilities such as molecular manipulation.

GOAL: To prove I can heat up cold water faster than normal.

METHOD:

Run the tap on the warm setting and time how long it takes for the water to heat up.

Repeat step one, placing my hand on the faucet, and time how long it takes to heat up again.

RESULTS: It took approximately thirteen seconds for the cold water to become hot under normal conditions. It took approximately four seconds for the cold water to become hot with my hand on the faucet channeling energy into the water.

CONCLUSION: The water heats up faster, indicating the presence of extra molecular energy—proof that my presence decreases the time it takes for the water to heat up. Caveat: Normal body heat may account for part of this faster time, and so does the fact that the tap had already heated up once before. So, only partial evidence for possible molecular manipulation.

TREASA

WHEN SCHOOL ends on Thursday, Jordan drags me straight to the music block, foregoing our usual shade sojourn. I've been miserable the whole day since last night's episode of *Project Blue Book* was preempted due to some American awards show. Now I've got another agonizing week of waiting ahead of me. The thought of seeing Gabriel today both alleviates the misery and adds to it.

"You shouldn't ask him until April," Jordan says.

"Ask him what?"

"To the dance. That gives you enough time to find someone else without making Gabriel think you're desperate."

"He's a Matric. He's not going to want to go to a grade ten dance."

"You could make it worth his while." Jordan grins and bites her bottom lip. I roll my eyes instead of saying something cruel that I'll definitely regret later.

"How's the art project?" I ask as we arrive at the music block. Someone's playing a familiar piano piece, the melody echoing down the corridor.

"It's going well, except I think I might get expelled for this one."

"You've said that before."

"True. Is that Gabriel playing?" Jordan bypasses the choir room, following the sound of the piano to a practice room near the toilets. There's a tiny window carved into each of the not-quite-soundproofed doors. She cranes her neck, smiles, and jerks her head for me to take a look. I stand on tiptoes and stretch my neck, only just managing to catch a glimpse of the boy at the piano.

He's playing without sheet music, his eyes closed as his fingers sweep across the keys. Beethoven. Sonata Pathétique. It's one of my favorites. Gabriel barely pauses as he finishes the first movement and starts the second.

"Impressive," Jordan whispers as she stands next to me, sharing the view. She jostles me deliberately, knocking my elbow into the door. Gabriel's head snaps around, his eyes wide. We step back from the door as he yanks it open, irritation scrunching up his features.

"Oh, hi." He rearranges his frown into a smile. "Am I late?" He checks his watch.

"Not at all. We were just enthralled by your playing," Jordan says.

"Enthralled?" He runs a hand through his hair, and seeing the way the strands fall back into his eyes makes my knees turn boneless.

"Well, Ree knows about music. You like this one, right?" She nudges me, and I unglue my tongue from my palate.

"Pathétique. The second movement. I… I love it." A blush meanders up my neck. I take a deep breath and send it scurrying away from my cheeks.

"One of my favorites too. Want to hear some more?" He barely glances at Jordan, his gaze focused on me.

"Sure she does. I'll see you in choir." Jordan gives me an ungentle shove toward the practice room and trots away, leaving me alone with Gabriel.

"The room's a bit small." He ushers me in, and I slip into the corner as he sits down at the piano. I stare at his head, at the way his hair parts and falls asymmetrically to either side of his face. He's not wearing the earring, but there's a scar on his left earlobe. He loosens his tie and pushes up his sleeves before closing his eyes. His fingers hover above the keys for a moment before he leans into the opening chord. I lean against the wall for support as he plays. The stool creaks as he shifts according to the music, accentuating the dynamics.

Far too soon, he slows it down and brings the movement to a delicate end. He turns on the stool and looks up at me with such expectancy on his face. I want to kiss him right now. I banish the impulse and stutter my way through praise of his performance.

"HOW COME you like Beethoven?" he asks as we leave the practice room.

"I always wanted to play piano, but I've got stubby little fingers." I splay my fingers and my heart catapults into my throat when he takes my hand and presses his palm against mine. His fingers are more than a full knuckle longer. He chuckles and releases my hand as goose bumps race up my arms. Must be my alien genes reacting so violently to his proximity.

"Long fingers aren't essential," he says.

"Short fingers don't help."

"Guess not."

"Did you know Rachmaninoff could play a thirteenth?" I ask.

He pauses to look at me with narrowed eyes. Did I say something wrong? "How did you know that?" Gabriel asks.

"I read."

He looks away, a smile on his face, and this one looks different, soft and genuine, turning his green eyes electric. "I can only reach a tenth."

"Still better than me. I can barely play an octave."

He chuckles and opens the choir room door for me. Jordan's chatting to Sibo and Lethi, their conversation interrupted by the sudden hush as we walk in. The Matrics and grade elevens give me death stares.

I scurry to my seat, not making eye contact with the older girls. Gabriel ambles over to the piano and runs through some scales.

"If there's some hierarchical order to these things, no one told me and no one called dibs," Jordan says so the whole room can hear. The grade eights giggle, the grade nines look bored, and the others snicker. Gabriel doesn't even look up from the piano where he's trying to stretch his fingers to reach a thirteenth. That makes me smile.

"So, you going for it?" Lethi sits next to me.

"We'll see."

"You should. He's cute."

"Thanks for the endorsement."

"Anytime, girlfriend." Lethi snaps her fingers as if she's from a ghetto and not a larny estate.

Choir practice is a blur. I try to concentrate on the material, try to sing as flawlessly as Gabriel plays, but my attention keeps shifting from "Adiemus" and Fauré to Gabriel's fingers. Finally, it's over, and a group of Matrics sashays over to him. More than one of them probably see him as Matric Dance material. Yeah, there's no way he'd agree to go to some corny grade ten Charity Ball.

Lethi and Sibo wave their good-byes, leaving Jordan and me waiting by the gate. "I still can't believe your mom took the whole earring thing so well," she says.

"You wanted me to get grounded?"

"No, but I thought she'd see me as a worse influence."

"You'll just have to try harder."

"I can do that." She grabs my skirt by the waist and hoists it up a few centimeters, exposing my thighs and the ends of my boxers.

"Jesus, Jords." I slap her hands away.

"You've got nice legs. You should show them off more," Jordan says, just as Candyce and crew arrive hot and sweaty from tennis practice.

"Are those boxers?" Jordan reaches for the ends of the boy's underwear Mom only buys me because I insist they're the most comfortable thing to sleep in.

"Oh, look, the Lesbian Sluts. Would you like a skirt with that belt you're wearing, Jordan?" Hannah's glossed lips curl up in a cruel smile.

"You know I slept with a guy, right? Not that I have anything against lesbians, but just to be clear." Jordan glares.

"Jordan, watch it," I warn under my breath.

"Look lesbian to me," Hannah sneers.

"Would you shut it? God, you're so immature." Candyce throws her sports bag down and turns her back on Hannah.

"You got cramps?"

"Thanks to you."

"You can be such a bitch, Candy." Hannah looks smug.

"Such a dirty mouth. No wonder the boys love you," Candyce shoots back, eviscerating her friend.

Jordan and I stare, gobsmacked, as we watch the verbal sparring between the cool-kid BFFs. "Now that's not something I would've expected." Jordan turns her attention back to me. "Lesbian or not, I think you should shorten your skirt."

"Is that allowed?" Gabriel sneaks up on me yet again.

"One should never miss an opportunity to break the rules." Jordan grins as she untucks her shirt and pulls off her tie.

Gabriel just shakes his head and slips on his blazer. I didn't think it was possible for him to look any hotter. What is it about boys in uniform?

"See you Saturday?" Jordan heads for the car park.

"There might be a change in time. I could let you know if I had a number to call."

A sly smile spreads across Jordan's face. "My cell's not working right now. Get Ree's number. I've gotta go. See you." She gives me a quick hug before skipping toward her mom's convertible.

"Should I call you 'Ree'?" Gabriel takes his phone out of his pants pocket. A Nokia, just like mine, except his is gray where mine's blue.

"Only Jordan calls me that. You can call me Resa if you want."

"Like the guy in *Project Blue Book*?"

Oh, kill me now. "Well, my parents have been calling me that for years." Even more lame. Here, call me by the nickname Mommy uses. I want to die. Is it too much to ask for a meteorite to land on my head right this instant?

"I prefer Treasa. What's your number?"

I call it out, trying not to focus too much on what might be considered a compliment of my full name. A moment later, my blazer pocket vibrates. I've got his number. Did this really just happen?

"Thanks," I manage.

"No problem." He studies my face. "Did you get your ears pierced?"

"Wow, you noticed."

"Sure." He rubs his own pierced lobe. "Noticed you singing too. You have a really lovely voice."

"Thank you." This is awkward. I don't know how to handle compliments, let alone from a guy I think I might be falling for. If this is a crush, then I've been reduced to shrapnel.

Hannah gawks at me as Gabriel says good-bye before sauntering toward his friend's Beetle. His friend waves to Hannah, and she gives the guy the middle finger. No idea what that's about.

God, I wish I had Gabriel's swagger, his confidence, his coolness. A smile stretches across my face, stretches so wide it hurts my cheeks, and I don't care. In my mind, I replay what just happened over and over. It was real. He asked for my number and gave me his. He complimented my name, my singing. Feeling as light as an up quark, I prance toward the Toyota and even kiss my mom hello.

GABRIEL

SHE KNOWS Rach's hand span. God, I don't need this. I don't want to get all gooey over a girl, even if she can name the sonata I'm playing and make decent comments about my musicality. I could've played for her all day. To have someone want to listen and genuinely appreciate my playing....

I've shot way past cloud nine.

Trying not to mess up the accompaniment, I steal a glance at her and tune into her voice, that bright tone with just a touch of vibrato that makes her a pleasure to listen to. I wish the rest of the choir would shut the hell up and let her sing. Maybe she'd appreciate the matinée on Sunday. It's not like anyone else will be in the audience for me, and the worst she can say is that she's got better things to do—which she probably has.

This is the last thing I need, and yet I can't stop my feet as I walk out of the choir room and follow the girls to the parking lot. My heart's beating so fast I'm pretty sure it's going to sledgehammer straight out of my chest. Playing it cool, I approach Treasa and Jordan. Maybe asking her to the matinée is a stupid idea.

"What's your number?" I ask before I have a moment to reconsider. It's just a phone number, not an engagement ring, and I do have a legitimate reason for needing it. Having swapped numbers, I feel lighter and heavier, as if the extra contact on my phone is a ball and chain that makes me oddly happy.

"Did you ask her out?" Dirk asks as he waves to some blond chick sitting on the steps. She gives him the middle finger and a glare.

"No. Just got her number."

"See that one?" He nods toward middle-finger girl.

"She looks familiar." At least the conversation isn't about me and Treasa.

"That's Hannah."

"*The* Hannah? Hannah who gave you a blow job in grade seven?" I never believed Dirk's story.

"That's the one. We had the same orthodontist. She wouldn't kiss me because we both had braces but she blew me just fine."

"Treasa has braces."

"Cute." Dirk grins.

"In grade seven, did you even have anything to blow?" I ask before I'm sure I want to hear the answer.

"Hey." Dirk looks insulted. "Skinny guys have the biggest dicks." He grabs his crotch for emphasis. "Besides, I hit puberty early, and so did she." We light cigarettes and drive with the windows down while Emperor blasts out of the speakers.

DAMN THIS sonata! My teacher said it was ambitious. I don't need such a huge composition for my portfolio. I could write a few songs and a couple of pieces of counterpoint and still pass. That's not the point. I want to compose this piece to prove I can do it. Mom used to compose easy pieces for me when I was just starting to play piano, but I loved them and remember them all by heart.

My fingers slam a dissonant chord on the piano in frustration, and my father yells his displeasure from the kitchen where he's fighting with a chicken casserole. The first and third movements are nearing completion. It's the second movement that's proving impossible. First movements are easy—introduce the theme, modulate, recapitulate. And it's easy to write flashy third movements requiring technical brilliance by adding a bunch of runs and triplets, by complicating the themes present in the first movement. The ending is easy too, just add a few resounding chords that drive home the tonic, à la Beethoven. Second movements are more complicated. They're a transition, a metamorphosis. They're the struggle from the promise of the first movement to the realization of the third, and I have no idea how to write it.

Nathan calls after dinner to let me know about the change of time for tomorrow. Now it's my turn to pass that on to Treasa. I didn't think composing an SMS of around four hundred characters could prove more difficult than composing an entire sonata! After typing, clearing, and retyping several times, I hit send, beyond caring if the nuance of my question might be misinterpreted. I'm pretty sure it was innocuous enough, but girls have a way of twisting the meanings of the simplest words. I guess I'm worrying for nothing, though. It's been five minutes, and she still hasn't replied. Maybe I'm the one who misinterpreted things.

TREASA

NORMAL GIRLS my age are out on dates on a Friday night, holding hands while pretending to watch a movie, really just waiting for the moment the boy leans over to kiss them. Mom and Dad are watching some British comedy show from the eighties, Jordan's on a date with Bryce, and

Lethi and Sibo are away this weekend with their folks at the Dam, so I'm alone in my bedroom with fictional characters, trying hard not to let my story turn into a porno rooftop make out session. Sadly, not even Resa and Tristan are making me feel better. They've got each other while I've just got an overweight cat snoring at my feet. I put on some Creed, hoping to drown out the posh TV voices emanating from the lounge, and open my battered copy of Stephen Hawking's *A Brief History of Time*. I've read the chapter on black holes three times, and I'm still not sure I understand it all.

My phone vibrates, and I grab it with lightning reflexes. An SMS from Jordan rating Bryce a five-star kisser. Fantastic. I get another two from her in quick succession, each an ode to some aspect of Bryce's hotness. When my phone vibrates for the umpteenth time, I ignore it. Thinking about Jordan kissing makes me think about kissing Gabriel, which makes concentrating on quantum mechanics impossible. I slam shut Hawking's tome and return to my Resa-Tristan epic.

I know guys are meant to get turned on by two girls kissing, but is it normal for a girl to be turned on by the idea of two guys kissing? Slipping low in my desk chair, I close my eyes and let loose my imagination. The boys are kissing, tongues dancing, pulses racing…. My fingers meander up my thigh as Resa removes Tristan's shirt. My phone keeps flashing, an obnoxious reminder that Jordan's out having a good time with a real boy diminishing the power of my fantasy. Reluctantly, I open the message. It's not from Jordan. It's from Gabriel.

Hi Treasa, class starts half an hour later tmw. Hope 2 see u there. What r u doing 2nite?

He sent the message twelve minutes ago. Does he think I'm dissing him by not responding?

How do I answer that without sounding pathetic? With sweaty hands, it takes me another five minutes to craft a response.

Hey, will see u tmw. Family nite 2nite. Lame. Wat u doing? There's no way I'll admit to spending my night writing homoerotic fan fiction and almost masturbating.

I hit send. For four whole minutes I'm in agony, chewing my nails to the quick and staring at my phone. Just when I'm sure I'll spontaneously combust, he responds.

Home reading 2nite. U doing anything Sunday?

Wat u reading? I'm free Sunday.

Whitley Strieber's Communion. I'm playing in a matinée Sunday. Wanna come?

Oh. My. God. I think Gabriel just asked me out. If he wasn't already the most perfect guy ever, the fact that he's home on a Friday night reading a book about aliens just elevated him to godliness. My fingers tremble as I attempt to type a response that's not all capital letters and exclamation marks. Gabriel responds and sends me into manic glee.

Great! See u tmw. Sweet dreams.

Sweet dreams? You bet! I dance around my room, much to Riker's amusement. He tries to catch my feet, and I scoop him up, swirling him around in a pirouette until his claws make contact with my bare arms. He runs out of my room, and I shut the door behind him. Feeling more alive than I have in my entire life, I switch CDs, replacing Creed with Beethoven's Complete Piano Sonatas. I lie on my bed staring at Liam St. Clare, who looks enough like Gabriel to fulfill the fantasy, and close my eyes as Beethoven's Pathétique causes every hair on my body to stand at attention.

I imagine kissing those lips, my hands under his shirt. My hands slide down my own body exactly as I imagine Gabriel's might, if we ever got past first base. My fingers meander between my legs, and I can't believe anything could feel this good. In my mind, I'm kissing Gabriel, nibbling his pierced earlobe and inhaling the scent of his shampoo. In my mind, I see both of us like a third person narration, only it's not me, it's Tristan. Tristan and Gabriel make out, their hands under each other's shirts, faces flushed, and it's the most exquisite thing I've ever seen.

"DOES AN afternoon recital really count as a date?" Jordan asks as we walk toward Hall C.

"It definitely does."

"You got an outfit to wear?"

"I don't even know where this thing is yet." What the hell am I going to wear?

"What did your Mom say?" Jordan studies her neck in the mirror of her compact and applies another layer of foundation to the hickeys on her throat.

"Haven't said anything yet. Waiting for the details."

"I could come over tomorrow and help you get ready." She dusts beige powder over the honey foundation.

"Thanks. I'll let you know about times."

Jordan smiles and drops the makeup into her bag. "So it seems we've both got dates for the ball, then."

"You going to stick with Bryce for that long?"

"Ouch. I'm not that bad." She feigns indignation.

"How many guys did you kiss last year?"

"Too many to count." She bounces down the corridor and I follow. Her ponytail swings in time with her hips clad in Lycra yoga pants. How does Gabriel even see me when I'm standing next to Jordan?

The class is great, another sweaty series of takedowns, and this time I don't hold back, pinning her every time.

"Maybe you are from Kazar," Jordan huffs as I help her to her feet.

"Kazar?" Gabriel says. I didn't see him come over, too busy tackling Jordan to the mat. He hasn't been ignoring me, exactly, but he's been showing a couple of others the moves today, and I've been busy pretending not to be jealous.

"Ja, Ree here thinks—ow!"

I whisk Jordan's leg out from under her before she can embarrass me.

"Nice one." She gives me a wounded look from the mat.

"Sorry, just thought I'd try a surprise maneuver."

"Just don't hurt each other too badly." Gabriel gives me a grin before jogging back to the sensei.

"That hurt, you know." Jordan dusts off her bum.

"You were about to tell him I think I'm an alien."

"Don't you think a guy should know something like that before getting involved with a chick who could spontaneously sprout tentacles?"

"Not funny." I fold my arms and watch Gabriel get knocked down by his teacher.

"It's a little funny. Like he'd even believe it."

I give her a withering gaze and say nothing. The last thing I want Gabriel knowing is that I'm a total freak.

"I'm pretty sure his interest in aliens doesn't extend to dating one." My tone is icy.

"You take yourself too seriously." Jordan tries a slow-motion headlock roll on an imaginary assailant.

Maybe, and being an alien is pretty serious. What if I do have latent superpowers and end up hurting Gabriel? Do I honestly believe I'm an alien, or is there some more terrestrial explanation for feeling so uncomfortable in my own skin?

After class, we meet Sheryl by the pool again. At least it's a bit cooler today, with the promise of an afternoon thunderstorm. The clouds are gathered thick as meringue on the southern horizon. They're white for now. By five o'clock they'll turn black, making Jo'burg look like Mordor.

"Hey." Gabriel saunters over to us. "You guys did great." Damn, even his walk is sexy.

"Thank you, Sempai." Jordan flashes him a flawless smile, and I want to rip her head off. She's not supposed to be flirting, least of all when she's in a tummy-revealing strappy top and micro-miniskirt.

"So about tomorrow?" I ask before Gabriel spends too much time looking at Jordan and realizes he chose the wrong girl.

"Ja, so the concert's at two at the Stormhof Anglican Church."

"Is it a religious thing?" Jordan lies back on the pool chair, and Gabriel's gaze lingers a little too long on her bare belly and long legs.

"No, it's just the best venue. Matric music students from the area are performing. Kind of like a rehearsal for prelims."

"Should I meet you there?"

"I can pick you up, if you like. Both of you. Jordan, you're invited too." My world starts to crumble.

"Nah, I'm out with the boyfriend tomorrow." Jordan turns her head. "But thanks for the invite."

"No worries." Gabriel doesn't look all that disappointed, so maybe he was just being polite, inviting her as well. "So, meeting there, or...?"

"I'll check with my mom and let you know."

"Cool." Gabriel gives us a toothy smile. "Chat later, then."

"For sure." My scalp prickles with warmth and anticipation as Gabriel lopes toward the parking lot. I watch him walk, the way the motion seems to come from his knees and not his hips. With practice, I bet I could walk like that too.

"So, you want me to come over around twelve, then?" Jordan asks.

"What about Bryce?"

"You can be super dense, Ree. I don't have plans tomorrow." She gets to her feet and rearranges her skirt.

"Thanks. I appreciate it."

"And?" She purses her lips and taps her foot.

"And, I'm sorry about before."

"Damn straight. I'm the best, best friend you'll ever have, and don't forget it." She slings her arm around my shoulder and gives me a hug. I love her, I love her with a clarity of emotion I've never felt for anyone else. Not the effervescent hyperventilating emotion I've felt for cute boys and am starting to feel for Gabriel, but that warm from-head-to-toes kind of love that makes her more like a sister than a friend.

GABRIEL

"IT'S A date," Dirk says.

"It's not."

"Do those hurt?" He jabs a finger into the bruise blossoming across my ribs from class yesterday.

I grab his hand and start squeezing. "Does this?"

"I know he's irritating, but please try not to break my son's fingers." Dirk's mom hands me my shirt. It's still warm from the iron. Apparently, no self-respecting young man can perform at a recital dressed in a creased shirt. My aunt's laundry lessons didn't extend to ironing, and I don't think we've owned an iron since Mom died, anyway.

"Thanks, Ma," Dirk says, only to get cuffed over the back of the head.

"Stop teasing him," she says. I button up my shirt, and she starts doing my tie before I can object. "You need a haircut, sweetheart."

"I like it like this."

"It's very Jimmy Eat World," Dirk adds.

"Thanks," I say with sarcasm so thick you could cut it with a knife and head to Dirk's bathroom in search of gel and a comb.

Ja, I've gone and done it. I stare at the guy in the mirror with slicked-back hair and a cleanly shaved face. It's only a matinée, but Dirk's right, this feels a lot like a date. The only thing that matters is my performance. Playing from memory can always be problematic. It's so easy to lose track of where you are, to mess up and look like a complete moron. Playing with music is worse. I hate having a page turner, someone literally looking over my shoulder and noticing every imprecision. Trying to play and turn your own pages is a different kind of nightmare altogether.

MY FATHER won't be there. I put a note on the fridge, marking the date and time of my concert with yellow highlighter. No way he could've missed it, though he's made no comment about it. Just once, I'd like him to lose the ego and listen to his moffie son play. Or does having a son who plays piano automatically diminish his manhood as well?

Dirk and his family can't make it today; they've got to trek out to Pretoria for his ouma's eightieth. At least my father let me borrow the bakkie—he's spending the afternoon fertilizing his precious flowerbeds—otherwise I'd be walking to and from the church.

"Hey, bru, we've got to go." Dirk bangs on the bathroom door. He gives me a stupid grin when I emerge. "Well, don't you clean up nice."

Marlize skips into the kitchen and stops short when she sees me. "Wow, when did you get so hot?"

I'm not sure how to take that coming from a twelve-year-old. Being Dirk's sister, she's probably more grown-up than most, even if she still plays sparkle pony PlayStation games.

"Don't you even think about it." Dirk shakes his fist at her.

"Maybe if you worked out more, you'd have a bod like that." She purses her lips and gestures to all of me with a wave of her pink-nailed hand. I don't know where to look.

"I better get going." Before Marlize can further embarrass me. The whole family comes to see me off, telling me to break a leg and knock them dead, et cetera.

I drive in silence, playing the sonata over and over in my head, visualizing the trickier passages and fingering them on the steering wheel. Inviting Treasa was a dumb idea. Now there's extra pressure on me not just to play well, but to play brilliantly, because as much as I might deny it to Dirk, I do actually want to impress her.

TREASA

THE STORM started yesterday afternoon, tearing through our garden and ripping Dad's carefully quaffed trees and shrubs to shreds. It hailed too, turning the lawn into a frozen carpet of projectiles. The rain lasted all night, thunder rattling the windows in their frames while lightning kept making the landline ping. When I was little, Mom used to tell me it was God playing marbles with the angels. Celestial war would've been more appropriate.

The storm has kept me awake, not that I was going to be able to sleep anyway. My alarm clock flashes 4:45 and lightning illuminates my room before another crash of thunder sends Riker scurrying up the bed in search of my face.

At least Mom said yes to the matinée. Of course, she's taking me and waiting in the car and driving me home. At least I'll still get to see Gabriel and hear him play. Taking it slow isn't a bad thing. I've never really had a boyfriend, unless you count Dennis in grade six. We dated for a whole eight hours before he told me he wasn't ready for a serious commitment. There was Trent in grade eight, my first kiss, and it was awful. He clearly didn't own a toothbrush, and the entire time he had his tongue in my mouth, all I could taste was the Bovril sandwich he'd had for lunch. Gabriel's older, and he's probably had plenty of practice kissing girls. I haven't had any practice. What if I'm a terrible kisser, and he tries to kiss me and I do the wrong thing? What if my braces put him off and he doesn't even want to kiss me? I fall asleep imagining all the horrible ways our first kiss might not even happen.

"YOU HAVEN'T been on a first date yet, and you're worried about kissing him?" Jordan sits on my bed, watching me fight with my hair.

"How do you know if you're a good kisser?"

"People tell you."

"I've only ever kissed one guy." I twist and pin a strand into place.

"Really?" She looks at me in the mirror. "Trent in grade eight?"

"Yup."

"That's depressing."

"Tell me about it." I examine my makeup. It's not much, but at least the foundation quiets the riot of freckles across my face, and the mascara accentuates my otherwise pale eyes.

"You need to practice." Jordan swings her legs over the edge of the bed.

"On who?"

"Me, of course."

"You want me to kiss you?" I do a final twist at the back and jam in half a dozen pins.

"Not particularly, but I'm willing to do this for the good cause of improving your kissing skills."

"Are you serious?"

She rolls her eyes and spins me around on the wheelie chair. "Stand up." Jordan places a hand on my waist and another on my neck. "Lean in slowly and just let your lips touch." She does, and her lips are sticky with gloss. "Then you pull back a little and gaze into each other's eyes." We do, and a startling warmth spreads up from my belly as she places my hands on her waist. "Then you go in for the real deal."

She kisses me, her lips slightly parted, and then her tongue slips between my teeth and she tastes of toothpaste and strawberry lip gloss. I pull her closer and kiss her back. Her fingers tighten on my neck, and we're getting really into it. Too into it. I'm not sure who freaks out first. We both pull away and don't say anything for a few awkward moments.

"You'll be fine," Jordan says as she twirls a strand of dark hair around her finger. "You're not a bad kisser. Definitely room for improvement, but certainly not bad." Her face is uncharacteristically flushed, and her hands are shaking as she reapplies lip gloss.

"Resa, we're going to be late." Mom walks in. "Wow, you look lovely."

"Thank you." In tight three-quarter jeans and a fitted T-shirt, I feel like a turkey dressed for the pot. Jordan wanted me to wear a skirt. Thankfully, the storm last night turned into set-in rain, and the day is too cool for bare legs. Not that I'd be caught dead in a skirt unless it's a school uniform. The bum-floss thong Jordan insisted I wear is already annoying me. Why can't I just be a guy and wear boxers and baggie jeans and not have to worry about matching my bra to my panties, or what the color of my underwear might reveal about my sex life when I have no sex life at all!

"Can I give you a ride home, Jordan?"

"Thanks, Mrs. Prescott."

It's been almost three years, and Mom still won't tell Jordan to call her Melissa. I pull on my All Stars and work the laces back into the shoe around my foot.

"Why don't you ever wear sandals?" Mom gripes as we head to the car.

"Because I like my takkies." Sandals? In what universe, Mother?

Mom thinks better of getting into an argument and swallows whatever comment she was going to make next. We drop Jordan off first, leaving Mom and me alone for the ten-minute trip to the church.

"How are your ears?" Mom asks over the Madonna song playing on the radio.

"Healing. Still a bit tender, but they'll be fine."

"Jordan was sweet to come over today."

"She's not the monster you imagine."

"I didn't...." Mom sighs. "Why is it that every conversation feels like I'm waging a war with you?"

I say nothing and keep staring out the window, watching raindrops slither across the glass. We pull into the church. There are a lot of people here.

"I should come in with you."

"Mom, I think I can manage a five-meter walk by myself."

Mom purses her lips. I fling open the door and dash through the drizzle into the church before Mom can change her mind and demand to walk in holding my hand like I'm a toddler.

There's a signpost pointing away from the actual church to an events hall. I pass several other teenagers, all wearing uniforms. Oops.

"Treasa." Gabriel separates from a group of Stormhof students and joins me outside the hall, under the dripping eaves. His hair is combed back and slicked down with gel. He smells like soap and aftershave, a dizzying combination.

"Was I supposed to wear my uniform?" Might as well have tentacles coming out of my butt since everyone's staring at me, the only one in civvies.

"I forgot to mention that, but don't worry. It's a government school thing, anyway, so you won't get into trouble. Here." He hands me a rain-spattered program. He's playing second to last out of thirty performers.

"They save the best for last, right?"

"Something like that." He grins, and there's a hint of arrogance in his stance I find kind of sexy. The Stormhof Matrics walk past, chatting in Afrikaans. I don't catch all of what they say, but there's a comment about Catholic schoolgirls that makes them all laugh, Gabriel included. The familiar warmth of a blush wends its way up my throat. I gulp in a lungful of rain-cooled air and banish the blood from my face.

"I've got to sit with the performers, but I'll see you after the concert." He touches my arm as he says it.

"Sure." His touch is like a brand.

He catches up to his schoolmates, and they disappear inside. Alone and feeling horribly conspicuous, I find a spot at the back, hoping no one will notice me. I actually wish Jordan had come today. For a moment I even consider going to get my mom so I won't have to sit alone. Then the first player gets up and performs something by Bach on the violin.

An hour and a half later, Gabriel goes to the piano. A hush falls over the hall as he raises his hands in preparation for the first note. For the next six minutes, I am enthralled by his fingers, by his body as it moves to the music, his shoulders bunching with every powerful chord. His fingers fly across the keys and his foot pumps the pedal. He closes his eyes before he starts the second movement, and so do I, imagining myself at the piano, imagining the keys beneath my fingers, what it must feel like to be that good at something, that flawless. Too soon, the heartbreaking movement comes to a close, and a few irritating members of the audience actually clap.

Gabriel cracks his knuckles before launching into the third. I close my eyes again, just listening. Somewhere in the middle of the piece, where the runs turn fiendish, the notes slip out of control, and my eyes flash open as Gabriel fudges a trill and ends on a dissonant chord. He clenches his jaw, his eyebrows gathered in a tight frown as he fights to regain control of the music. He recovers, and the rest of the piece is pure perfection. He brings the sonata to a crashing end, and the audience bursts into applause, some even whistling. Despite the audience's approval, Gabriel bows and leaves the stage without even the faintest wisp of a smile.

The final performer steps up, a black girl who's singing an aria from *The Magic Flute*. My attention is on Gabriel as he sits dead still amongst his peers. The girl's voice slices straight through me as she nails the super high notes of the aria. The audience gives the girl a standing ovation. Gabriel rises too, and so do I, if only to keep him within my view.

Afterward, I wait for him under the eaves. The rain has stopped, and the sun is prying its way through the clouds.

"Hi." He sounds deflated, his shoulders sagging.

"You were brilliant."

"No, I wasn't." He stuffs his hands into his pockets.

"Oh, come on, you made one tiny mistake." My attempt at lightening his mood is met with a scowl.

"Now you know why I'm second to last." He turns and walks away.

"Wait." I run after him and grab his arm. He tenses, and my heart lurches. "I just meant that one wonky trill shouldn't take away from the perfection of the rest of it. Interpretation and expression is more important than technical precision anyway, right?"

He regards me for a moment with eyes far too green. Then his lips twitch up into a smile. "You want to go for coffee or something?"

"You're not with your friends?"

"No."

"Wait, my mom's here. I can't just leave."

"Oh, okay." Dejection mars his face.

"Would you mind coming with me while I ask her?"

"Why not?"

We pick our way past puddles to Mom's Toyota, and I tap on the window, startling her from a nap. Gabriel waves, and Mom rolls down the window.

"Mom, this is Gabriel, the pianist."

"Nice to meet you, Gabriel."

"Afternoon, ma'am." Gabriel shakes Mom's hand through the window.

"I hear you're quite the star—black belt karate, pianist, and academic, I see."

Star? Where does Mom get this stuff, and why do I tell her anything when all she ever does is embarrass me? Gabriel, however, seems to be preening in the wake of the compliment.

"I was wondering, ma'am, if it would be all right with you for me to take Treasa for coffee."

"Oh, now?" Mom looks at me and I nod, hoping she says yes. "You drive?"

"Yes, ma'am. We'd only be going to the Mugg & Bean up the road."

Mom looks at me again, and I hope she can read the pleading I'm trying to etch into my expression.

"Sounds lovely, but she needs to be home by six."

Six? Really? My usual curfew on school nights is eight. I'm not going to throw a tantrum in front of Gabriel, and Mom knows it. She reaches for her wallet and hands me a twenty-rand note. We've only got two hours; it's better than nothing.

"Thanks, Mom."

"You're welcome, Treasa." There's an edge in her voice I don't understand, even as she smiles and watches us walk over to an old bakkie before pulling out of the parking lot.

"This your car?" I ask as Gabriel opens the passenger door for me.

"My father's. Just borrowing it for the day."

"Oh, where are your folks?"

"Not here." There's finality in his response, and I don't press the matter. The bakkie smells like pine air freshener. Bar-One wrappers and an empty Fanta bottle litter the floor.

"Sorry about the mess." He chucks the bottle into the back seat. "Pick some music."

The CD wallet he hands me is faded and scuffed. I flip through the albums, mostly rock and heavy metal by bands I don't know. Half the names I can't even read. The last CD is Marilyn Manson's *Mechanical Animals*. I've never listened to Manson, but it's probably the safest choice. I slip that into the CD player, and moments later, eerie guitar reverberates through the car before the strained vocals start. I actually like it. Gabriel grins and pulls a cigarette box out of his blazer pocket.

"Do you mind?"

I shake my head as he lights up.

"Won't you get into trouble, being in uniform?"

"Ja, but that's only if someone sees me... or reports me." He gives me a sideways glance before putting the car into reverse.

"I'm not going to," I promise.

"I hardly ever smoke, anyway. It's a disgusting habit."

"Why smoke at all, then?" I roll down my window to escape the pall of nicotine.

"Because...." He pauses. "I think it helps relax me when I'm feeling pissed off."

"Does it?"

"Not as much as taking pretty girls out to coffee." He gives me a cocky grin and blows smoke out of his window.

Even though he kind of just called me pretty, I can't help wonder how many girls he's taken out for coffee, and if I'm just the Catholic schoolgirl conquest to be checked off his list. What bugs me even more is that I'm not sure I care if I am.

BY THE time we get to Mugg & Bean, I'm in love with Manson's voice and lyrics. The chorus of "Great Big White World" keeps playing in my head, and it's comforting to know that another person on the planet gets the way I feel, like there's this haze obscuring the world, and I wish I had a gigantic bottle of turpentine to wash away the grime and see the truth behind the veil.

We sit at a table in the back. I head for the corner seat and so does Gabriel. Propriety wins, and he pulls the chair out for me. He orders a latte and asks me if I want to share a muffin. I'd share anything with him right now.

"So, tell me something." He gouges his fork through the colossal blueberry cake.

"Like what?" I take a sip of cappuccino.

"Something about you. I know you sing in the choir and that you like aliens." He smiles, revealing a sliver of inner lip stained blueberry purple. "You read about composers, and I guess you're Catholic, being at St. Bridget's."

"Um...." I take a moment to collect my thoughts, to quash the impulse to tell him I think I'm an alien, to resist the urge to ask him if my being a Catholic schoolgirl is the only reason I'm here. Although the idea of fulfilling some sordid fantasy of his doesn't sound too bad. Bobby socks and pigtails? For Gabriel, I'd do that.

"I used to play piano," I say.

"How far did you get?"

"Twinkle Twinkle."

He laughs, and the tension keeping his shoulders bunched seems to drain, letting him slide lower in his chair.

"You going to study music next year?" I stab a blueberry with my fork, hoping they won't become permanent fixtures in the wires on my teeth. Gabriel doesn't say anything, his expression clouded by ineffable emotion. "Sorry, did I say the wrong thing?"

"No, it's just...." He slurps up latte and licks froth from his upper lip dusted with the shadow of stubble. Damn, he's gorgeous. "I'd love to study music, but...."

"But?"

"My father doesn't approve."

"But you're like the next Ashkenazy!"

"I'd rather be the next Horowitz." He fiddles with his serviette, shredding the logo printed on the corner.

"So, what are you going to do, then?"

"Engineering, probably." He doesn't look happy about it, and I don't know him well enough to press the issue.

"I'm thinking of doing a BA."

"Bugger all?" He grins.

I snort my coffee and cough up a blueberry. So sexy. Don't think I've ever laughed this much with anyone, let alone a guy.

"Is that what they call it?"

"So I hear." He takes another bite of muffin before pushing the plate and last few pieces across the table to me.

"I'd love to do astronomy, it's fascinating, but I suck at actual science. I'm good at history and languages, though." Don't want to sound like a complete idiot in front of Mr. Academic Colors here.

"So BA history, then?"

"Anthropology, maybe."

"You want to study people?" He seems surprised.

"It might help me understand why we're all so messed up."
Awkward. He studies the shreds of the serviette and makes no comment.
"So how come you're doing a licentiate, then?"

The question makes him cringe. Great. I'm on such a roll. He shreds
some more of the serviette before answering. "I'm not actually doing it,
more like preparing to do it. I don't have the theory grade to take the
practical exam yet. Maybe I'll be a teacher one day. Reckon if I can find a
teaching job, then I can ditch engineering and support myself doing what I
want."

"You're too good to teach. You're a performer."

His sardonic laughter makes me wish I'd never opened my big fat
mouth.

"I could be a performer if I had more time to practice, but between
academics, karate, and rugby next term, I don't get enough time."

"You play rugby?" Not a game I've ever understood the allure of.
Looks like a bunch of troglodytes running around in spandex after a
misshapen egg. Dad wasn't impressed when I told him that, and I'm not
going to tell Gabriel that either.

"It was the deal. If I play rugby, I can play piano." He crushes the
remains of the serviette in his fist. "Would've preferred playing cricket,
but that's not manly enough or something."

"That's a pity. You look so good in white." The words slip out of my
mouth. "I mean, you know, in karate. It's just—" I bite my tongue hard to
shut myself up.

Gabriel gives me a smile, the soft one that actually touches his eyes.
"Thanks," he says. "You play a sport?"

"Tennis, sort of. And hockey. But I'm not that great at ball sports."

"Me neither, much to my father's embarrassment." There's a dollop
of bitterness in his voice.

"Parents don't get it at all," I say.

"No, they don't."

We share a long look across muffin crumbs, and there's a lot more
going on behind his emerald eyes. There's sadness there, and anger, and a
sort of longing I can relate to even though I don't completely understand
it. Gabriel longs to play piano and study music; what am I longing for?
My alien space daddy to swoop down in his spaceship and warp-speed me
to some distant planet?

He checks his watch. "It's five thirty."

The waiter brings the bill and I take out my wallet.

"Ag, don't be silly." Gabriel pays, leaving a generous tip.

"Thank you, but—"

"Next time it can be on you." He gives me that smile I'd like to believe is reserved just for me, and my blood turns to sherbet, fizzing happiness into every extremity. There'll be a next time. I can't help smiling as we walk out together, the left side of my body acutely aware of his presence, with mere millimeters and two layers of fabric separating our skin. He takes my hand, and the world tilts on its axis as my knees turn to marshmallow. By the time we get to the car and he releases my fingers, my pulse thunders in my ears and my whole body feels like it's on fire in a tingly, pleasant kind of way.

ON THE drive home, he smokes another cigarette and we chat about *Project Blue Book*, about Stephen Hawking, quasars, Graham Hancock, and the chances of government conspiracies hiding evidence of alien life on earth. Our conversation makes me less certain about my extraterrestrial origins, which is a good thing because I'm already imagining kissing Gabriel, and maybe more, and would hate to spontaneously sprout tentacles from some embarrassing orifice.

Too soon, he pulls into my driveway.

"Thank you, Gabriel. I had a really good time."

"I love the way you say it."

"Say what?"

"My name. Gay-briel," he mimics. "I hate being *Ghar*-briel."

The Afrikaans pronunciation makes it sound harsh and guttural. Not a name for an angel, and definitely not for the boy sitting beside me.

"It's a beautiful name."

"Thanks." He gives me that smile I think I'm falling in love with, never mind the rest of the boy it's attached to. "So I'll see you Thursday?"

"Absolutely." I hesitate as I open the door, on the off chance he may want to kiss me. He looks down, and I guess that's a sign there'll be no kissing today, or ever? Of course, I'm totally gross, having just eaten. I run my tongue over my braces, hoping to dislodge remnants of muffin. Good, my teeth are crumb-free.

Feeling deflated, I get out and traipse toward my front door.

"Wait!" Gabriel lopes after me. "You should have this." He hands me *Mechanical Animals*.

"Have it?"

"Let's call it indefinite borrowing. I've got three other Manson albums, but this is his best so far."

I take the CD, and our fingers brush together before he ambles back to the bakkie. No kisses for me, then. Maybe he doesn't want to kiss me; maybe I'll be relegated once again to friend status as he pursues prettier, skirt-wearing, normal girls. Still, he gave me his CD, and that counts for something, right?

GABRIEL

TREASA UPSETS my equilibrium in ways I can't even begin to quantify. She's beautiful in that classic, almost mythological kind of way, like a teenage Boudicca. More than that, I actually want to talk to her. Usually, I'm just happy to sit around listening to girls babble about the mundane before they're ready to make out. With Karla, we'd sit around listening to metal, commenting on the riff or drumming, then we'd make out or have sex, and it never got more personal than that. I didn't want it to. Treasa is different. Even though our time together was brief, I feel like I can tell her things. I want to tell her things, and I want her to tell me things, meaningful things, the things that make her who she is. What the fuck is wrong with me?

I could've kissed her, cigarette breath and all. She would've let me too. I just couldn't. Not in my father's bakkie in her parents' driveway. She deserves better than that. She deserves someone better than me. The way she looks at me, like I'm the only person in the room, like I'm the only boy she's ever been with, like she's seeing not who I am, but who I could be; it's terrifying.

Maybe pouring all of this onto paper will help me figure out what's going on inside my messed-up skull.

Dear Mom,

I've met a girl, and I don't know what to do about it. She scares me, in a good way, I guess. I think you'd like her. She has a really good voice, and she's easy to talk to. I never thought I'd say a girl gets me, but this one seems to. It's early days still. Maybe she'd be happy just being friends. More than that and I don't think I'll cope. I wish you were here to talk to because....

My father knocks on my bedroom door and opens it before I get a chance to answer.

"I thought I told you to mow the lawn," he says. He glances around my bedroom, his gaze lingering on the poster of Manson before focusing on my face. I stuff the letters back into their shoe box and shove it under my bed before he asks what I'm doing and demands to see the pages and discovers the photographs.

"I was busy."

"You sure as hell look it." My father raps his knuckles against my doorframe.

"I was playing at a concert today. There was a note on the fridge about it."

He stares at me, a vein throbbing at his temple.

"That grass won't cut itself."

"Did you even hear what I said?"

"What I heard was another excuse about why you can't do your chores." He points a finger at me.

"I'm not your slave."

"You want to live under my roof and eat the food I put on the table, you can damn well mow the flippin' grass. Now!" He takes a menacing step toward the bed.

"But it's after eight on a Sunday night."

"Now." He waits while I pull on my takkies.

"Mom would've been at my concert." We're standing face-to-face, the difference in height negligible. My father might've been a brawny rugby player once, but now all that muscle has turned to flab and *beerboep.* "Why weren't you there?"

"Watch it, Gabriel. That piano would make good firewood."

"That was Mom's piano." I can't believe he'd ever do anything to damage the piano. "Did you even remember that? Do you even remember your dead wife at all?"

He slaps me twice. Palm and backhand. My lip splits across my bottom teeth, and I taste blood. With cheeks smarting and involuntary tears welling in my eyes, I push past him and sprint to the garage. Sure, I'll cut his fucking grass. I drag the lawn mower out into the dark garden. The tank is full, and the engine starts with three tugs on the crankshaft. Amidst a haze of petrol fumes, I push the mower around the lawn and across the flowerbeds my father so fastidiously tends. Mom loved these flowers too. I don't care. I just need to destroy something beautiful.

AM I AN ALIEN, TREASA TEST #04

HYPOTHESIS: Extraterrestrials possess superhuman abilities such as controlling electrical circuits.

GOAL: To prove I can control electric circuits such as the lights at robots—red to green.

METHOD:
>   While in car, pull up to red robot.
>   Concentrate on changing the red light to green.
>   Change should be almost instantaneous to qualify.

RESULTS: On the drive home from school with Mom, three red robots were encountered. Of those, only one successfully changed immediately after concentration of energy was aimed at it.

CONCLUSION: Partial evidence for control of electric circuits under certain conditions. Caveat: Lights may have been about to change anyway, and multitasking (concentrating on conversation with Mom and controlling the traffic lights) may place too much strain on my abilities.

TREASA

OF COURSE he didn't kiss you, Jordan informs me by scrawling a pencil message in the margin of her French book.

Why? I write back, trying to concentrate on the conversation we're meant to be listening to.

He smokes. Did he have mints?

No.

So he had ashtray breath. Therefore no kissing! She goes over the exclamation mark several times to drive home her point.

I didn't think of that. Poor guy was just being considerate, which only confirms his godliness. Can a guy really be this perfect?

Buy some Tic Tacs, Jordan scrawls, and I make a mental note to do just that, in case another opportunity for kissing should present itself.

How do you know if you're in love? I write.

Jordan turns her chuckle into a cough as our hawkeyed French teacher gives us a disapproving glare.

You just know, she writes.

Make a list?

Jordan turns to a clean page in her book, and I tune into the conversation between a kid and his mother. Something about what he should buy at the grocery store. I've missed most of it, and who can think about tomatoes and bananas when there's an angelic boy to daydream about? Angels. They could be aliens. The way the angel Gabriel appeared to Mary is a lot like how people have described close encounters of the third kind. Bright lights, strange beings—does that mean Mary was impregnated by aliens and that Jesus walked on water because he was really from another planet?

Jordan nudges my arm with the corner of her book, ending all heretical speculation. I read the list:

Warm fuzzies?—check

Guy seems perfect?—he is

You feel weird around him (weak, dizzy, warm etc.)?—of course

You can't stop thinking about him?—check

You dream about him?—check

You're counting the seconds til you see him again?—check

You type sms's to him, but can't decide whether to send them or not?—maybe

You check your phone twenty times a minute waiting for an sms?—maybe

He's the hottest thing ever and you'd like to do bad things to him?—Jordan!

You feel all floaty and giggly for no apparent reason?—check

I pass the list back to her, and she smiles as she whispers, "You're in love, Ree."

The conversation about tomatoes ends, and I waft through the rest of the lesson. Not even the never-ending list of verb conjugations can get me down. Gabriel. I'll only see him again in three days. The waiting is the worst. At least there's an episode of *Project Blue Book* to look forward to in the meantime.

I'VE PRACTICED the walk for two hours and still can't get it right. Are guys' legs even connected to their hips at all? How do they walk from the knees without getting that swaying movement in their hips? It's impossible. My thighs and bum muscles burn from pacing up and down my bedroom in guy mode and listening to Manson when I should be doing homework. Even when I concentrate on altering my center of gravity, sinking low and flicking out my feet, I end up looking like a Neanderthal with a limp. It's not even remotely close to how Gabriel walks, how effortlessly he carries himself, all broad shoulders and straight back and narrow hips that don't go sashaying all over the place. Damn hips, damn boobs, damn double-X chromosomes!

Too sore to keep it up, I collapse in my chair and open up the Word document I've been working on. It's not even a coherent story anymore—and definitely not something I can hand in to my English teacher—just a collection of scenes I wish would manifest in real life. I'll have to write something more PG for school.

"WHAT IF we get caught?" Tristan scanned the corridors for prowling teachers. The whole point of being on Earth was to blend in and

disappear, to act human, to stay off the intergalactic radar until the political situation cooled down on Kazar and an extraction team was sent to retrieve the emperor.

"What are they gonna do? Scramble our DNA and exile us to some primitive planet?" Resa grinned and grabbed Tristan by the shirt, dragging him into the janitor's closet.

"But—" Tristan's protests were silenced by a crush of lips and tongue. Resa tasted like orange Tic Tacs (do they have Tic Tacs in America?), sweet and fresh and not at all like the menthol cigarette he'd insisted on smoking before class to solidify his bad-boy status in front of the cheerleaders. But the cheerleaders weren't the ones getting dragged into a closet for a make-out session, and that made Tristan smile as his hands slid beneath Resa's shirt....

"WHAT ARE you listening to?" Mom startles me as she walks into my room with a pile of clean laundry.

"Um, just a CD Gabriel gave me." Surreptitiously, I slide the surreal, genderless album cover under a pile of papers so Mom won't see it and freak out. She cocks her head, listening to lyrics about drugs and suicide. I save and close the scene I've been writing. Best Mom doesn't read my homoerotic fan fiction.

"You like this?" She folds her arms, clearly unimpressed.

"It's not bad." I shrug. Like it? I bloody love it.

"And this is the music Gabriel listens to?" Her eyebrows form perfect arches.

"When he's not listening to Beethoven and Chopin."

Mom sits on my bed, and Riker joins her. "Do you like this boy?"

"I think so."

"He's older."

"He's only just turned eighteen." His birthday's January tenth, making him Capricorn, which is a great match to my being Cancer, or so says the Zodiac Matchmaker column in one of Mom's magazines.

"And eighteen-year-old boys have one-track minds, Resa."

I roll my eyes. We haven't even kissed yet.

"Treasa, this is serious. I don't want you to throw your life away over some boy."

"How is having feelings for Gabriel throwing my life away?" I fold my arms over my chest.

"I don't want you pressured into something you can't handle. That's all."

"You mean pressured into sex? And of course I'll end up pregnant, because that's what happens to all ignorant teenagers. Mom, I've known about condoms since grade four."

"Are you sleeping with this boy?" Mom's voice is choked, and her eyes shine as if she's about to cry.

"No!" Not that I wouldn't. I mean... would I? And just how does Mom think we've wrangled the logistics to find somewhere private enough to have sex? Like I'd do it on school property or in the back of Gabriel's bakkie, because that's just so bloody romantic. Honestly, mother!

"Has he asked you to?" Mom's fingers wrap around the edge of my duvet.

"He hasn't even asked me to kiss him. I think my virginity is safe, possibly forever."

Mom exhales a relieved breath that only irritates me. Doesn't she want me to be in love and have moonlight kisses and possibly, maybe, one day make love to some perfect boy with beautiful eyes and a ripped body like all the pop songs suggest I should?

"I just don't want you to be in a situation you can't handle, sweetheart."

"I'm fine, Mom. I go to self-defense training, remember?"

A fleeting smile sprints across her face. "You're enjoying that?"

"A lot."

"I'm glad." Mom gives Riker a final pat before standing up to leave.

"Mom?"

She pauses at my door.

"I was wondering if I could start taking piano lessons again."

"Really?" She arches a single eyebrow at me this time.

"I know we don't have a piano anymore, but I could practice at school."

"Does Gabriel have something to do with this?"

"Listening to him play just made me miss it, is all."

"And how much would that cost, Resa? You're already taking the martial arts class." Jordan only paid for the first one.

"I know." I chew on my bottom lip when an idea goes supernova. "What if I asked Gabriel to teach me? He's doing his teacher's licentiate, so he probably wouldn't charge as much, if at all." I exaggerate a little.

Mom gives me a long, hard look, and I know she must be thinking this is just a ploy to spend more time with him, which it isn't, although I'll hardly complain about that if she says yes.

"Let me discuss this with your father and we'll see. Fair?"

I nod and listen to Mom's footsteps retreating down the passage, headed toward the kitchen. I check my phone for an SMS. Nothing, so I turn up the volume on Manson and return to my blushworthy descriptions of Resa and Tristan making out in the janitor's closet. It's a real pity we have neither boys nor janitor's closets at St. Bridget's.

GABRIEL

MY FATHER won't even look at me since I annihilated the geraniums. He hates me, probably as much as I hate him. I guess we deserve each other.

Jean-Pierre got a car when he turned eighteen. A crappy old Nissan. At least he still had wheels and freedom. Not me. Apparently, it's because my father can't afford it, given my expensive extramurals, but I bet it's his passive-aggressive way of punishing me. If I made it into first-team rugby, I'd probably come home to find a brand-new car waiting for me in the driveway.

Dirk had to take his ouma to the dentist this afternoon, so I either had to walk twenty kilometers to the dojo or skip karate. I really could've done with an hour of letting people hit me. Maybe I'll pick a fight with my father when he gets home and let him give me a black eye this time.

My lip is still a bit swollen, but doesn't look half as bad as it felt. No one even asked me what happened. I do karate—injuries are inevitable.

With my father still at work, I turn to the piano and run my fingers over the wood, tracing the grain. The piano is ancient. It was Mom's when she was a child, and now it's mine. It used to have old-fashioned candelabra on the front. Mom had those removed and the holes filled in.

She said she hated the idea of fire anywhere near the wooden instrument or her sheet music.

I start with Bach but can't stay in control of the fingering. I move on to Beethoven; disaster. Next is Schumann, and I give up on the first crescendo. My heart's not in it, my thoughts totally *deurmekaar*, and it's all Treasa's fault. I want to SMS her, though that seems a bit desperate. Last thing I want to do is to encourage her, to lead her on and make too much of this, whatever it is. I don't want a girlfriend. I've never been in love, and if it is as ridiculous as all those Hollywood movies make it out to be, then I don't think I ever want to be in love. Focus, that's what I need. Focus and two hundred sit-ups....

At midnight, I remember I've got a physics test tomorrow. Even if I fail it, I'll still end up with at least a B average since I've had As all year. I turn on my lamp and drag my schoolbag onto the bed. I wonder if Treasa's still awake? Focus, damn it.

At 2:00 a.m. I slam my textbook shut and pull out my sonata instead. If Treasa refuses to get out of my head, then I might as well make the most of the distraction and let her inspire the chaotic harmony of the second movement. I let the music flow chromatically until the section comes to a close on a Tristan chord, the augmented intervals exquisitely painful to my ears. My music teacher is going to hate this. I think Treasa might love it.

Treasa

So sick of this school! Now it's all roses and hearts and squeals of delight as girls place their orders for Valentine's Day. Every year it's the same torturous event for people like me, people who don't know any boys, let alone plan on sending or receiving a Valentine.

Candyce and Hannah hog the order sheets pinned to the board at the front of the classroom, discussing whether to send chocolate hearts or fake roses to their crushes at St. Adrian's and Cosmas and half a dozen other boys' schools on the list. Whatever caused the rift between them a few weeks ago, they seem to be BFFs again.

"You sending Bryce anything?" Lethi asks Jordan as we grab our lunch bags and head out for some fresh air.

"If I was, it certainly wouldn't be this cheap-ass cheesy crap." Jordan gestures to a poster of the items available for the interschool Valentine's Day swap.

"Think he'll send you anything?" I ask as we wend our way toward the shade. A rain bird warbles ominously, as if it wasn't a foregone conclusion we'd have a storm by five o'clock today.

"He better." Jordan grins. "I expect at least a dozen roses. Real ones. Delivered to the school."

"Seriously?" Sibo raises her eyebrows.

"Girl can dream, can't she?" Jordan shrugs, and the conversation thankfully turns from Valentine's Day to the English test we've got next week.

I hate Valentine's Day. It should be a day of mourning, considering the poor dude got martyred on February fourteenth. Instead we scrawl inanities on cards and eat chocolate; how worthy you are of love defined by how many roses some boy at some school sends some silly girl who thinks that even matters. Still, I wish I were one of those girls, the ones with flowers from boys, and not the girl in the back row with a melting chocolate heart courtesy of her best friend.

GABRIEL ARRIVES a minute late to choir practice. He looks exhausted, with purple rings under his eyes, which seem less starry than usual, and dark stubble along his jaw. His lip is a bit swollen, and his shoulders are slumped, making him look shorter than his 180 centimeters. He still plays beautifully, and Mrs. McArthur is all smiles and compliments.

Afterward, I walk with him to his friend's car. The tar is so hot my feet are burning. Hot enough to fry an egg on, Dad would say. Dirk plays imaginary drums on his steering wheel, completely ignoring us. Metal by a band I don't know spills out of the rolled-down windows, reverberating around the parking lot. Dirk doesn't seem to care that he's disturbing the parking lot gossip and getting death stares from half the PTA.

"You want me to teach you?" Gabriel says.

"Only if you want to." I fiddle with my tie, acutely aware of the sweat dripping down my neck and soaking my collar.

"It's not that I don't want to." He drags a hand through his hair, slicking back the unruly waves. "It's just I don't know when I'll find the time." He stifles a yawn.

"How you doing with everything?"

"It's been rough. I was up til late last night cramming for a physics test." He seems about to say more when he presses his lips shut.

"How did it go?"

"Won't be an A." He frowns and looks crushed. Damn, I'd be delighted with a C for physics.

"Don't worry about the lessons." I feel defeated. After an agonizing discussion with my parents, promising to improve my math grade if it meant I could take piano lessons, they'd finally said yes, and now Gabriel's saying no. I could find another teacher, but that's not the point. I want Gabriel to teach me so I can play like he does.

"No, wait." He loosens his tie and undoes a couple of buttons. It's painful tearing my eyes away from the exposed sliver of collarbone to focus on his face. "Maybe we could do a half-hour lesson after choir. Would that suit you?"

"Absolutely, but only if you think this might help with your licentiate preparation."

"It would and then some." His eyes regain some sparkle. "But we can only start in a couple of weeks. I've got a bunch of tests coming up." A whole two weeks until I get Gabriel all to myself for half an hour in a room the size of a janitor's closet. I can wait.

"How much should I pay you?"

He shakes his head and opens the car door. "No way, you're doing me the favor, letting me practice my teaching skills. No charge, Resa."

He called me Resa. Dragons roar in my belly and my blood turns to lava. I'm definitely in love. "Thanks," I squeak.

"No problem. Hey, are you busy this weekend?"

Oh my God, is he asking me out on a real date? And so close to Valentine's Day! Maybe this year I won't be that girl sitting at the back of the Valentine's Day assembly sans roses or hearts. Maybe Gabriel will make me feel less of a freak this year. I'm about to say I'm absolutely 100 percent free to watch paint dry with him if he wants to, but instead I channel alien Resa and play it suave. "I don't think so. Why?"

"Maybe we can hang out."

THE OTHER ME | 85

"Sure. Just let me know when and where."

Gracefully, he slides down into the seat and closes the door.

"Howzit, Treasa?" Dirk starts the engine.

"Hi." I haven't technically been introduced to the guy. I guess Gabriel must've told him about me. I wonder exactly what he's said and how Matric boys might discuss a grade-ten girl who's clearly smitten with one of them.

"Chat later." Gabriel fastens his seat belt, and they drive off, leaving me floating in the stratosphere with the blood thrumming through my veins.

GABRIEL

"YOU KNOW what you just did, right?" Dirk says as we pull out of the parking lot.

"We're just hanging out."

"On the weekend before Valentine's Day."

"Ah shit," I groan. How could I forget the pseudo lovefest when the shops are decked out in hearts and lovey-dovey slogans that make me want to hurl?

"You know the rules."

"Your rules."

"My system is rock solid, bru." Dirk slows to a crawl as we approach a red robot, ignoring the irate hooting from the guy behind us. The lights change before we have to come to a stop and I exhale the breath I was holding.

"Your system is flawed."

"*Kak.*" Dirk lights a cigarette. "Don't ever ask a girl out before or around Valentine's Day. It's simple. A week either side of the fourteenth is toxic, man."

"And do you deliberately break up with said girl in January just to avoid Valentine's Day?"

"Ja, fine. That can be a problem, like if you meet a chick in December and things are good, and then February happens."

"Like I said. Flawed."

He punches me in the arm. "So is Treasa your Valentine?"

"No." Definitely not. God, I hope she isn't expecting anything like roses or chocolates. Just asked her to hang out. Nothing remotely romantic in that suggestion, is there? Maybe I should cancel.

"Bru, if you see her this weekend, I guarantee you she's going to think you want to be her boyfriend, like she'll be practicing her signature with your surname."

"That's absurd."

"That's women for you, man. Crazy, the lot of them."

Dirk hands me the pack of cigarettes, and I light up, needing the burn down the back of my throat. What the hell am I doing?

TREASA

GABRIEL CALLED to cancel our hanging out. Said he had schoolwork and studying and… whatever. I'm the idiot for thinking he liked me in that way. Or maybe this weekend's proximity to Valentine's Day freaked him out—or so hypothesizes Jordan. At least he called. He could've just SMSed me, but the fact that he called means something, right?

God, will this assembly never end! No roses again for me this year, just an eternity spent at the back of the hall waiting for all the bleach-blonde sporty girls to collect their Valentines from boys with names like Josh and Travis. The cacophony of squeals and giggles makes me want to vomit. Jordan sits in the lotus position with her eyes closed, zoning out of it all. Lethi has to shake her shoulder three times when they call her name. She yawns and ambles up to the podium to fetch a bunch of plastic flowers.

"Fake," she says when she returns and folds herself back into meditation.

"At least you got something." Sibo pouts.

"Patience, Sibs," Jordan says.

"Nothing from Gabriel?" Lethi asks me.

"Stormhof wasn't on the list," I say, sounding more dejected than I'll admit I feel.

"Stuck-up bitches, they never list the government schools." Jordan looks truly disgusted. I can't help but envy the dozen roses she's so casually tossed behind us. Once again, I'm Valentine-less, and the box of chocolates Mom gave me this morning definitely doesn't count.

"WHAT'S WITH the walk, Scotty?" Hannah follows me to the bathroom. Thinking I was alone in the deserted corridor after Valentine's assembly, I was practicing my boy walk en route to the loo.

"Nothing." I unbend my knees and return to my girly hip sway.

"Looks like you shat yourself." She disappears into a stall.

Great, just when I thought I was finally getting into the rhythm of it and not looking like a spastic duck anymore. Having locked the door and double-checked the security of the bolt, I lean against the partition and take a moment, trying not to listen to Hannah peeing or opening what can only be the packaging on a sanitary pad. Periods. The bane of my existence. Why would anyone want to be a girl and bleed once a month? The only way to stop is getting pregnant. Terrific. Who actually wants to get that bloated carrying a human-shaped parasite? Not me, that's for sure.

The toilet flushes and the door slams open.

"You enjoying yourself in there?" Hannah turns on the tap. "Or are you just going to have a good cry since no one sent you anything for Valentine's Day?"

Before I can formulate an appropriately sarcastic comeback, Hannah leaves the bathroom and I'm left muttering my brilliant ripostes to the graffiti on the walls. They're mostly just ballpoint pen inanities or swear words. Someone's been really rebellious and drawn an upside-down cross above the loo paper. Above that, someone's written "R&G" with a heart around it in green Koki. It's a sign from the universe. Resa and Gabriel— we're meant to be.

GABRIEL

MONDAY MORNING, I arrive at school to a locker festooned with paper hearts, each deliberately cut from pink and red cardboard. Embarrassed doesn't even begin to cover it.

"Who's your boyfriend, Gabe?" Kelvin saunters past with a stupid grin plastered on his face. I grab my textbooks, and a glitter-smeared heart-shaped card falls at my feet. Curiosity gets the better of me, and I peel it open.

"That a joke?" Dirk leans against the wall beside me.

"Hope so." I hand him the card.

"'Dear Gabe. Let's work things out. Love, Karla,'" Dirk reads in a whisper so only he and I can hear. "Told you she loved you."

"Can't imagine why." I slam shut the locker and rip off several Prestiked hearts. Doesn't she have better things to do with her time?

"You should talk to her." Dirk hands me the card, and I drop it in the nearby bin.

"I made it pretty clear we were over months ago."

"Have a heart, bru." He puts a hand on my chest, his face twisted in mock pain.

"I'll *donner* you."

He removes his hand. "But seriously, can't you guys be friends?"

"You're the expert. You tell me."

Dirk ponders this in silence as we stalk through the corridors toward Afrikaans, my gaze scanning left and right. Last thing I need is to run into Karla now.

"Maybe being friends with an ex is wishful thinking," Dirk says as we traipse into the classroom. "Besides, you've got Treasa now."

"I don't have anyone." My voice is devoid of emotion, even though the truth in that statement hurts more than I imagined possible.

TREASA

FINALLY, THE heat wave breaks, and we can all breathe easier. It's been raining for three days. The spiderweb-fine consistent drizzle turns the world into a giant swamp.

Too cool for umbrellas, we don our blazers and head for the music block. My hair is going to frizz. Rather that than look like a dork with a brollie.

"Irish weather," I say, echoing my mom.

"More like bed weather." Jordan picks her way past a puddle. I can't resist. Taking a run up, I jump and land with both feet squarely in the puddle.

"Treasa, what the hell?" Jordan yells.

"It barely touched you." I, on the other hand, have drenched socks and a mud-splattered skirt.

"This is so gross." Jordan uses the sleeve of her blazer to wipe down her legs.

"It's only water," Gabriel says, coming up behind us, and my heart ratchets up my throat. I'm a little miffed he canceled our weekend plans, but there's no way I can stay cross with his face wearing a lopsided grin like that.

Jordan folds her arms and purses her lips. Gabriel chuckles and taps his toes in a puddle, creating tiny splashes.

"No, like this." Maybe it's seeing Gabriel again, maybe it's the weather or hormones or some weird affectation of my alien DNA, but I have the overwhelming urge to puddle stomp. I launch myself with bent-kneed fury at the minipond and land with a magnificent splash. Jordan screams and backs away. Gabriel laughs, and the sound makes me warm and tingly despite being dripping wet.

"You asked for it, Treasa." Jordan runs at me, grabs my arms, and lands with her feet on either side of mine, ensuring we both get soaked.

"My turn." Gabriel leaps into the air, holding his music file high above his head, and sprays us with muddy water. The game begins, and for a few liberating minutes, we charge around the music block, jumping in puddles and kicking water at one another.

"Ladies!" Mrs. McArthur bellows from the safety of the choir room. "And Mr. du Preez. You are late." She says nothing about our once-white socks now stained brown or our flushed and water-smeared faces. She does, however, insist Gabriel clean himself up and dry off if he plans on being anywhere near the piano.

AFTER CHOIR, I'm hoping there'll be round two of puddle-stomping hysterics. Alas, the sun dismantles the clouds, casting a faint rainbow across the sky. Jordan says good-bye and heads back to put in a few more hours on her art project, while Lethi and Sibo wave before stepping into their mom's black BMW.

Damp strands of hair dangle in front of Gabriel's eyes. I want to reach up and tuck them behind his ear. Would that be overstepping the invisible boundary between us? He flicks his head, clearing his eyes.

"That was fun." He changes weight between feet, his shoes squelching. "We should do it again sometime."

Dirk's Beetle chugs into the parking lot. My time with Gabriel is almost up.

"Listen." He runs a hand through his hair. "Dirk's having a *braai* on Sunday. Thought you might want to go."

I can't breathe, yet somehow manage to ask, "Who'll be there?"

"Dirk, a few school friends. That's it."

"Sounds good." Sounds positively terrifying. "And you won't cancel this time?"

"Sorry about that." He squirms and flicks hair out of his face. "And no, I won't. Promise. Just let me know if you need a lift."

"Thanks. I'll ask my folks and SMS you, if that's okay?"

"No problem." He smiles, and not even the sunshine parting the clouds or the rainbow hanging in the sky comes close to the radiance of his expression. "See you later, Treasa."

I watch him slip into Dirk's car and ride away. Now to convince my parents to let me go to a braai with a bunch of Matrics.

MOM AND Dad are not a united front. If I want something, like a new cellphone or computer or to go to a braai with Gabriel, approaching Dad first is the way to go. He's out on the patio nursing a beer, watching the weaver birds shred the leaves of his prize palm tree.

"Bloody buggers just won't stop." He picks a pebble out of Mom's potted plant and lobs it at the palm tree. The birds flutter away, only to return moments later for continued destruction. I bring a dish filled with salted peanuts, Dad's favorite, onto the patio with me.

"Want a nut?"

"Thanks, my girl." He grabs a handful, and I give him a moment to chew and savor before I start.

"Daddy." I sit next to him. "You know that guy I told you about? Gabriel?"

"Afrikaans lad, the piano player."

"Yeah, well, he asked me to go to a braai on Sunday. You think I could go?"

Dad gives me a knowing look as he swigs his beer.

"At his house?"

"A friend's place."

"Hm." Dad'll need some more convincing.

"It's a friend of his from the rugby team." I'm reaching.

"Gabriel plays rugby?"

"He's a kicker." I hope there's such a position. "Like Percy Montgomery," I add since that's the only name I know from the sport, because that's the only player who is even remotely good-looking.

"Does he play cricket?"

"If he had the time, he'd prefer to play cricket. He thinks cricket is the better sport." And so does Dad, so let's hope he says yes to the braai now.

"So it's a team braai?"

"Something like that."

"These boys'll be drinking?"

"Only the ones over eighteen."

Dad seems to consider this for a moment, so I hastily add, "But Gabriel won't be drinking and neither will I, obviously."

"Obviously." Dad throws another pebble at the palm tree. "A rugby-playing pianist? Wonders never cease." Dad smiles, and I know I've almost got this one in the bag.

"So can I go?"

"Why not? If it's okay with your mother, it's okay with me. I'll take you, though, suss it out. You know, the usual Dad stuff."

"Thank you, Daddy." I lean over and give him a kiss on the cheek. One down, a mother to go.

"Absolutely not," Mom says while chasing stir-fry veggies around the wok with an egg lifter. "I don't know these people, and I'm not relinquishing my daughter to complete strangers."

"Dad said he'd take me and suss it out first."

"Did he, now?" Her eyes narrow into lizard-like slits.

"Please, Mom. Even if it's for a couple of hours."

"I'm not happy about you hanging out with this older government school crowd. You stank of cigarette smoke after that concert."

"So, Gabriel smokes on the odd occasion."

"Does he make you smoke too?" She's turning into a velociraptor over nothing.

"No."

She's not even listening. "First the piercings, now cigarettes. What's next?"

"Mom, please calm down. Seriously. It's just a party."

"I said no." She adds too much chili to the vegetables.

"Don't you want me to have a social life, or would you prefer I stay at home every weekend with Mommy and Daddy?" I slam the knife into the carrot I'm chopping for the salad.

"Resa, of course I want you to have a social life, but I want you to be safe." She softens.

"Dad will drop me. He can even come in and meet the parents." Not that Dad will, because he's more introverted than I am.

"Is it a bring and braai?" Mom adds onion to the pan.

"I think so."

She chases the vegetables around the wok aggressively. "Do you want to take *boerewors* or *sosaties*?"

"So I can go, then?"

"But you'll have an eight o'clock curfew. It's a school night."

"Thank you, Mommy." I throw my arms around her, and she pats my shoulder.

DINNER SEEMS to take forever. My dad spends the entire meal extolling the virtues of Mark Boucher's ability to defend the wickets and Hansie Cronje's brilliance as a captain, asking me what Gabriel thinks of this spin bowler or that Indian batsman. I duck as soon as I'm done, leaving Mom with Dad to discuss his predictions for the upcoming test series.

I race to my bedroom to SMS Gabriel. While I'm waiting for him to reply, I SMS Jordan the good news, hoping she'll offer to be my personal stylist again. Gabriel replies first, saying he'll pick me up at 3:00 p.m. A lengthy and somewhat embarrassing SMS conversation about why my dad wants to drop me off ensues. Gabriel sends me a smiley face and Dirk's address.

Jordan finally responds with a series of smiley faces and exclamation marks and the promise to help me pick out what to wear. I lie on my bed with Riker curled up beside me, vibrating against my ribs with every purr. I stare at my walls, at Liam St. Clare, and can't help wondering if replacing all my posters of the celebrity with pictures of Gabriel would be weird. Ah, Gabriel, with his bright eyes and square jaw and floppy hair and kissable lips.

Worry knots my insides. In this week's episode of *Project Blue Book*, Resa finally kissed the human girl he's been in love with the whole season—personally, I think he and my Tristan make a better couple—and in that moment of passion, the girl glimpsed images of Kazar. Rust-colored sand dunes and crimson cacti, a city of glinting spires rising from the dust, and Resa's real face—which they didn't actually show. I guess his true form isn't quite as sexy as Liam St. Clare's. The girl completely freaked out, calling him a monster and telling him not to touch her, which broke Resa's heart. What if Gabriel tries to kiss me Saturday night, and I am an alien and he sees something weird and terrifying? Will he be disgusted? Will he hate me? Will I end up on the run for my life with a bunch of government agencies wanting to stick me in a lab for testing?

Maybe I do need therapy, or maybe I just need him to kiss me and then I'll know for sure. If he doesn't see anything weird, I'm just a girl with issues, and if he does see purple oceans and three-headed aliens, then at least I'll know I have a legitimate reason to feel like such a freak.

GABRIEL

MARLIZE IS only too delighted to paint my nails. She offers to give me a complete manicure, and while I'm curious why all women seem to like someone fussing over their cuticles, I'd rather not spend the whole afternoon entertaining Dirk's little sister.

"Can I at least file them?" She wields an emery board like it's a sword.

"If you have to." I squirm in my chair, fingers splayed on the kitchen table as Marlize continues her ministrations. Dirk's wiping down the outside furniture in preparation for the party. Sanding complete, Marlize dips the brush into black polish and starts painting.

"So...." She draws out the word. "Dirk says you have a girlfriend?"

"Dirk's telling fibs."

Marlize looks at me with her huge brown eyes and grins. She has blue-and-pink elastics around her braces, giving her a kaleidoscopic smile. Treasa has braces too, but hers are barely noticeable, with transparent elastics.

"So who's this girl that's coming today, then?" She uses the corner of a tissue to wipe away varnish on my skin. My father would kill me if he caught me wearing nail varnish—more proof of apparent homosexuality. I guess that makes all rock stars gay too.

"Just a friend."

"Lize, when can I schedule a pedicure?" Dirk's dad walks in, totally unfazed by the nail polish party happening at the kitchen table.

"I'll have to check my schedule." She flicks blond fringe from her eyes.

"Watch out she doesn't put pink glitter hearts on your fingers too," Dirk's dad says.

"You liked those pink glitter hearts." Marlize pouts.

"On you, sweetie, not on me." He kisses her forehead and heads out onto the patio to give Dirk the latest cricket score.

Being at Dirk's house always feels like I'm in some parallel dimension, one where a dad can have his daughter paint his nails pink while he watches a rugby match on TV. Maybe it's just par for the course when you're married to a drama teacher. But then, Dirk's dad is a bit left field himself, being a fulminologist. What my music teacher mom saw in my business administrator father, I'll never know.

MARLIZE'S PRISTINE paint job lasts precisely four minutes, until I pop open a can of Coke and chip my right index finger. I'm saved from her admonishment by the gate bell. Tank and Bullet are already barking at the new arrival that could be Treasa, and my stomach lurches. It's not. It's Karla dressed like a slutty vampire, with a crimson smile plastered across her face. I can only imagine what she's got stashed in her *Nightmare Before Christmas* backpack.

"Sorry I'm early." She brushes past me, smelling of cherry tobacco, and breezes up the driveway as Dirk emerges from the house. If this was his idea, I'm going to kill him.

"Karla." Dirk looks as shell-shocked as I feel. "What are you doing here?"

"Nandi said you were having a braai."

Dirk catches my eye and gives me an apologetic look. He should've known—invite Nandi, invite Karla. The two have been joined at the hip since they were thirteen.

"Where is Nandi?" I ask.

"She'll be late. She was at some great-aunt's funeral." Her gaze rakes up and down my body, and she smirks, the way I imagine a female praying mantis might look at her mate before biting off his head. "I brought hubbly," she says and sashays into the house with a flutter of black lace.

"Bru, I didn't invite her. I swear, man." Dirk fumbles with a box of cigarettes and lights up.

"Well, she's here now."

"Just play it cool. It's not like Treasa even needs to know."

Now I'm pissed, firstly that Karla has the audacity to show up uninvited and turn what should've been a pleasant evening into something awkward. Secondly, that Dirk presumes my sexual history is something Treasa would even care about. We are not dating. Karla being here shouldn't matter—in fact, maybe it's a good thing. Maybe it'll get Treasa to take a step back from… from what? I invited her to this party. If anyone should be backpedaling, it's me.

TREASA

THE MOISTURE clinging to the mirror obscures my reflection. I open the bathroom window and release the steam from my shower. Slowly, the mirror clears, revealing a voluptuous redhead I'm still not convinced is me. Maybe if I dyed my hair brown like Resa's—like Gabriel's—I'd feel less conspicuous, although hair color isn't the only thing making me stand out.

Jordan says I should be grateful for having the boobs so many women pay a fortune for. I squish my C-cups flat and stand sideways, trying to imagine what I'd look like flat chested, breastless, even. My boobs are too big and bulge out beneath my hands like grotesque tumors. If I squish them just right and look at myself straight on, I can kind of create a guy's chest, a gym-bunny guy's chest with sculpted pecs, but male nonetheless. Now if only I had a kilometer of bandage to wrap around my body and keep these udders in place.

"You enjoying yourself in there?" Jordan knocks on the door.

"Just a minute." I release my breasts with a sigh, mentally cursing my hormones.

Jordan, still in her yoga pants, has laid out several possible outfits for me. Only one involves a dress—she knows better than to force me into frills.

"It's just a braai." I flick aside the dress I've never worn in favor of acid-wash jeans and a T-shirt.

"I don't get you, Ree. You've got this killer bod, and you just wanna be a bag lady."

"Bag ladies don't wear Sissy Boy jeans." I wriggle into a G-string and pull on my only pair of brand-name jeans, which I got for Christmas from an aunt who thought I liked clothes that had the labels on the outside. Despite the label, the jeans are super comfy and are this perfect shade of washed-out blue without looking secondhand. I can't wear boxers, though. They'd only bunch and make my bum look even bigger.

"I'm just saying you've got assets and shouldn't be afraid to show them off." Jordan's gaze drops to the towel I've got wrapped around my bare chest.

"I'm thinking about getting a reduction."

Jordan spins me around, hands on my shoulders, and gazes into my eyes. "Are you serious?"

"Seriously." I fold my arms self-consciously.

"Can I get your offcuts?"

"That's gross." I chuckle and reach for the T-shirt. Jordan snatches it away and hands me a purple halter neck that's somewhere between being sexy and casual.

"It would save on having to buy all these extra-padded Wonder bras." Jordan touches her elbows together to create some cleavage as I lay the halter top on the bed, not quite convinced I should wear it. There's no way I'll get a sports bra under that, which means wearing the underwire lacy thing Mom bought me.

Jordan tightens the straps for me, making sure my "assets" don't bounce free. I'm sure there'll be a pool, and I'm sure others will swim. There's no way I'm getting almost naked in front of Gabriel and his friends.

"I wish we could just swap bodies," I say.

"I'm not sure I could pull off all those freckles."

I snap my wet towel at her legs. She dodges and arms herself with my hairbrush.

"Are you ready?" Dad knocks on the door. He's got to get me there and back between innings.

"Almost." Reluctantly, I pull on the purple top and study myself in the mirror. I look far too girly, far too curvy. "Gabriel will like this look?" I ask.

"For sure. You look hot." Jordan's gaze runs up and down my body, and she gives a satisfied nod.

We spend another five minutes trying to tame my hair, looking permed after a wash. Nothing works, so I push it all back with an Alice band and hope it behaves. Mom scrutinizes me when we walk into the kitchen. She hands me the cooler bag with a packet of chicken sosaties and two Cokes in it.

"You going to swim?"

"No."

"Probably for the best," she says, eyeing my cleavage.

"See you later." I give her a quick hug and follow Jordan out to the garage, leaving Mom and Dad to have a quick confab about me.

Ten minutes later, we're in the car, with me up front holding the map book open to where Dad's marked the address. The cricket commentator's going on about Hansie's captaincy and Boucher's catches and Kallis's batting, and I'm bored as hell.

"You seeing Bryce tonight?" I turn in my seat to ask Jordan.

"Nope, but we're doing dinner tomorrow," she says. "He still owes me a Valentine's date."

"Oh." That stupid rose-giving, chocolate-munching, make-all-the-lonely-girls-feel-like-crap day lingers on.

Dad gives me a sideways glance but doesn't comment. He seems to understand me a lot better than Mom does.

AFTER DROPPING off Jordan, we drive for several minutes up a long dirt road before finding number ten. The house is a large double story nestled at the top of a sprawling plot. A few other cars are parked in the driveway, and two Rottweilers the size of small horses come bounding up to the gate, barking and snarling. What the hell am I doing here?

"Tank, Bullet, *voertsek*." A man in cargo pants and a Meatloaf T-shirt claps his hands, and the dogs start wagging their docked tails as he opens the gate.

Dad gets out of the car with me and introduces himself as David Prescott. He only ever uses his full name when he's trying to make an impression. The dogs sniff at us and bash my hands for attention. I ball my hands into fists in case they decide my fingers look tasty.

"Hey, you want to grab a beer? Got the cricket on."

I give Dad a "you-are-going-home-right-this-minute" look, and he declines the offer.

"So you'll be here all evening?" Dad asks.

"Ja, for sure, man. We'll get the Weber going just now," Hannes Joubert assures my dad. "They're all out by the pool." Hannes ushers me up the driveway, and Dad waits for my nod, giving me one last chance to back out. If I want the dream of being with Gabriel to ever become more than fantasy, I'll have to get to know his friends at some point.

Dad drives off, and Hannes takes my cooler bag, then guides me through the cluttered house toward the patio and swimming pool. I feel more like an alien standing on that patio, searching for Gabriel in a sea of unfamiliar faces, than I ever have before.

"Are you Treasa?" asks a younger girl in Afrikaans. She's in a blue bikini with a tie-dyed sarong wrapped around her waist. The family resemblance is unmistakable.

"Yes, I'm Gabriel's friend," I answer in English. "Are you Dirk's sister?"

"Ja. He's in the kitchen." She jerks her head back toward the house before slip-slopping toward a pool chair. I wait, unsure whether to navigate my way to the kitchen or find somewhere to sit outside.

"Treasa." He's standing so close, I feel his breath on the back of my shoulder. I whirl around, and Gabriel grins. He's transformed. His usually floppy hair is combed up into a mohawk and there's a big silver ring in his ear. He's wearing a Marilyn Manson T-shirt with the sleeves cut out over black board shorts. He's got a spike-studded armband around his left wrist, and his nails sport chipped black polish.

"Wow."

His grin widens, and he hands me a can of Creme Soda. "Is that a good wow?"

"Yes… um… no, I mean…." My gaze strays from his face to his bare biceps. "You look great."

And nothing like a rugby-playing jock or a classical pianist, for that matter.

"You look pretty." He turns away and clenches his jaw as if he hadn't meant to say it. Maybe he just doesn't want to be caught using the word "pretty" by his friends. It doesn't matter, because something inside me melts.

We stroll out into the garden, where maybe a dozen guys and girls are hanging out on pool chairs and picnic blankets spread out in the shade on the grass. Dirk hops out of the pool and comes over to us, not caring who he drips on. He has a tiger tattoo clawing its way up his ribs.

"Don't think you've officially met Dirk." Gabriel mock-punches his friend on the shoulder.

"Nice to meet you."

"Do you know Hannah McKenzie?" Dirk asks.

"Yeah, she's in my grade."

"Nice girl." The smile on his face makes me shudder. "Huge nipples."

"I wouldn't know." And wow, has Dirk just let slip the Cullinan Diamond of gossip.

"Don't you girls compare tits in the bathroom or something?" Dirk's gaze drops to my cleavage.

"Only in pubescent male fantasies." I don't usually manage such brilliant ripostes, but this guy deserves it.

"Nice one." Gabriel smiles at me.

Dirk chuckles and whips his hair back and forth, showering all of us with pool water. "Want a drink?" he asks.

"Got, thanks." I hold up my can.

"I mean a real drink." He saunters over to a cooler box some other shirtless guy is using for a footstool. He shoves the feet aside amidst a chorus of four-letter words and pulls out a beer.

"Ah, no thanks. I don't drink."

"Suit yourself." He tosses Gabriel a beer and cracks one open for himself. "Make yourself at home, Treasa. Braai'll be ready soon as Pollock takes care of Tendulkar."

I know the names, just not their significance. I nod anyway as if it all makes sense. Gabriel rattles off more introductions as we pick our way past girls suntanning in barely there bikinis. They're more interested in soaking up the sun than meeting me, which doesn't bother me in the slightest. We settle on a picnic blanket at a safe distance from the pool, and one of the dogs trots over to lie down next to Gabriel, offering him its belly.

"You like dogs?" he asks.

"These aren't dogs. These are monsters."

"Nah, they just act all tough. Don't you, Tank?" Gabriel lies back, resting his head on the Rottweiler's shoulder. He looks so different with his hair gelled up—harder, older, not at all like the type of boy who can play Beethoven's Sonata Pathètique. He slips on his Ray-Bans, takes another sip of beer, and sighs in contentment.

"You always dress like this?" My gaze meanders from his mohawk down his torso where his shirt has pulled up, revealing a sliver of belly. His legs are fluffy, and I almost reach out to feel them, but I sit on my hand instead. Maybe I should let my leg hair grow, just to see what it would be like to be that hairy. Feminists and hippies don't shave, so why should I?

Somewhere inside, there's a celebratory roar, so I guess the right team is winning. I sip my drink and wonder what to talk about when two girls approach. They're like yin and yang: a pale white girl in a black bikini top and ripped-up skirt held together with safety pins, and a black girl in a white bikini with beaded sarong. They're both tall and beautiful and intimidating. They saunter over with a hookah already filled with water.

It takes me a moment to realize the white girl, Karla, I think, isn't deformed, and that what appear to be three nipples straining against the fabric of her bikini must in fact be nipple piercings. She has a silver bar skewering her navel too.

"Treasa, right?" Karla sits down beside us, and Nandi follows.

I nod and watch her long fingers as she shapes a piece of tinfoil and balances a single oval coal on top.

"You go to St. Bridget's?" Nandi asks.

"Yes. You all go to Stormhof?"

"They do, but I go to the NSA."

"Music?" I ask.

"Visual Arts."

"Nandi paints." Karla snaps her fingers, and Gabriel pulls a lighter out of his pocket. The stab of jealousy at their familiarity feels like a laser burning through my chest.

"Ever smoked hubbly?" Gabriel sits up as Tank goes bounding off to help Bullet demolish an old car tire.

"Nope."

"Oh, Gabe gets to pop your hubbly cherry." Karla grins, and Nandi rolls her eyes. Gabriel glares at her, and she bites her bottom lip, giving him a seductive smile. There's something going on between them; there must be. I'm the idiot—of course Gabriel isn't single. How could a guy like that not be taken?

"It's overrated." Nandi lies back and closes her eyes.

"Only try if you want to." Gabriel shuffles forward, his knee touching mine. "It's not like smoking. No tar or anything."

"This is strawberry vanilla." Karla taps the glass with a long fingernail. Gabriel detaches one of two pipes and takes a long pull as the water inside the pot bubbles. Karla does the same and exhales smoke rings at Gabriel.

"You used to be able to do really *kif* smoke rings with that tongue of yours." She gives him a look that shreds my insides.

"Karla, *pasop*," Nandi says.

"What? It's true." She giggles, but Gabriel doesn't look impressed. He hands me his pipe, and I take a tentative slurp.

"You've got to really suck it, like this." Karla demonstrates.

"Are you done?" Gabriel's tone is venomous.

"Like this?" I wrap my lips around the pipe as suggestively as possible and suck in a deep breath. This time I taste the tang of strawberry and sweet vanilla. It's not half-bad and makes my head feel kind of buzzy. Karla scowls, clearly not amused as Gabriel pries the pipe from my fingers and takes another hit.

"So, Treasa, are the stories about St. Bridget's true?" Karla narrows her eyes.

"Karla," Nandi warns.

"It's a fair question. So?" She looks at me.

"Depends on the story." I take another slurp of hubbly. The buzz in my head turns to a consistent pressure, and the world seems to soften around the edges. I blink a few times to clear my vision. The haze remains.

"I've heard you take cucumbers to school to practice giving blowjobs."

"Jesus, Karla. Enough already." Gabriel picks a leaf up from the grass and starts tearing it into tiny pieces.

"That's not what you used to say." She stares at him, her gaze nuclear.

"Honestly, I wouldn't know," I say before Gabriel gets annihilated. My arms feel heavy as lead. It feels like I've sprouted roots, and they're pulling me into the ground. Maybe this is what happens when an alien smokes hubbly.

"About blowjobs or the cucumbers?" She takes another pull of hubbly.

"Either."

Karla chuckles. "You picked the wrong one, Gabe. You should ask for your money back. Unless you're into virgins now."

Is my lack of experience that obvious? I expect a verbal barrage from Gabriel, but he ignores her and studies the contents of the pot as I suck in another lungful of hubbly.

"Shit, you put weed in this?" His eyes burn with anger.

"Just a pinch. Picked it up in Mozambique last weekend. Isn't it great?"

He shouts at her in Afrikaans. The words have lost all meaning.

"Treasa, are you feeling okay?" He brushes the hair from my face.

"It's dagga, not crack. She'll live." Karla scowls.

Weed in the water? "Am I stoned?" I ask. My tongue feels thick and heavy.

"Very." Worry creases Gabriel's forehead.

"She only took two hits." Karla laughs. "Not a tough cookie, are you?"

"*Hou jou bek*," Gabriel snaps, and Karla stops laughing before gathering herself and the hubbly off the blanket. She stomps away, giving both of us a filthy look. Nandi gives us an apologetic shrug before following her friend.

"I think I just need a nap." I start lying down. Gabriel places his hands on my shoulders and keeps me upright.

"Not out here."

He stands and helps me to my feet. It's like I'm wading through *mieliepap*, each step requiring more energy than the last. Faces blur around me as we traipse inside; their voices sound hollow and distant in the veil of mist descending over my brain. Gabriel's arm is all that keeps me from falling as I stumble up the stairs.

He sets me down on a bed, gently guiding my head toward a pillow. My eyes won't open, but I know he's still there. I feel his presence.

"You'll be okay," he says.

"Sorry," I mumble.

He chuckles, and the sound is a rustle of dry leaves.

"Don't apologize. I should've known better." He settles beside me and eases the Alice band off my head, dragging his fingers through my hair. His touch gives me goose bumps and makes my toes curl in a good way.

"It's because I'm an alien," I whisper.

"That's the dagga talking." He sits next to me. I reach out with jelly fingers to trace his jaw, his lips, and end up poking him in the belly button.

"Stay with me." Is that really my voice?

He hesitates, and after what might be hours of deliberation, he slides down to lie beside me. He folds my hand against his chest and an army of tingles march up and down my spine. I can feel his heartbeat beneath my fingers. The layer of fabric between us irritates me, and I wriggle free from his grip. After a few fumbles, I manage to slip my hand beneath his shirt, resting it on his chest above his heart. His whole body tenses, and I've probably crossed some line, but I don't have the energy to care.

"Treasa, we shouldn't." He inches away and I follow, wanting to feel his breath like butterfly kisses on my closed eyelids. I fight the soporific tides threatening to pull me under. I'm losing the battle even as Gabriel changes position and places a tentative arm around me. I want to be conscious if he tries to kiss me or otherwise take advantage of me—not sure I'd even mind if he did right now. I need to stay awake; the rhythmic thumping of his heart and his steady breathing lulls me into sleep.

GABRIEL

THE THC makes my thoughts as sticky as wet tar. It makes muddling through the chaos of my mind like trying to pry apart the strands of a colossal spider's web. Damn Karla. I should've known she'd do something spiteful. That's what happens when you accidentally break a girl's heart—or so Dirk says, who got it on good authority from Nandi that I was an idiot for ever thinking Karla didn't love me. Love—what is that, anyway? A chemical stew in the brain making us idiots.

Treasa's breath wuffs against my shirt as she snores, and it feels far too nice.

"She okay?" Dirk whispers from the doorway.

"Just passed out."

"Don't let her upchuck on my duvet."

"She wasn't drinking."

"Greenies can still get you, man." He sidles up to the bed and stares down at her. "What you going to do about this?" He gestures to her hand still under my shirt. Her fingers are curled in sleep, her head resting on my chest. No denying the fact that I like the feel of her body pressed against mine, that our skin on skin makes my heart beat faster and the blood pump away from my brain into certain extremities.

"No idea."

"She'll be fine. You can leave her for a while."

"Don't want to. Karla might shave her head or something."

"Karla's just miffed." He sits on the edge of the bed.

"About what?"

"You using her and discarding her. I warned you that whole friends-with-benefits thing never works out for the guy."

"You could've told me that instead of encouraging me to sleep with her."

"Didn't think you'd be that dumb." Dirk shakes his head sadly.

"So if I listened to you constantly telling me to nail Treasa, that would make me dumb too?"

"An absolute idiot, but it would get you laid." He grins, and I thump him in the arm, not nearly hard enough for fear of waking Treasa.

"Come on, man. We're starting the braai."

"In a minute."

He shrugs and ambles out of the bedroom.

I run my hand through the spill of red hair across my chest. The curls are tight spirals around my fingers, soft and springy. She must use coconut shampoo, and I breathe deeply, savoring the scent before placing a kiss on her forehead. I'm not sure why I do it; it just seems right.

Extricating my limbs from her grasp takes a minute. She stirs, shuffles into the pillows, and doesn't wake up. At least I learn from mistakes; there's no way I'll do to Treasa what I did to Karla.

TREASA

THERE'S A poster of a topless woman with pointed elf ears straddling a dragon on the wall. Where the hell am I? My head throbs, and my mouth is as dry as the Karoo. My gaze drops from the poster to the figure beside the bed. His hair is wet and tousled. And he's shirtless. I count the knobs of his spine visible above the bed frame. Old bruises mottle his ribs yellow and green. I wonder if any are a result from my takedowns in self-defense class.

I try saying hi. It comes out more like the dying croak of a bullfrog.

Gabriel turns and slides up onto the bed, ditching the Carl Sagan novel he was reading. "Feeling better?" he asks.

"Yup," I manage, although I can barely breathe with him so almost naked and close to me.

"You were asleep, so I went for a swim." He shakes his head, showering me in chlorinated water. I don't mind, even if it makes my hair go frizzy.

"Thanks for... before." *For rescuing me* would sound like I can't handle some hubbly, which I can't because I'm an alien, but there's no way I'm telling him that.

"If I'd known there was weed—"

"It's okay." I cut him off. It's not, really, and how very not okay it is, is only just starting to sink in. Getting stoned at a party with total strangers is moronic. Even Jordan would agree. "You smoke it a lot?" I hold my breath, waiting for his answer.

"Not anymore. It causes memory loss, and that sucks for me."

"Because you'll forget how to karate chop?"

"Because I'll have a memory lapse in the middle of a sonata."

"You don't look like a typical pianist." Boys who play the piano are usually nerdy and skinny and wear glasses. They don't listen to heavy metal, paint their nails black, and do karate.

"You don't look like an alien." He gives me that secret smile. My study of his face is interrupted by my cognizance of the word "alien."

"What?"

"When you were high, you said you were an alien." He grins and gives me a wink that turns my blood to syrup and spawns a weyr of dragons in my belly.

"Oh my God." Another reason why drugs are super dangerous for someone like me. I should've known better. There was an episode of *Project Blue Book* last season where Resa got drunk, and his powers got all confused, and he ended up spontaneously changing hair color and almost blew his cover.

"Your secret's safe with me." He stretches across the bed and passes me my Alice band. "Hungry?"

I nod, unable to speak. He helps me to my feet, and I let my hand linger in his. Damn, he's gorgeous. He's lean and muscular, with a six-pack and those tapering V muscles that disappear teasingly beneath the band of his shorts.

"I saved you a plate of food." Gabriel leads the way out of the bedroom, which I presume is Dirk's, naked elf maiden and all, and downstairs into the kitchen. It's dark outside, and only a couple of people are still sitting at the pool. Karla is not among them, and I breathe a sigh of relief.

Gabriel walks with his shoulders back and head high, his muscles rippling beneath his tanned skin, his shorts hanging perfectly on his hips just below those two awesome dimples in his lower back on either side of his spine. He looks so content in his skin, and I'm envious.

"What's the time?" I ask as he hands me a plate of potato salad and a boerewors roll.

"Around seven."

"Sleeping Beauty's awake." Dirk strolls into the kitchen. "Those sosaties you brought were *lekker*."

"Glad you enjoyed them." I stare at the ketchup-smeared sausage on my plate, dreaming of honey-drizzled chicken kebabs.

"I tried saving you one, but these guys are pigs." Gabriel leans onto the counter, hair falling into his eyes. Dirk pretends to punch Gabriel. Gabriel reacts and has him in a headlock in seconds. Watching them laugh and wrestle, I wish I were a boy.

GABRIEL BORROWS Dirk's car and drives me home. He puts on Metallica, and I roll down the window, letting the cool night air breeze through my hair.

"You should put the window up," he says and slows to a crawl as we approach a red robot.

"Does this car have aircon?"

"No, it's just…." He scans the road, his gaze flicking left and right to the foliage flanking the pavement. The lights turn green and he accelerates, loosening his white-knuckle grip on the steering wheel.

"You okay?"

"Fine," he says, although he clearly isn't. The scenario repeats itself every time we approach a red traffic light.

"Are you always this paranoid?" I ask as we roll toward the fifth intersection on red.

"It's the weed."

Somehow I don't believe him, but I don't argue.

We pull into my driveway a full fifteen minutes before curfew. He lowers the volume on Metallica screeching from the speakers and turns to look at me.

"I had a great time," I say.

"Despite getting drugged?"

"Wasn't so bad."

"My friends...." He bites his bottom lip. "I'm sorry."

"What for?"

He looks down and picks at the stitching on the steering wheel cover. "Like that whole cucumber thing with Karla."

"Oh. That." I'm blushing.

He flicks damp hair off his face. "We have a bit of a history."

"That much was obvious."

Gabriel gives me a long look, and I think he's not going to say anything more when he eventually starts talking. "We were sort of together for a while last year, and it didn't end well."

"I see."

"Sorry."

"It's okay. Not like I don't have a few exes in the closet either." Why am I lying?

"Really?" He looks curious.

"No, actually," I blurt, and thankfully Gabriel laughs, dispelling the tension.

"I only have two, and that's definitely two too many," he says.

He's only had two girlfriends? I'm not sure if I find it reassuring that Gabriel isn't a slag, or intimidating that his standards are clearly so high he's only dated two girls. Although high standards wouldn't explain Karla. Is that the kind of girl he likes, pierced and safety-pin clad? Why did he go for me, then, and not Jordan?

"Treasa...." He bites his lip as if he's about to say something, then changes his mind. We share a look, and I'm pretty sure we're about to kiss when the kitchen light flicks on and there's a silhouette in the window. Probably Mom making sure I'm not being impregnated. Trust her to ruin this moment when I could've had fireworks and shooting stars and Gabriel's lips on mine.

"I should go." I crack open the door, but he leaps out and insists on holding it open for me.

"I'll SMS you." His voice is double-chocolate fudge. "And I'll see you Thursday for the piano lesson."

"Absolutely." Part of me is still worried he might cancel, like tonight is too good to be true.

He smiles and flicks hair out of his eyes. "Good night, Treasa."

"Night." On winged feet, I skip toward my front door feeling floaty and light-headed, only the world isn't hazy, it's limned in neon.

Gabriel waves to the figure in the kitchen window before reversing out of my driveway, taking a large chunk of my heart with him.

"You're late," Mom says when I walk into the house. From the sound of the juddering pipes, Dad must be in the shower.

"We've been in the driveway for fifteen minutes."

"Your curfew was 8:00 p.m."

I roll my eyes. The digital clock on the microwave reads 20:06.

"Treasa." Mom's about to go all Gorgon on me.

"I had a great time, thanks for asking." I stomp past her and head down the passage to my bedroom. God, I hope she doesn't detect the marijuana in my bloodstream. She follows me, stepping across the threshold before I can close the door.

"I want to talk to you, young lady."

"About what? How Gabriel is obviously going to get me pregnant? Come on, Mom. I'm almost sixteen. Can't I just be in love?"

"You're in love?" She looks horrified, like she might throw up, even.

"Is that so terrible?"

"Not at all." She sits on the edge of the bed, taking a minute to recover. Riker's fast asleep on my pillow. "I just want to know more about this boy, who he is, and who his family is."

"You're being stifling."

"I'm being a mother."

"I'm tired. Can we do this tomorrow?" I need some time to process the almost kiss before I start trying to explain things to my mom.

"Fine, but I want to meet this boy. I have a right to know who my daughter thinks she's in love with."

God, she can be so condescending. Of course I just think I'm in love because I'm just a teenager, and no one under the age of forty-five could possibly understand their emotions well enough to know what they're feeling is love! I'm fuming, even though I smile and promise to tell her everything tomorrow so she'll leave me alone. She kisses me on the forehead and says good night. An hour later, I'm showered and in pajamas. Dad says good night, and I turn off my lights, shove the cat off my pillow, burrow under the duvet, and wait for Gabriel's SMS.

GABRIEL

DIRK DROPS me off before midnight. The house slumps at the end of a potholed driveway, dilapidated and unloved. Mom loved this house and spent her weekends tending flowerbeds, filling bird feeders, or making clay figurines for the garden. The gnomes she made, and which I helped her place in the flowerbeds along the driveway, are caked in bird shit. One of them lies in ceramic shards where Jean-Pierre reversed over it at Christmas. Only I seemed to care.

Lights flicker through the lounge window. My father must still be awake or passed out in front of the television. I stalk around back, through the darkness-drenched garden to the kitchen door. From there, maybe I can sneak up to my room.

My father's in the kitchen making a sandwich, and I'm caught like soon-to-be-roadkill in headlights. "There a problem with the front door?" he asks, and pops a slice of polony into his mouth.

"No."

"Good party?" he asks as if he cares, smearing Mrs. Balls across the bread.

"Ja, I guess."

"You been drinking?" He turns to face me.

"Why, have you?"

He takes three steps toward me and grabs my shirt, sniffing around my face.

"Jesus, I haven't been drinking." I shove him off me, and he grabs my wrist, inspecting the chipped varnish on my fingers.

"What the hell is this?" He squeezes so hard it hurts.

"It's nothing." I try to pull away, but his grip is a vise. "Marlize did it, just for fun."

"Playing dress up with little girls now?"

What the hell is this about? So I usually remember to soak my fingers in acetone before my father sees any trace of polish. I never thought he'd freak out like this.

"It's just nail polish. It doesn't mean anything," I say, still trying to wiggle free.

"No son of mine...." His favorite phrase these days.

"I wish I wasn't your son." Somewhere inside me, a dam breaks, and the words rush in a torrent I can't control. "You should've been in the car that night. It should've been you with a bullet in the head bleeding out on the side of the road. You should've died." I shove him away, but he's still got my wrist. Instinct kicks in, and I go through the motions of practiced defense movements.

Despite my father's extra weight, taking him down should be easy enough. Part of me registers the hard kitchen tiles and the damage they'll inflict if I use full force to pin him down. My hesitation results in a moment of imbalance. We go down together, and my father's flailing fist catches me square on the cheek. I squirm and roll away as he lies winded on the floor. My face throbs. Gingerly, I explore my cheek. It's going to leave one hell of a bruise.

My father grunts as he rolls to his knees. He meets my gaze, and there's genuine surprise in his eyes. Guess he didn't expect so much fight from a moffie piano player. I peel myself off the floor and head to my room. I lock the door behind me, his shouts fading.

The reflection in the mirror has a lopsided face already swelling up on the right. I should put ice on it, but I want it to hurt. I need the pain. No matter how much I wish my father hadn't had one too many beers that night, no matter how much I wish it was him in the car attacked by hijackers, no matter how much I wish he could trade places with Mom, none of it matters because it's not my father's fault. It's mine.

I was a selfish and stupid kid, sneaking out to a party all the cool kids were going to. After a week of arguing with my parents, they still said no to me going to a party where there'd only be older sibling supervision. So I lied, told them I was going to Dirk's house for a sleepover, and instead I wrangled a lift from a friend's older brother to Claudia's birthday party. Claudia was my first real crush, and I wanted to prove to her that I wasn't the class nerd, that I could be cool like the rest of the boys fawning over her. Truth is, the party was terrible. I spent most of it sitting in the corner wishing the party would end. Claudia didn't even know I was there.

Apparently, I forgot my pajamas, and Mom called Dirk's mom and found out where I was. My father was over the legal limit and couldn't drive. My folks had an argument, and Mom ended up driving out to Claudia's house alone. There was no way I could've known three guys in balaclavas would be waiting at that deserted intersection for the lights to turn red, no way to know they'd shoot my mom for her car keys, only they did, and it was Dirk's mom who eventually came to pick me up. The rest of that night and the next few days are a blur I'm happier not remembering.

I quit pacing and rifle through my desk drawer for the Bic lighter I know I've got buried in there. The flame dances above the spark wheel, and I roll up my shorts, revealing a cluster of scars on my inner thigh. It's ironic they call these smileys.

TREASA

JORDAN PINCHES my arm, and I snap out of my daydream. An illicit one involving Resa and Tristan, except that in my fantasy it's Gabriel and Tristan who end up in the janitor's closet with their pants around their ankles.

"What?"

"You've been in a *dwaal* the entire week," Jordan says.

"Sorry."

"Girl's in love." Lethi fans herself with her dog-eared copy of *Julius Caesar* and bats her eyelashes.

"And it's annoying." Jordan sounds genuinely peeved.

"I think it's sweet. Tell us again about the almost kiss," Sibo teases me.

"And all the SMSs." Lethi grins.

I've already told them the kiss story at least a dozen times, recalling that night in blow-by-blow detail—except the part about me being an alien. Only Jordan got to hear that bit. I didn't tell any of them what Dirk said about Hannah either, since news like that spreads like a veld fire and can be even more destructive.

"I'd really rather you didn't." Jordan slams her book shut as the bell rings. One more lesson, a whole fifty-five minutes to get through until the end of the day, then another wait before choir, then choir…. What should I say to him? That I'm in love with him and that I'll happily lose my virginity to him? I'm not sure it's not the truth, and that's terrifying.

"You got PMS or something?" Sibo asks.

"No, I'm just tired of little miss infatuated here." Jordan leaves, not waiting for me to catch up.

"What's her problem?" I ask.

"Something to do with Bryce, I think." Lethi packs up and heads toward home economics as I follow in the wake of Jordan's turbulent exit to science.

She ignores me when I join her at our usual desk. "What's wrong, Jords?"

"Nothing." She stares straight ahead.

"You're obviously upset."

She gives me a withering gaze. "Thanks for finally noticing."

That stings, because it's true. I've been so wrapped up in thoughts about Gabriel, I haven't paid any attention to anything else. I even spaced out during English yesterday and got an embarrassing B on a test that should've been a piece of cake in the one subject I'm actually damn good at.

"I'm sorry. But I'm here now."

Our physics teacher walks in and switches on the overhead projector. There's a collective moan as we start copying notes from the screen. While annoying, it's also the perfect opportunity for a scribbled margin conversation.

Please tell me, I start.

Bryce! He gives me fake roses and then tries to go to third base with me.

What's third again?

Below the belt.

And you said no.

Which apparently came as a shock because bitchface Hannah has told the WHOLE of Cosmas that I'm a guaranteed screw.

What!?!? I don't understand girls.

Yeah so now that that's a no, he's lost interest.

Is this what'll happen with Gabriel? Is he only interested in me because of rumors like this one? But why pick me?

Typical. What a dick. You're better off without him. Words of comfort, I hope.

I liked him. :(

I'm sorry.

I just need a hug.

I put down my pen and wrap my arms around her. Her shoulders shudder, and I think she might be crying, but Jordan's tougher than that. She won't cry at school, especially not over something like this. Candyce and Hannah are sitting two rows in front of us, having a whispered conversation. Hannah glances over her shoulder, skiffing us.

"Urgh, lesbo skanks," she sneers.

Jordan tries to pull away, and I hold onto her a moment longer.

"Thanks," she says and returns to her notes. I tear a piece of paper out of my exam pad and contemplate what I'm about to do. Hannah deserves it. She's been a bitch to Jordan for no reason and picks on me relentlessly. I'm sick of it. The words run and smear across the page as fury clouds my vision.

Dirk Joubert wants to know if you still have huge nipples. Who's the slut now?

I fold the piece of paper and write "Hannah" on the front before handing it to Tina behind me and telling her to pass it along. The note traverses the classroom, and more than one girl stops to read it, snickering and "oh my goshing" as they do. Eventually, the note gets handed to Hannah. Her face turns red, then purple. She whips around in her chair, searching for the culprit. I meet her gaze, and she scrunches up the note, probably wishing it was my head. Mission accomplished. Maybe now she'll leave Jordan alone and concentrate her vitriolic attacks on just me instead.

LETHI, SIBO, and I head to choir without Jordan, who's decided to work out her angst in the art room. Her Stigmata Martyr project is almost complete and scheduled to be unveiled in the library next Tuesday as part of culture week. Apparently, she's putting the Minora blades to good use.

Gabriel arrives late and flustered. There's a bruise on his left cheek, which, combined with his messy hair, makes him look more rugged and badass-sexy than ever before. He catches my eye and gives me a tiny smile before Mrs. McArthur ruffles her tie-dyed skirts and rehearsal starts in earnest. Since we almost kissed, it hasn't exactly been a Romeo and Juliet whirlwind romance. He did SMS that night, only to say he enjoyed the evening and that we'd talk soon. I managed to control myself and not SMS him all week, even though I desperately wanted to. He finally SMSed around midnight last night saying he'd see me today—that was all.

An hour later, I follow Gabriel to the last practice room in the block, offering us a smidgen more privacy than the others. I really don't want anyone gawking in at us through the window, or standing outside laughing at my pathetic attempt to play "Chopsticks."

"How are you?" He drops a music file onto the piano.

"I'm so sick of teenage girls." I settle on the creaking stool.

"Why?"

"Because they're mean and bitchy. Sometimes I wish I was a boy."

"So you could just punch each other and move on?" He raises an eyebrow at me.

"Is that how it works?"

"Sometimes." He's still standing by the door.

"Is that what happened to your face?"

"Karate." Gabriel doesn't elaborate, and there's a guarded look in his eyes that makes me think maybe it didn't happen at the dojo.

"Aren't you meant to be on holiday now?"

"Ja, but Mrs. McArthur insisted I wear uniform to the practices."

Probably because she's afraid he'll arrive in a vest or something equally sexy and create a hormone storm in the choir room.

"Don't you have better things to do in the holidays?"

"Not really."

Awkward.

"So where do we begin?" The black-and-white keys feel cool beneath my sweaty fingertips.

"Actually, I wanted to talk to you about this." He rakes his fingers through his hair. "I'm not sure this is such a good idea."

"If you want, I can pay you."

Gabriel shifts under my glare and jams his hands into his pockets. "That's not what I mean."

Oh, I get it. "Would you teach me if I slept with you?" I trace my fingers across the piano keys without looking at him. After an excruciating minute of silence, Gabriel perches at the edge of the piano stool.

"Christ, Treasa. No." His voice is low and rich as treacle. "Not even at all."

Great, so I disgust him. "Good to know."

"Sorry, I didn't mean it...." He closes his eyes for a moment and shakes his head. "Treasa, my life is complicated enough without a girlfriend. I just don't think I should lead you on."

"Oh." My world starts disintegrating, as if some giant hand holding sandpaper starts scrubbing out everything good and beautiful, beginning with Gabriel.

"Could we be friends?" he asks and plays a trill as if it's nothing.

Friends. Yay. Nothing better than just being friends with the boy of your dreams. But if I say no, then that's good-bye Gabriel, and not having him at all would be worse than having him only as a friend.

"Sure," I say without conviction. "Friends." I give him a wan smile, and he shuffles closer, giving me a good whiff of his deodorant. This is torture.

"Can you still read music?" he asks, apparently relieved the conversation is over.

"A bit." I avoid meeting his gaze. "The treble clef, the time signature, key signature. Not sure where these notes are on the piano, though."

He opens the music file and taps a note. I squint at a black squiggle that could be an E or a G.

"Big Dogs Fight All Cats," he says.

They're just five notes, not even music, and yet, I can't stop staring at his fingers as he plays each note according to the rhyme. I can't stop thinking about what he said. So whose life isn't complicated? It doesn't mean you shouldn't even give being with someone a chance, does it?

"Treasa?"

"Yeah?" I try to focus on the piano. "I remember a different one, about cows eating grass."

"That's for the left hand." Gabriel gestures for me to put my hands on the keyboard. He nudges my right hand up a few notes, his touch igniting every nerve ending in my body.

"This is G position. G, A, B, C, D." He plays the notes with my fingers. "Now the left hand."

He reaches around the back of me and presses the keys down with his fingers on top of mine. His chest is pressed against my back, his body heat soaking through my clothes and skin. I want to concentrate on the musical alphabet, but it's impossible with his face so close to mine. Screw it. Life is too short not to kiss a beautiful boy when he's practically on top of you anyway. I turn toward him, our lips almost touching. I angle my kiss higher, brushing my lips across the bruise on his cheek.

I thought he'd pull away, run for the door, but he doesn't.

"Why?" There's a war raging behind his eyes. He fixes me with his emerald gaze, and I almost cower from the intensity of his stare.

"Why what?"

"Why me?"

Has he looked in a mirror lately? Is he that oblivious to his own awesomeness?

"Because you're perfect." I grab his tie, tugging him closer, and then my lips are on his. I remember Jordan's instruction: brief touch, pull back, share a look, then go in for the real deal. I pull back and meet Gabriel's gaze. His eyes aren't just green; they have these little flecks of brown in them and a black ring around the edges. His fingers leave a lava trail up my arm as he reaches behind my head and slips his fingers into my hair. He pulls me forward, and we kiss again as heat spools through my veins.

This time our lips meet, and his mouth opens, just like Jordan's did, and I let him kiss me, I even kiss him back, and our tongues do this darting dance like I've seen in movies. As his grip tightens in my hair, I place my own hand on his cheek, fingers hovering above the bruise. Our bodies press together, and I'm pretty sure Gabriel wants to do more than just kiss me. His pants don't do much to conceal that fact. His kiss makes me feel like a quasar, emitting enough energy to incinerate us both.

This is it, my first real kiss. So the lightbulb above us doesn't explode, and I doubt he's seeing a sunrise on Saturn. It's still a great kiss. Even so, I don't want to be me right now. I want to be a boy in the janitor's closet with him. Without thinking, I splay my fingers on his chest, running my palm across his well-defined pecs. What I want is a body like his and hair and eyes.... I want to unzip his skin and crawl inside of him.

He pulls away first and runs a hand through his hair, his forehead creased with concern.

I gulp down a lungful of air, my face ablaze. We share a long look, and I'm sure he's about to tell me how we're still just friends. The tension between us is palpable.

"Nobody's perfect," he says.

I shrug and lick my lips, still tasting his kiss.

Gabriel surreptitiously rearranges his pants and coughs a little. "You still want to play?"

"Fine. Let's get back to the G-spot."

He laughs, a full-on belly-rumbling laugh that leaves me mortified even as it dispels the tension.

I try to place my trembling fingers in the correct place. My blood's going to turn into red steam if I blush any hotter, so I'm going to pretend I didn't just say that and keep breathing.

"It's the G position, Treasa." He shifts my hand up a few notes. "Let's try again."

Yes, please, let's. Let's just keep kissing and let everything else fade away. At least when I've got my eyes closed and my body pressed against his, I can almost believe I'm not Treasa, not an alien, and not this girl I don't want to be.

GABRIEL

WHEN SHE asked about sex, I should've said yes and either chased her away for good or been able to score. It was a win-win situation for me, and instead I sat down and taught her to play C major. Now she thinks I'm perfect. Perfection doesn't even exist. It's some imagined perceptual construct designed to drive people mad in the search for this nonexistent ideal.

No piece of music, no matter how exquisite the melody, no matter how complex the harmony or detailed the dynamics, can ever be perfect. A person is like that too. Sure, you can have perfectly straight teeth or a face free of acne, you can have symmetrical facial features and Michelangelo-like muscle definition, but that's superficial. If you start deconstructing the whole, you'll start seeing the tiny imperfections—the parallel fifths in the chords, the stray sharps or erroneous slurs… the scars and shame and guilt, the conceit and selfishness, ego and eccentricities.

I'm not perfect, and while it might seem flattering to have Treasa think I am, it's really terrifying. If she only knew the truth about my mom…. Treasa's got me on a pedestal, and I'm getting vertigo. The problem with being put on a pedestal is that when you tumble off it—and you will—you don't just break. You shatter.

AM I AN ALIEN, TREASA TEST #05

HYPOTHESIS: Extraterrestrials possess superhuman abilities such as telepathy or the ability to share images from memory or thought during sexual contact.

GOAL: To prove a telepathic connection is possible during sexual contact, specifically kissing.

METHOD:

Kiss Gabriel—with tongue.

Gauge reaction—shock or disbelief may indicate visions occurred during kiss.

Ask Gabriel if he saw anything—without sounding too weird.

RESULTS: Kiss was successful. However, there was no evidence to suggest Gabriel was shocked, creeped out, scared, or otherwise surprised during or after the kiss, suggesting he saw/felt nothing out of the ordinary. Step 3 was deemed unnecessary.

CONCLUSION: Since this alien power may require certain chemicals in the brain (serotonin and oxytocin) in order to occur, kissing alone may not be enough to produce desired effects. Inconclusive.

Will have to try again.

TREASA

I SPEND Friday afternoon with Jordan under the pretense of studying for a math test on Monday. So far there's been no apparent backlash over the note I sent to Hannah, although word has spread throughout the grade that a Stormhof boy has seen her naked. I've heard various versions of the story, and they all have one thing in common: little miss perfect is sleeping around. Hannah did her best to ignore the comments today, neither confirming nor denying the rumors. I almost feel bad for her, guilty about what I did, but after all the nasty things she's said about Jordan, Hannah deserves it.

I'm bursting to tell Jordan about my kiss with Gabriel. Given her reaction to the previous almost-kiss discussion, I'm going to play it cool.

"You think I could ask Gabriel to the art expo?" I ask Jordan as we float around the swimming pool on lilos.

"Why not?" She drags her fingers through the water and flicks droplets at me.

"Do you think I should sleep with him?"

Jordan pushes her sunglasses up her forehead and meets my gaze. "Does he want you to?"

"I think so."

"You haven't even kissed yet."

"Well...."

"Did I miss something?" She sits up on her lilo and peers at me over the rim of her sunglasses.

"We did kiss. Yesterday."

Using her hands like spades, she chucks water at me until I'm begging her to stop. "Why didn't you tell me?" She gets just as drenched as I do.

"Because...."

"Bryce? I'm so over that." She wrings her hair out. "Soooo, tell me about this kiss."

And I do.

"Do you want to take it further?" she asks after I've described the kiss in extreme detail, twice.

"I think so."

"I don't think you should." She paddles closer to me and grabs hold of my lilo. "It's not something you can take back. Once you do it, that's it. No undo button."

"Do you regret doing it with Callum?"

Jordan sucks on her lower lip. "Ja, I do. I liked him, but I should've waited. There's no rush, you know?"

"I know, it's just…."

"He's in Matric and you think he expects it?" Jordan raises an eyebrow at me.

"Kind of."

"That's the wrong reason to do it. You barely know this guy. If he's still around in six months, then maybe you should consider it. But definitely not now, especially not with Hannah on the warpath." Jordan hands me her sunglasses and slips into the water. She's right, but without giving him more, I'm not sure Gabriel will be around in six months, and I don't want to lose him.

"Let's get ice cream." Jordan emerges at the steps and grabs a towel.

Fifteen minutes later, we're in the Spar up the road, contemplating the virtues of ice cream on a stick. I've made my decision and leave Jordan trying to decide between mint and caramel as I make my way to the toiletries section. The shop doesn't have much to offer by way of hair dyes, only three different browns. Maybe I can't change my eye color or my biology, but what I can change, I will.

"If you want to dye your hair, I've got tons of henna at home." Jordan comes up behind me. "It's better for you and not so permanent."

"Brown, though. Not black."

"Think I can manage that," she says, and I amble over to the nail polish to find the darkest color they have. Deep burgundy. That'll do.

"Will you dye my hair for me?"

"When?" We head to the cashier. Jordan says nothing about my nail polish purchase.

"Today."

She gives me a measured look, her eyes narrowed. "Why the sudden decision?" We walk out of the air-conditioned store into the blistering sun.

"Been wanting to for a while. Just haven't had the courage." I shrug. I'm not sure Jordan would understand why I want to look less like me and more like Resa, more like Gabriel.

"Your mom's going to have an apoplexy." Jordan grins through a mouthful of caramel ice cream.

"That's her problem." I'm done asking for permission to be the person I want to be. If Mom doesn't like it, then she can just give me back to the adoption agency. I'm not sure they have a return policy, but if Mom really can't handle me being a brunette, I'm sure they'll make a plan.

An hour later, I've got my now dark hair piled atop my head as we wait for the color to set. We're watching a daytime rerun of *Project Blue Book* and painting our nails. I coat mine with several layers, trying to make the color darker, while Jordan paints hers with a single layer of bright blue. The episode is from last season, the one where Resa gets drunk and switches hair color.

"I wish I had that power." Jordan studies a strand of her own hair. "How cool would it be to be able to look different on a whim?"

"I'd kill to have that kind of ability."

"What's up, Ree?" Jordan turns down the volume on the TV.

"Nothing."

"Come on. I know you better than that. Piercing your ears, dying your hair, painting your nails." She snatches the polish out of my hand before I can start applying a fifth coat. "You're changing."

"No, I'm not."

"Ja, you are, and you're changing for him, aren't you? Did Gabriel say something about your hair?"

"No!" Her assumptions are a little too close to the truth for comfort. "Just want to try something different."

"As long as it's not for him. Do it for yourself." She studies my hair and pats down a loose strand.

"Do you ever wish you were someone else?" I ask.

"Like who? Nicole Kidman or Alanis Morissette or something?" She gestures for me to follow her to the bathroom, and I do, not answering until she starts rinsing my hair over the bathtub.

"No, I mean…. Just like a normal person, only not yourself."

"I like being me."

"I don't."

Jordan puts down the shower spray and hands me a towel. "You don't like being you?"

"Not all the time. Sometimes I wonder what it would be like to be someone else."

"Like who?" She turns me to face the mirror. So I've still got a freckle infestation, but at least the orange hair has been replaced by shiny chocolate brown.

"This is perfect, thank you." I give Jordan a hug before I start tugging a comb through the damp strands.

"Like who, Ree?" She perches on the edge of the bathtub, studying my reflection as I work out tangles.

"Do you ever wonder what it would be like to be a boy?"

Jordan crinkles her nose in disgust. "Dirty, sweaty, horny, and prone to erections at inappropriate moments? No, thanks. Being able to pee standing up is not worth body hair and prostate exams."

Tears prick my eyes as I study my reflection. "So you want to be a girl?"

"I am a girl." Jordan gives me a puzzled look. "It's who I am. Who we are."

"I guess." I force a smile. I must be the only person on the planet who feels cheated by God or whomever decided on my double-X chromosome. No one ever gave me the choice, and if they had, I sure as hell wouldn't have picked this body.

MOM SAID nothing when she saw my hair, which was almost worse than if she'd started ranting. We drove home in stiff silence. Mom focused on the road, and I focused on the Chopin étude pouring out of the radio tuned to Classic FM and wondering if Gabriel can play Chopin as well as Beethoven.

"Is it henna?" Mom asks as we pull into the driveway.

"Yes."

"Does it damage your hair?" Mom turns off the engine, making no move to get out.

"It hasn't damaged Jordan's."

Mom's lips are pressed into thin white lines. "Why are you doing this, Resa?"

"Doing what?"

"Is this because of that boy?" Mom grips the steering wheel, her knuckles paler than her lips.

"No." Yes, only not in the way Mom thinks. "I just didn't want orange hair anymore."

"And the earring and nail polish?"

"Just wanted a change." I shrug.

"Are you done, or will you come home with a nose ring next week?"

"Urgh, Mom." I roll my eyes and get out of the car, slamming the door behind me. Mom stays put, and I stalk into the house.

"Wow, Resa." Dad's in the kitchen making his signature coleslaw. "What happened?"

"I dyed my hair, that's all."

"But why?" He puts down the knife, wipes his cabbage-smeared hands, and comes toward me, reaching tentatively for my dark strands.

"Because I was sick of being a carrottop."

"Oh, sweetheart, your hair was lovely. It suited you. This...." Dad hesitates. "It makes you look different."

"Different good? Different bad?"

"Just... different. It'll take some getting used to." He kisses my forehead and returns to the chopping board. "Where's your Mom?"

"Still in the car recovering from the shock."

Dad nods. On my way to my bedroom, I hear the front door open and shut. Dad's probably gone out to console my mom. If she's going to have a meltdown about my change of hair color—just wait til I mention I want a breast reduction. Maybe all these little changes are good for her, gradually easing her toward accepting the bigger changes yet to come, and they're not going to be a bloody nose ring.

Mom looks as if she's been crying but says nothing about my hair or her bloodshot eyes at dinner. She burns the steaks. Something must be really wrong because Dad doesn't complain, and he usually would've given Mom a lecture about how to cook the perfect sirloin the way his mother did. It's my turn to do the dishes. Dad tells me he'll do them and gives me a wink. Leaving my parents to their whispered conversation and soapy water, I retreat to my bedroom and stare at my phone.

To SMS or to call, that is the question.

Twenty minutes later, I've typed and deleted umpteen versions of the same SMS, so I take a deep breath and call him instead. Gabriel answers on the second ring. I cut right to the chase, hoping to avoid any awkward discussion about G positions and kisses.

"There's an art expo at the school next Tuesday evening. Only the best works from grade ten to twelve will be on display. I was wondering if you wanted to come. It's a uniform event."

There's a moment where all I can hear is his breathing. "I have karate. What time?"

My heart shrinks two sizes. "Starts at six, but you can come anytime before nine."

"Is your work going to be on display?" he asks.

"No, I don't do art."

"Oh." He sounds disappointed.

"But Jordan's will be." Not sure why Gabriel would care about that.

"Okay, I'll be there, but I'll only make it closer to seven."

"That's great. See you then." I'm about to hang up when he says my name. "Yeah?"

"You coming to class tomorrow?"

"Sure."

"Good. See you tomorrow." He hangs up, leaving me wishing we'd spoken about the piano lesson, because now I have to face him with the kiss hanging over us like a guillotine.

GABRIEL

I'VE SKIPPED karate practice this week, partly because of my face and partly because I don't want to get naked in front of others with fresh burns on my leg. Scars people can ignore. Fresh wounds are harder to pretend don't exist. I lean against Nathan's car, squinting up at the ultramarine sky. Not even 9:00 a.m. and it's already spiking above twenty-five degrees. Will this summer never end?

Nathan dumps his gear in the back before studying my face. The bruise is yellow now, barely visible except to those who are used to giving and receiving punches.

"You didn't get that at the dojo," he says.

"Wouldn't be the first." I turn away. He grabs my chin and pulls my face toward his so we're eye to eye.

"Who's hitting you?"

"It was an accident."

"Someone at school? Are you being bullied?"

"I'm a black belt, remember?"

He releases my chin. "Your father, then?"

"It was an accident." I look down, studying the pockmarked tar.

"Is that what he told you to say?"

"No. It's the truth." This time, at least.

"You should at least defend yourself, or do you let him hit you too?"

I meet his gaze, hating the look of pity in his eyes. "What the hell do you know?"

"Nothing, Gabe, except what I see in my dojo week after week. You think I'm the only one who notices Sempai getting the crap beaten out of him?"

"So what?"

"Nothing." He opens the door and slides in behind the wheel. Reluctantly, I get into the passenger seat. "But," he continues, "I know when one of my students is in trouble. I let you take it at the dojo because it's controlled and I can stop it if it goes too far. Knowing you get hit at home, that's different." He starts the car.

"It's not like I'm being abused or anything. Tons of kids get smacked around."

"Sure, my dad used to take off his belt and tan our backsides if we so much as put our elbows on the table. Doesn't make it okay."

I stare out the window, watching the street vendors setting up their roadside stalls: wood-carved giraffes and rainbow-colored beanbags, pirated DVDs and ethnic jewelry made in China. I can't help feeling nervous every time we stop at a robot. Even in broad daylight, I half expect men with masks and guns to descend, and I wasn't even in the car with my mom when it happened.

"Have you got someone to talk to?" Nathan asks.

"Like a shrink?"

"No, I mean like an adult who isn't your dad."

"I am an adult. Ag, it doesn't matter."

Muscles tighten along his jaw. "Of course it matters. Have you spoken to anyone since your mom died?"

"Jesus, when did you get a degree in psychology? So I let people hit me. I'm not going to kill myself." Although throwing myself out of the car right now is rather appealing. I'd be crushed instantly by the taxi in the lane beside us. Probably wouldn't even feel the breaks and abrasions before the tires crunched over my skull. My hand finds the door lock and pops it open.

"How's piano going?" Nathan asks, catching me off guard. "When's that big exam again?"

"Whenever I'm ready."

"When's that?"

"Who knows?" The practical part is easy; the theory and everything else is not.

"How many pieces have you got?"

"Four."

"Mozart, Beethoven, Bach, and?" A sly smile spreads across his face.

"Beethoven and Bach, yes. Then Schumann and Rachmaninoff." I lock the door again and take a deep breath before going into detail. Not that Nathan knows much about art music, but he listens, and that's enough.

TREASA DYED her hair. She's destroyed the one thing that made her truly magnificent, making herself ordinary instead. Goodbye Celtic princess; hello bad dye job. The dark hair is at odds with her pale eyebrows and gingerbread freckles and just looks wrong. She's not my girlfriend. We kissed once. If she wants to dye her hair or even shave it all off, it's none of my business.

"You like it?" she asks. I don't know how to answer that when we're surrounded by a dozen others in the gym hall about to start tossing one another onto the mat.

"It's different."

"I think it looks awesome. Makes her look older, sexier." Jordan winks at me, and I want to smack her. Older? A little, maybe. Sexier? No. Just harder and less like the lovely girl I've been pretending not to like as much as I do.

"She looks more like you." It comes out more bitter than intended, and Treasa looks confused while Jordan narrows her eyes at me and purses her lips.

"What's that supposed to mean?" Jordan asks.

"Older, sexier." I shrug, hoping it's enough of a backpedal.

"I'm thinking of cutting it too," Treasa says as she rakes back her curls into a ponytail.

"Don't."

"Why not?" She cocks her head, waiting for an answer.

"Because...." I open and close my mouth, not sure I'm even entitled to an opinion here. Sensei summons me, and I give her an apologetic smile before slinking away. Would her having shorter hair make any difference to me? Would it change how I feel about her? No, because I don't have feelings for her.... I do... but I don't want to, and.... Easier to just let Sensei throw me to the ground repeatedly than think about Treasa.

DEAR MOM,

I wish you were here. I need some advice about this girl. She's different and a little odd, but I like that about her. She's smart and sings and isn't half-bad at karate. She's a bit young but doesn't seem immature at all. Thing is, there's a lot she doesn't know about me, and she called me "perfect." How do you tell someone you're not without disappointing them? I don't want to disappoint Treasa, but I feel like I should tell her the truth, that I'm the reason you're dead. I'm pretty sure she wouldn't look at me the same way if she knew. I don't deserve her looking at me in any way.

Better to just forget all about Treasa, but I can't. She makes my world seem less gray and crappy. When she had her red hair, she was a literal splash of color on the world—not so much anymore, but she's

still got those sad eyes and ginger freckles. Part of me
wants to be perfect for her, and that's what's killing
me.

My hand cramps up from pressing too hard with the pen. I let my
gaze linger on a photo of Mom sitting on the beach near Durban, where
we went every holiday, the wind whipping her hair into a blur in the
background. She's smiling. Looking at her so alive and happy hurts
catastrophically.

I bury the shoe box and memories under my bed and turn to my
unfinished sonata instead. The second movement is finally taking shape,
thanks in part to Treasa and the music she conjures in my mind. Maybe
being with her wouldn't be such a bad thing. Maybe we could take it slow.
No harm in holding hands and the occasional kiss, right? Maybe she won't
hate me that much when I tell her the truth.

TREASA

JORDAN'S NOT nearly as nervous as I am, and I'm not the one baring my
soul to the world by exhibiting my art. We've been busy all afternoon in
the main library, clearing away tables and setting up the installations.
Hannah and her posse have ignored us, speaking in monosyllables only
when they need something like an extra easel or more duct tape, content to
skiff us the rest of the time. Candyce is conspicuous by her absence.
Thought she would've been here cheering on Hannah, but it seems she's
left that to Gillian.

Lethi, Sibo, and I pin up charcoal sketches on the backboard,
forming winglike extensions on either side of Jordan's central work—the
one I have yet to see.

"These are amazing," Sibo says. "This girl can draw."

"It's all from her head?" Lethi asks.

"You think someone would've posed for this?" I pin up a detailed
drawing of a girl masturbating with a crucifix.

"You think she'll get expelled?" Sibo's forehead puckers with
concern.

"The art teacher never said anything, so I doubt it. Besides, this school needs some progressive thinkers." Lethi pins up another drawing, this one of three naked men, the last more ephemeral than the others.

"Oh my God, is that the Holy Trinity?" I ask.

"Yup." Jordan beams and carries a huge canvas to the central easel.

"You are going to be in trouble, Jords."

"Wait til you see this." She places the painting, fussing over the alignment, and once happy, beckons us to look at her display head-on.

"Eish." Sibo sucks in a breath.

"Girl, you've got sack." Lethi high-fives her, and I stand gobsmacked. I'm blushing just looking at it. The painting is beautiful at first glance, a perfect replica of the Virgin Mary statue in the main corridor of our school. Except, instead of a crown of roses, Mary has a crown of razor blades cutting into her forehead. She's also got razor blades protruding from her wrists and ankles. And what should be a bleeding heart is actually, well, it could be a flower, but I know Jordan, and what she's painted is a vagina.

"What are the lyrics again?" I ask, my hands shaking at my friend's audacity. Jordan unrolls paper made to look like an old-fashioned scroll complete with ink smudges, charred edges, and a broken wax seal. She pins it up above Mary's head, just like the INRI scroll present on many crucifixes. As we read, my blood cools and fear knots in my belly. How could the art teacher let her do something like this?

"Crimson orifice?" Lethi asks and Jordan points at the heart-flower bit.

"And the naked guys?" Sibo asks with a flick of her braids.

There's a mischievous glint in Jordan's eye. "Father, Son, and Holy Ghost," she says.

"That's disgusting!" Hannah stands behind us with her hands on her hips. "Like, I may actually lose my lunch right here. It might improve your installation."

"Oh, blow me," Jordan shoots back.

"I bet you'd love that," Hannah sneers.

"I've heard you give great head." My words are bullets.

"And I bet you're doing both those Stormhof boys." Hannah's shaken—I must have hit a nerve—and her accusation lacks conviction.

"I think they're messing up your display." Sibo points at Hannah's setup and her friends, who are struggling with a giant fishtank for who knows what.

"No, not like that!" Hannah bolts as her friends slosh water all over the carpet.

"An hour til parents and everyone else start arriving." Jordan rubs her hands together gleefully.

"If you want to stay a pupil long enough to have this seen by anyone, maybe you should cover it up." Lethi gestures to spare tablecloths lying on an unused desk.

"Great idea." Jordan grabs one, and we all help her enshroud her painting before going in search of free tea and biscuits. If nothing else, the reveal will certainly be dramatic.

GABRIEL ARRIVES on time, his hair hanging in damp waves that brush his blazer collar. I'm surprised they haven't ordered him to cut it yet. He flicks strands from his eyes and fiddles with his tie, searching the crowd.

"Up here." I wave from the top of the stairs, and he takes the steps two at time.

"Hi." He gives me that smile, and my heart kicks up two gears.

"You're on time."

"Ja, thought it would be impolite to show up late."

"I'm glad you're here." I tuck an errant curl behind my ear, and his gaze drifts from my face to my hair.

"I preferred it the way it was."

"Really, you liked my orange hair?"

"It wasn't orange, and it reminded me of Boudicca." He leans against one of the pillars lending our library Grecian elegance.

"Like the Queen of the Iceni?" He knows history too. Could this guy be any more perfect?

"That's the one. You look Irish."

"I am, sort of." He doesn't even know I'm adopted. I wonder if that'll change anything?

"Hey, Gharbriel." Jordan pronounces his name with the guttural Afrikaans G. I glare at her.

"I've heard you're a fantastic artist." He charms her, and I'm a little jealous until he takes my hand. Our fingers are entwined, our palms pressed together. I cannot breathe.

"Flattery will get you nowhere, mister." She smiles, and I know he's forgiven for last Saturday's hair comment. "You coming? Time for the great reveal." She skips into the library, and we follow. I hope everyone sees him holding my hand. I want to hold it high above our shoulders and do a victory dance.

I manage to restrain myself, leaning into his shoulder. He smells so good. I can't wait to kiss him again.

Parents and teachers are gathered around the artworks, some already tittering about the contents of Jordan's sketches. Sibo and Lethi join us, and after introducing them to Gabriel, we all help Jordan peel back the tablecloth. There's a collective gasp from the onlookers and Jordan suppresses a grin of satisfaction.

"Um, really?" Gabriel looks shocked, and so am I when I turn around to face the painting.

"No, no, no."

Jordan's painting is destroyed. Sure, it was subversive and blasphemous to start with, but it was still a brilliant work of art. Not anymore. The word "SLUT" has been daubed over the canvas with thick black paint, ruining the piece. Parents and teachers stare aghast, not knowing whether this was intended or some horrible prank.

"Jordan." I lay a hand on her shoulder. She wrenches away. Jordan takes another look at the painting, tears welling in her eyes. "Jords, we'll find out who did this."

"We know who did this." She glances over her shoulder at Hannah, who's not doing a good job of feigning innocence. Jordan strides toward her.

"Jordan, don't," I call after her, but she ignores me and has already reached Hannah's installation by the time I catch up. Lethi, Sibo, and Gabriel follow.

"You did this." Jordan's voice is low and deadly.

"What? I would never." Hannah smirks.

Jordan stares at her, and I can almost hear the cogs grinding in my friend's head. Jordan's gaze drops to the fish tank. Hannah has got tiny figurines suspended in glass bubbles at various depths in the tank. It's clever and really pretty, and I know Jordan's about to break it.

"Jordan, please." I grab her arm too late as she kicks the tank with the full force of her newly acquired karate skills. Hannah screams as water, varicolored angelfish, and her glass bubbles scatter across the carpet.

"You bitch." Hannah claws at Jordan, but Jordan evades her fingers and gives her a bloody nose instead. Parents and teachers stare, dumbfounded. Jordan pulls back her fist, and I'm frozen to the spot, knowing she's going to keep hitting Hannah until someone stops her, and I still can't seem to get my limbs to move. Gabriel steps around me and grabs Jordan's arm. She tries one of the defensive moves, attempting to buck Gabriel. He anticipates her movement and folds his arms around her even as she screams. Meanwhile, Hannah starts spitting invective at Jordan, calling her four-letter words I've never heard before.

"Hannah Walters!" Mrs. Owen swoops in in all her intimidating, bowel-loosening, headmistress fury.

"She started it." Hannah points at Jordan.

"And I will end this."

"She broke my nose!"

"If you can swear at these decibel levels, I highly doubt your nose is broken." The principal has spoken.

"Hannah, darling, what happened?" The woman who can only be Hannah's mother joins the fray, dabbing at the blood on Hannah's face with tissues. "Who did this to you?" the woman shrieks.

"She did." Hannah points at Jordan.

"Mrs. Walters, I'd like you and Hannah to meet in my office, immediately. Please. As for you—"

Mrs. Owen turns to Jordan, who is hysterical, sobbing into Gabriel's chest. The principal looks at her with what might be sympathy before gesturing to me.

"Calm her down and then bring her to my office. Bring your friends as well, anyone who might've been involved." She gives me a stern look that turns my innards to water. "Got it, Treasa?"

"Yes, Mrs. Owen."

"Good. And you can thank that young man for me too. Get hold of Jordan's mom, please." The principal then orders a bunch of grade eights to clean up the spill, and the crowd returns to relative normalcy. Lethi and Sibo have the good sense to cover up the ruined painting before joining me as we escort Jordan to the bathrooms.

I turn to Gabriel. "I'm so sorry about this."

"Don't be. Just take care of your friend."

"Call me later?"

"You don't want me to stick around in case you need help with anything?" he asks.

"You really don't have to. I'll call you later. Thank you, though. For everything." I could kiss him if it weren't for Jordan's renewed sobs echoing from the bathroom.

I say good-bye and hurry into the to help Jordan, cursing Hannah and humanity in general for ruining what could've been an awesome night for all of us. I wish I could reverse time like Resa. I'd take us back to before Hannah ruined the painting, and I'd stop her from doing it. Maybe I'd unravel time even farther and stop myself from sending that bloody nipple note to Hannah in the first place. This is all my fault.

AM I AN ALIEN, TREASA TEST #06

HYPOTHESIS: Extraterrestrials possess superhuman powers such as the ability to suspend or even reverse time.

GOAL: To prove I have control over time.

METHOD: (*Spontaneous experiment carried out without specific methodology.*)

Decide on specific moment to freeze or amount of time to alter reality by (freeze moment before Jordan hit Hannah—reverse time to before Hannah damaged Jordan's painting).

Concentrate on given moment and alter time.

RESULTS: Time neither froze nor reversed.

CONCLUSION: This spontaneous situation was one of immense emotional duress, and this may have affected my ability to perform a temporal shift. Results are therefore inconclusive.

GABRIEL

"IT COULD'VE been worse," Treasa tells me Thursday afternoon while we're sitting at the piano. "Jordan could've really done damage if it weren't for you. They're lucky Hannah's not pressing charges, but then, of course, Jordan could press charges for destruction of property since Hannah's friends admitted they helped her destroy the painting."

"Why do any of it in the first place?"

"It's complicated." She bites her bottom lip as a look of guilt settles over her face.

"So what's happening to Jordan?"

"They've both been suspended pending a disciplinary hearing next week." She drags her fingers along the piano keys.

"Think they'll be expelled?"

"I hope not." Treasa wrings her hands and squirms in her seat. "This is all my fault." Her shoulders sag and tears roll down her face. I hate it when girls cry—I never know what to do. Would comforting her seem patronizing? Would not comforting her make me an asshole? I slide closer on the piano stool but don't touch her.

"It's not your fault."

"Oh, it is." She chokes back a sob and looks up at me with such heartbreak in her eyes that I can't help but put my arm around her.

"How is it your fault?"

She rests her head on my shoulder and takes a wobbly breath. "Jordan and Hannah have always been at each other, name-calling and so on. Recently, Hannah spread a nasty rumor about Jordan around Cosmas, so I...." She shudders. My shirt is wet with her tears.

"So you what, Treasa?"

"Remember what Dirk said about Hannah?"

"How could I forget?"

"Yeah, so I sort of started a rumor of my own to get back at Hannah for Jordan."

"And then Hannah destroyed Jordan's art?" Girls can be passive-aggressive bitches.

"I thought she'd get revenge on me, not Jordan. This is all my fault." She hiccups and starts crying again.

"No, it's not." I kiss her hair, wishing it was still red. "You didn't force Hannah to do what she did. You didn't even know she'd do it. The situation was beyond your control. Totally not your fault."

She presses the heels of her hands into her eyes. "I should've known, though."

"You couldn't have known she'd do this." I don't know what else to say to make her feel better.

"Maybe." Treasa eases away from me. Her eyes are puffy and bloodshot, her cheeks pale, making the freckles stand out more than usual. I kiss her gently on the lips, and she smiles. "I don't think I can play today." Her hands are shaking.

"Actually…." An idea ignites. "Do you think I could play something for you?"

"Sure." She scoots off the piano stool to stand in the corner. "A new piece?"

"Just let me know what you think, honestly."

"Always."

She chews on a cuticle, and I turn to the keys. Somehow, memorizing my own compositions is never a problem. As soon as I've got the music written down, that's it. It's locked in my memory. The first movement goes smoothly, even though I take the syncopated sections slower than my own tempo indication. The piece goes well, and the modulations sound as good out loud to an audience as they did in my head and empty house. Treasa even claps at the end.

"More?" she asks.

"The second movement isn't finished yet."

"Wait, this is your own composition?" She stares, wide-eyed.

"Ja." Now it's my turn to squirm as I rub the back of my neck. My hair is too long. It's making me sweat.

"Even if it's not finished, could you play me just a little? Second movements are my favorites."

With a smile, I turn back to the piano and start playing. The music unspools beneath my fingers and snatches of melody coalesce into a theme I haven't written yet, unraveling from the dissonance of the Tristan chords peppering the movement. Must be Treasa's presence inspiring me. The music runs out a section before the end, and I diminuendo toward the last unresolved chord.

"Play it again." She perches next to me on the stool. I do, and Treasa starts to hum a descant over the notes of my right hand. Why is the most beautiful music always so sad? She continues to hum, and I scramble to accompany her with chords. She trails off after an augmented fourth.

"Should've recorded that."

"If you forget it, I can just hum it again." She smiles. "Your piece is beautiful. Does it have a name?" There are fresh tears in her eyes.

"Not yet."

"I love those dissonant chords."

"Tristan chords."

"What?" She stares at me with eyes the size of flying saucers.

"Tristan chords, named after the leitmotif used by Wagner in *Tristan und Isolde*." I play the notes of the chord. "Augmented intervals."

"*Diabolus in musica,*" Treasa says.

"That's an augmented fourth. This is an augmented sixth." I play both intervals, illustrating the difference. "But I think the augmented fourth is my favorite."

"You are so talented. God, if I had a quarter of your ability." She bites her bottom lip and looks at me with something close to awe, and it makes my skin prickle.

"This is nothing special. Not compared to Scriabin or Rachmaninoff."

"Stop being so self-deprecating. You're brilliant and you know it."

I wish I had her confidence in me. Before I can stop myself, I lean in and kiss her. She kisses me back, opening her mouth to mine. She tastes like tears, and I wrap my arms around her. I get hard and ease away from her before I embarrass myself. I smile and she licks her lips. All I want to do is spend the afternoon with Treasa, composing while she sits next to me, fueling my muse. Now I can understand why that guy in *The Red Violin* could only compose when surrounded by beautiful women.

"Can I ask you something?" she says.

"Depends."

Her forehead puckers in a frown, and she fiddles with the hem of her skirt. "When you kiss me, do you, I don't know… feel different? Weird? Like maybe see stuff?" She keeps her gaze on the piano keys.

"Um, see stuff?" The penny drops, and I chuckle. "You mean like how the girls Resa kisses see stuff, alien stuff?"

Her scarlet face is answer enough.

"You really think you're an alien?" Sort of cute, mostly troubling. Please let Treasa not be a head case.

"Forget it." There's unexpected bitterness in her tone, and I grab her hand as she stands up to leave.

"Hey, wait. I'm sorry. Just sit for a minute." She slides back down, keeping her gaze averted.

"So you really think aliens walk among us?" I ask gently.

"You've read Strieber's books, Hancock's. You think they're making it all up?" She glances at me, her blue eyes twin cobalt marbles.

"Honestly, I have no idea. I guess it's possible."

"Sometimes I just feel like that's the only explanation for…." She catches herself and clenches her jaw.

"For what?" Bells and whistles shrill in my ears that Treasa might've forgotten to take her meds this morning.

"For sometimes feeling like I don't belong."

"At St. Bridget's?"

"At school, in this country, in this body, on this planet!" She wrings her hands then turns to me and forces a grin. "You must think I'm crazy."

I take a while to answer, wanting to frame my words just right. She's opened up to me, and I should return the gesture, but there are some things I just can't talk about.

"I feel like that too sometimes. Like I should be someone else and not me."

"Exactly." This time her smile is genuine, and I want to kiss her again. We're about to take a giant leap toward being in a relationship, which means sharing truths and secrets about ourselves, which means telling Treasa the truth about my mom, which means toppling off that pedestal and turning into splinters. I can't do it.

"Treasa, I've got to go."

"Gabriel." She tugs on a strand of her hair nervously. "Would you like to come over for lunch on Sunday?"

"You mean, like, to your house?" To meet the parents? I never even met Karla's parents.

"My mom has this thing about wanting to get to know you better. It's stupid. Forget about it." She heads for the door.

"No, it's okay." I hold the door open for her and follow her out into the afternoon sunshine. The southern horizon is black with storm clouds.

"Really?"

"Why not?" Because this brings us precariously close to being an official couple.

"I'll SMS you details."

"Perfect." I choke on the word as we stroll toward the car park together. "Did you watch *Project Blue Book* this week?" I ask while we wait for our lifts.

"Oh my God, yes. How cool are Resa's new powers? Imagine being able to project a force field like that. If I were an alien, I'd like to be one like that and not a Klingon or member of the Borg."

"You're into *Star Trek*?"

"If you give me a Vulcan salute, I'll punch you."

I laugh, and she squints up at the sky.

"You think Resa'll ever get back to Kazar?" she asks.

"I think the big irony of the story is that by the time he can go home, he won't want to." We share a complicated look, her gaze boring right through me. I'm about to apologize for saying the wrong thing—even though I'm not sure I have—when she sighs and turns her attention back to the parking lot as her mom's Toyota pulls up.

"See you Sunday," she says with a wave.

"What about Saturday?"

"Jordan's grounded," she calls over her shoulder, as if that explains everything.

A blue Honda Civic pulls in as the Toyota turns out of the gate. I'm still waiting for Dirk's Beetle, so it takes a minute to realize why I recognize the car. Jean-Pierre. Seeing him annihilates all thoughts of Treasa and aliens. It takes me another minute to get over the shock of seeing my brother and command my feet to walk.

"Howzit, *boet*?" JP says as I open the car door.

"What are you doing here?"

"Get in and I'll explain."

At least JP's car is air-conditioned, although I'd rather have to suffer the cigarette swelter of Dirk's Beetle if it means avoiding the techno crap JP insists is music.

"Did something happen to Dad?"

"Nothing like that. Don't worry." JP offers me chewing gum and I accept. Better to be chewing on something rather than grinding my teeth together.

"How's life?" he asks.

"Fine. Yours?"

"Can't complain." He gives me a sideways glance and punches my shoulder. "Looking good, boet. You been hitting the gym?"

"Karate."

"Girlfriends?"

"No. You?" I say it too quickly, and JP grins.

"Ja, still with Michelle. How's school?"

"Why are you here?" There's no way my brother drives up from Stellenbosch just to play catchup with me, considering our shared DNA is the only thing we have in common.

"Dad called."

"About what?"

"You." He pulls up to a red light, and I try to keep my hypervigilance to a minimum, but he notices. "You still freaking out at robots?"

"No."

"Let's go get a drink." He does an illegal U-turn and heads in the opposite direction of home.

"I'm in uniform."

"No one will see us."

FIFTEEN MINUTES later, we park outside the NG Kerk cemetery. JP grabs a bottle of wine out of a bag on the backseat and saunters through the gates, like coming here is as easy as going to the Spar.

"Come on, boet. The ghosts won't bite."

I haven't been here since Mom's funeral. I can't. I don't want to be here. "Please, just take me home."

"Nope. I've got a bottle of merlot, Mom's favorite. I missed the anniversary, so we're going to go share a *dop* with her now."

"I can't."

"You will."

I try to get back into the car. The doors are locked, and JP's holding the remote.

"I will drag you if I have to." That's no idle threat, coming from a rugby forward.

"I haven't been here...." The words catch in my throat.

"That's part of your problem." His tone softens, and I catch a glimpse of the protective big brother I used to know. He loops an arm around my shoulders, and I let him guide me through the cemetery gates.

TREASA

GABRIEL IS a saint. I don't think too many guys would've let some girl bawl on their shoulder like that. I'm amazed he agreed to meet my parents after my magnificent display of emotional restraint and all the alien weirdness. At least he seems to get me and didn't call the men in white coats.

For all his pretty words about Jordan, it still feels like this whole thing is my fault. No, I didn't know Hannah would retaliate like that or that she'd take it out on Jordan instead of me. That doesn't make me feel any less guilty.

"Want some coffee?" Mom pops her head into my bedroom.

"Mom, can I talk to you for a minute?"

"Sure, sweetheart. Something wrong?" Mom settles on the bed, and Riker leaps onto her lap.

"It's just...." I abandon the French Revolution essay I should've finished by now. "I don't understand girls."

Mom cocks her head and gives me a peculiar look. "How so?"

"Well, like Hannah. She's always been deliberately nasty to Jordan. I just can't figure out why."

"Teenage girls are catty."

Catty seems a little euphemistic. "Do they ever grow out of it?"

Mom puffs air into her right cheek, which means she's thinking hard. "As you grow up, you'll learn how best to deal with people in the least damaging way. That doesn't mean people won't be petty or nasty, but handling them will get easier."

"Mom." My throat closes up, making the words razor blades on the back of my tongue.

"What is it, Resa?"

"I invited Gabriel to lunch on Sunday." Better to change topic. Mom will be mortified if she knows I was part of the rumor mill. I owe Jordan an apology first, and that's a conversation I'm not looking forward to.

"This Sunday?"

"You said you wanted to meet him."

"Just wish you'd checked with me before inviting him."

"I can cancel." Relief.

"No, don't." She's adamant. "We'll braai. Three o'clock." The oven alarm sounds in the kitchen, and Mom hurries out of my room after transferring Riker to my lap.

If a bunch of half-starved peasants can storm the Bastille and overthrow the powers that be, then I should be able to pick up the phone and talk to my best friend. I dial and hang up twice. What would Resa do? He would've fixed the painting with a wave of his hand. Despite my best efforts, particle manipulation seems a bit beyond my possible alien genetics at the moment, so an apology will have to do. Sheryl answers after three rings.

"You know she's grounded and not supposed to take phone calls."

"This is really important. Please. It's about what happened to her painting," I say.

"Fine. You've got five minutes."

My palms are so slick with sweat, I almost drop the receiver.

"Hey, Ree, what's up?"

"Jordan, I...." Deep breath, count to ten. "There's something I need to tell you."

"I'm listening."

"That thing about Hannah's nipples." I lower my voice in case Mom hears. "About her being a slut. That was me."

Silence.

"I heard it from Dirk, and I just thought that after all she'd said about you, she deserved some of her own medicine. I thought she'd come after me, not you. I'm so sorry." The words tumble out of my mouth and I keep apologizing, a broken record stuck on sorry.

"Treasa. Stop it," Jordan finally butts in. "I know."

"Know what?"

"Know that the rumor started with you."

"You didn't say anything." I squeeze Riker's tail too hard and receive a scoured hand as punishment.

"Because I knew you had good intentions. Also, what difference would it have made?"

"Did you find out why Hannah even took it so far?"

"That girl has some mega issues. Her mother is hysterical in the unfunny and totally crazy kind of way. I almost feel sorry for her."

"Are you all right?"

"Fine. Catching up on homework. Hearing's on Monday. I'll see you back at school on Tuesday."

"Okay, Treasa, time's up." Sheryl picks up another phone somewhere in their house. I say my good-byes and hang up. So Jordan doesn't hate me for what I did, not that it makes me feel much better. I almost feel like I owe Hannah an apology too. Almost. If only Hannah and Jordan had had this dustup months ago and gotten it out of their systems, maybe they wouldn't both be facing expulsion.

I don't know what I'll do if Jordan gets expelled. I love Sibo and Lethi, but we only have two classes together, and they have each other. I'll just become a third wheel without Jordan. Without her, surviving St. Bridget's will be a nightmare.

GABRIEL

CEMETERIES SHOULD be eerie, replete with the blackened boughs of gnarled winter trees providing perches for croaking ravens. It should be overcast, preferably with drizzle, and cold. Cemeteries should have the decency to be somber. Not this one. Here the tombstones lie dotted between rainbow flowerbeds. Pansies and marigolds, geraniums and daffodils—all alive with the constant hum of bees. There are even butterflies flitting between the blooms. It doesn't seem fair to the bodies rotting below us, providing the fertilizer for the flowers.

JP leads the way; I can't actually remember the exact location of Mom's grave. The sun glints off a vase of white lilies next to the tombstone bearing the simple inscription: Katherine Marlena du Preez, Beloved Daughter, Wife & Mother.

"Who brings the flowers?"

"Dad."

JP drops into a crouch at the edge of the grave, demarcated with a border of white daisies, and pops open the wine. He takes a generous swig before pouring some onto the grass and handing the bottle to me.

"To Mom," he says, and I echo it. I crouch down beside him and pick at the brown petals of a sun-dried daisy. We stay in silence for a while, feeling the wind against our faces. There's a storm coming.

"I can't believe Dad brings flowers," I say after another gulp of merlot that tastes like vinegar. How did Mom ever drink this stuff?

"You think he only goes to church every Sunday?" JP squints at me.

"It doesn't make sense."

"Why? Because he gives you a *klap* when you deserve it?" JP studies my face.

"Did Dad tell you?"

"Ja. Told me he's been drinking too much and that you've been giving him a hard time." He shifts into a sitting position, elbows on knees, and I do the same. I haven't spoken to my brother like this since before Mom died. We were never that close, but we'd talk. Mostly he'd talk and I'd listen.

"He won't let me study music."

JP closes his eyes against the glare. He looks so much like my father.

"He won't even listen to me playing piano, practically ignores my very existence, and he says I'm being difficult?"

"Gabriel." JP runs a hand over his shaved head. "Have you looked in the mirror lately?"

"What do you mean?"

"Would you just get a bloody haircut already."

"You're going to tune me about my hair now? Why does it even matter?"

"You're seriously thick." He rips up one of the daisies and shreds the petals onto the grass.

"Does having longer hair make me moffie too?"

He shakes his head. "You look like her." His words are barely audible over the cacophony of *hadedahs* in flight. The birds pass over us, their squawks fading.

"Look like who?"

"Like Mom, you dipstick." His gaze strays to the tombstone and stays there. "I'm not the most sensitive oke, but even I can see Dad's hurting. I know I couldn't stand it."

"Stand what?" My heart beats jackhammer syncopations as I wait for the answer.

"You. Being in the same house when everything you do reminds me of Mom. And you only look more and more like her. Same eyes and smile, and the way you play that bloody piano. It was a relief, getting out of the house. Did you ever stop and think what it does to Dad that you still play those pieces Mom wrote for you?"

I open and close my mouth. Words fail me as my chest constricts and my stomach flips painfully.

"You think you're the only who loved her, who grieves?"

"Of course not." My voice is hollow.

"Well, then, give him a break. He's a single Dad, and you're not making it easier." JP hops up and dusts grass off his baggies. "Dad's making us *bobotie* tonight." He offers me his hand, but I get up on my own. He walks back to the car, leaving me alone with the ghosts.

"I'm so sorry," I whisper to the bees and flowers and to whatever's left of my mother beneath my feet.

TREASA

WHAT THE hell do I wear? I stare into my cupboard, hoping an outfit will leap out at me and look perfect. I could do baggy shorts over my boxers and a T-shirt over my chest-flattening sports bra. I'd be more comfortable like that, but I don't think Gabriel would be impressed, and I need to impress him.

Can't wear my Sissy Boy jeans again, and there's no flipping way I'm wearing a skirt.

"Resa, some help, please," Mom yells up the passage. I'm meant to be making potato salad.

"Coming," I yell back as I grab a fitted T-shirt and pair of less-baggy shorts that will actually require panties. Do I wear black or blue? What are the connotations of blue undies?

"Treasa Rae!" Mom's losing her cool. Gabriel will be here in less than hour. Dressed and with my hair scrunched up in a bun, I head to the kitchen and start work on the potatoes.

"You look nice." Mom bastes the chicken legs.

"For once I bet you're glad I'm not wearing a skirt and sandals, right?" I mean it as a joke. Mom purses her lips, unamused. The oven buzzer rings, and Mom retrieves a perfect milk tart.

Keeping an eye on the clock, I watch the minutes tick closer to three. Everything's ready, leaving me a full three minutes to double-check my face and hair. I'm touching up a dash of concealer on my chin where pimples are rearing their ugly heads when Dad shouts, "He's here."

Gabriel gets out of a blue Honda, firing off a volley of Afrikaans at whoever is behind the wheel. The driver waves at me and gives me a huge smile before reversing out of the driveway. Gabriel walks toward me. He's wearing camo shorts and a navy-blue T-shirt. I was a little nervous he'd arrive with a mohawk and black nails. I'm also a little disappointed he looks so respectable. I would've loved to see Mom's face!

"Hi," he says and hands me a Tupperware container.

"What's this?"

"Fudge. It was either that or toast." He gives me a strained smile.

"Thank you." He is too sweet. The gesture will go down well with Mom as well. "Who was that in the car?" I ask.

"My brother, JP." He drags his long fingers through his hair.

"Oh. He's on holiday?"

"Taking a break, ja."

"Thanks for doing this." I lead the way into the house. "I hope it's not too awkward."

"It'll be fine."

Introductions go as well as can be expected. Dad shakes Gabriel's hand harder than is necessary, and Mom scrutinizes every inch of him before nodding in greeting. Dad offers him a beer, and Gabriel respectfully declines, passing the first test. He and Dad head out to the braai while Mom and I pour soft drinks and empty chips into a bowl.

"You play rugby," Dad starts.

"A bit. I prefer cricket, but don't have the time for it." I give Gabriel a thumbs-up behind my Dad's back. "Did you hear about this Hansie Cronje debacle?"

"Of course."

And their conversation becomes an animated discussion about the match-fixing accusations brought against the Proteas. I sit on the patio with Mom, a ball of nerves still wreaking havoc in my belly.

"He seems like a nice boy," Mom leans in to tell me in a hushed voice.

"Told you so." I crunch through half a bowl of chips before the meat is ready and we can eat. We're halfway through the meal when Mom starts firing her questions at Gabriel about school and future aspirations, and then she asks about his family.

"You've mentioned your father. What about your mom?" Mom sips her glass of white wine.

"Ah...." Gabriel impales a chunk of potato with his fork. "She's dead." His says it with such finality. I hope my mom takes the hint and leaves it at that, but of course she's about as sensitive as a tree trunk.

"Oh, I'm so sorry. How did it happen?"

"Mom," I hiss between clenched teeth and reach for Gabriel, placing my hand on his knee. I didn't know his mom was dead. He has a right not to tell me and not to have to blurt out every detail of his life over chicken kebabs and coleslaw.

"Car accident," he says, and carries on eating.

The conversation dies after that, no one really sure what to say. We eat in silence and Gabriel helps me clear away the dirty plates afterward.

"I'm sorry about your mom," I say when we're elbow to elbow, dropping dishes in the sink.

"Everyone always says that, but there's nothing for you to be sorry about."

"I mean I'm sorry you lost her, sorry you hurt."

Gabriel turns to me, his eyes shiny green. I'm pretty sure we're about to kiss when Dad walks in with a dish full of leftovers and ruins the moment.

Mom serves milk tart, ice cream, and fudge for desert.

"This is delicious," Dad says between mouthfuls. "Who taught you to make this?"

"My mom. She loved condensed milk," Gabriel says. I take a piece of fudge, savoring the grainy texture and creamy taste. It's the best fudge I've ever eaten.

"Damn, this is good."

Mom glares at me, because in her books, "damn" is a swear word.

"I'm glad you like it. It's easy to make." Gabriel gives me that soft little smile that makes me melt.

"Would you teach me?"

"Of course."

"You seem to be teaching my daughter quite a lot." Mom gets violent with the ice cream server and ends up with double the amount she usually eats.

Gabriel looks at me, clearly not sure what to make of Mom's tone.

"Piano, karate." If I had alien powers, I'd be using them on Mom right now, giving her a few wrinkles around the eyes and a streak or two of gray.

"Treasa's a natural at karate," Gabriel says, and I swell with pride.

"Really?" Dad seems totally surprised.

"Ja, she throws me down no problem." Gabriel smiles, and both my parents raise their eyebrows.

"And piano?" Mom had to ask.

"Less of a natural, but not terrible." Gabriel gives me a sideways glance and sneaks a hand under the table to squeeze my fingers.

The phone rings and Mom excuses herself to answer. With her gone, Dad and Gabriel start chatting about cricket again and migrate indoors to catch the news in case there's any more information about the match fixing.

Just after six, Gabriel's brother arrives.

"Invite him in," Mom insists. Gabriel politely refuses, saying they're in a hurry. We've learned more about his family today then he probably intended us to. Mom almost follows me out to the car. Thankfully, Dad grabs her arm and leads her back inside, giving us a modicum of privacy. No chance of a kiss today, with my parents hovering in the background and JP grinning at us from behind the wheel.

"On a scale of one to ten, how'd I do?" Gabriel asks.

"You're at least a ten."

"Your parents think so too?" He grins.

"Not sure I care what they think."

He bites his lip and studies his feet for a bit.

"Thanks for today and for the fudge."

"No problem." He lifts his head, meeting my gaze, and now's my chance.

"There's something I wanted to ask you."

"More questions?" He looks nervous.

"Not like that. It's just…." I take a lingering look at the stitching on the collar of his shirt. "Would you go with me to the grade ten dance?"

"Treasa—"

"It's in May, so there's still time."

"Treasa." He runs a hand through his hair and shifts his weight between his feet. "I'm not sure what this is, what we are." His voice is almost a whisper.

"That's okay. Me neither." I force a smile.

JP hoots at us, and Gabriel swears. "Sorry, I should go. See you Thursday?"

He sort of leans forward as if to kiss me, but he seems unsure and I hesitate, the moment lost to awkwardness.

"Chat later?" he says.

"Sure. See you Thursday," I echo as he gets into the car. I watch them drive away, and Gabriel waves before the car slips out of view. What are we? Excellent question, Gabriel. I wish I had the answer. And what about the dance? He didn't say no; he sure as hell didn't say yes. In what world would a guy like that go with a girl like me to a ball?

GABRIEL

"HOW WAS it?" JP asks as we cruise along the Sunday-quiet roads.

"Fine."

"They give you the third degree?"

"Sort of."

"They like you?"

"Why do you care?"

JP chuckles and shrugs his bulky shoulders. "Just curious. She's not the sort I'd thought you'd go for."

"What sort would that be?"

"The Karla type."

"You only met her once."

"Once was all it took. So is this chick good in bed?"

"Fuck off." I sidle up to the window, getting as far away from my brother as possible. He laughs as we pull up to the lights.

"Ag, I'm just teasing you, boet."

We're the only ones at the intersection. Movement out the corner of my eye catches my attention. A guy runs toward us. There's something in his hand and my body goes rigid.

"JP, drive."

"It's red, man."

"Just drive. Drive!"

The guy reaches us, and I scream at JP as black hands start smearing our windscreen with soapy water.

"*Jislaaik*, calm the hell down, boet." JP puts a hand on my shoulder. I jerk away and grab his hand, twisting his arm and tugging back his fingers.

Blind panic overwhelms me as the window washer gives me a white-toothed grin and starts with the squeegee. Pain bursts across my face, and my head whips back, connecting with the seat.

"Christ, Gabriel." JP rolls down his window and gives the guy five bucks.

"You hit me?"

"You nearly broke my bloody fingers." He accelerates through the intersection. "You need help, boet. I'm serious. Like real, proper help."

I spend the rest of the drive trying not to hyperventilate, hiding my shaking hands by sitting on them. Maybe JP's right. Maybe I do need help. And I thought Treasa was the head case.

When we get home, I scoot straight to my bedroom and lock the door. JP shouts his good-byes an hour later. This weekend has been hell. I shouldn't have gone to Treasa's: the scrutiny from her father, the third degree from her mother, and Treasa's adoring eyes when she doesn't know the truth, doesn't know I lied to all of them about my mom. It's too much.

Without Jean-Pierre here, the house is back to its regular morgue-like state, with my father passed out in a beer coma. For the past three days I've watched my father come alive. He and JP talked about rugby and

Michelle, they pottered around the garden together, they shared beers, and Dad even laughed. I haven't touched the piano once. Maybe I should've been the one who left.

My brother might be gone, but his words ricochet around my head. I put on Immortal, hoping to drown out everything he's said to me since Thursday. Charging around my room headbanging to the relentless bass isn't enough. Guilt settles like an anvil in the pit of my stomach, the despair nauseating. This is all my fault. I'm the reason Mom was in the car that night, I'm the reason JP couldn't wait to get out of the house, and I'm the reason Dad can barely even look at me, let alone listen to me play.

I totally get where Treasa's coming from. More often than not, I wish I was someone else too.

Why did she ask me to the dance? I wanted to take things slow. The last thing I need is the pressure of some school dance, all fancy suits and ball gowns and inevitable disappointment when the night isn't the dream event it should be. I don't know why I didn't just say no. Such an idiot. Now she'll think there's still a chance I might say yes. This is a lose-lose situation: say no now and hurt her feelings, or say yes to the dumb dance and disappoint her then, hurting her even more. Either way, Treasa gets less than she deserves.

I retrieve the lighter from my drawer and thumb the spark, watching the flickering flame. Once the metal's hot, I press it into my thigh and hold it down. My flesh sizzles. With my leg smoldering and tears blurring my vision, I thumb the spark wheel, wait for the metal to heat up, and do it again… and again….

TREASA

WHAT'S WRONG with me that he can't bear to call me his girlfriend or even say yes to a stupid dance? I knew I shouldn't have asked about that alien stuff. He must think I'm a total freak.

After assembly—in which the sports prefect gave a heartfelt speech about why Hansie Cronje was a hero and wouldn't ever be involved in anything nefarious—I make a beeline for history, wishing I could generate a force field like Resa to protect me from the skiff looks. One minute I'm walking, the next my face smacks linoleum and I taste blood. Gillian and crew stand laughing at my expense, my skirt flipped up revealing my ultranerdy *Star Trek* boxers.

"Now I know why Hannah calls you Scotty," Gillian snickers.

"Aren't those boy's undies?" Gillian's BFF Tanya makes the observation as I struggle to regain composure. My lip is split along the inside where flesh made contact with my metal braces. I pick myself off the floor and glare at them, struggling not to cry.

"Hannah was right." Gillian's face crumples in disgust. "Freak."

Candyce hangs back, and there's pity in her eyes I wish wasn't directed at me. I want so badly to be an alien right now, to distance myself from the human race, to be able to say I'm not one of them. I don't have Resa's superpowers either, so there's no rewinding time or erasing Gillian's memory. Leaving my dignity in shards on the floor, I shoulder my backpack and slink into the bathroom, their laughter echoing down the corridor. Having double-checked the lock on the bathroom door, I sit on the closed toilet and wrap my arms around my legs. I sob. Not dainty little tears that can be rather endearing, no, these are gigantic, shoulder-shaking, snot-spewing convulsions.

I'm so far gone in my saline-soaked misery that I don't hear anyone else in the bathroom until someone knocks on my door.

"Go away," I gasp.

"Treasa, please let me in. I want to help." What the bloody hell? It's Candyce.

"Yeah, right." I get my sobs under control and use half a roll of toilet paper to dry my face.

"Please, Treasa."

"Not interested."

I think she'll go away. Instead she walks into the stall next door and closes the toilet lid with an audible clink before sitting down. I glance at her shoes: black baby dolls with scuffed toes.

"I'm sorry about this whole thing with Hannah and Gillian."

"What?" My brain is still fuzzy from crying. My ears must be blocked.

"Truly, this is sort of all my fault. I'm really sorry."

"I don't understand." This must be some cruel joke.

"If I tell you something, do you promise not to tell anyone?"

"I guess." Damn, now I'm curious.

"I'm trusting you not to spread more stories."

Ouch, I deserved that. "I promise."

She's quiet for several long moments before she takes a deep breath and starts talking. "That story about Jordan and me fighting over some boy is a total lie. The truth is...." Her feet shift as if she's squirming. "The truth is that I kissed her at that social in grade seven. It wasn't that I kissed a boy she liked. I kissed her."

My brain goes supernova. All other thoughts have just been obliterated.

"I was too young to really understand, and it just kind of happened. She seemed into it, but then she wasn't." Candyce's voice cracks with emotion I didn't think she possessed. "Later that night, I saw Jordan grabbing some random boy, and she made sure I saw. I was hurt and confused, and that's when all this nonsense started."

I unlock the stall and follow my feet until I'm standing in front of Candyce. Her face is pale and streaked with tears.

"You could've stopped it."

"By what? Admitting I kissed a girl and don't ever want to kiss another boy?"

"You're lesbian?" I stare in disbelief.

"I hate that word. It's like a scarlet letter or a brand or worse."

"I've kissed Jordan." I clamp my mouth shut too late.

She blinks at me a few times before an almost smile tweaks up the corners of her lips. "So you two are together."

"No, oh no. I very much like boys, but we... well, she taught me how to kiss."

Candyce makes frothy noises that are half crying, half giggling, and smoothes back blonde hair from her face. "You learn from the best." She stands up, and I join her at the basin. We both splash water on our faces before I peel back my lower lip to inspect the damage. It's not so bad.

"Hannah doesn't know?" I ask.

"She'll never know." Candyce dries her hands and fixes me with a stare. "Right?"

"I'm not telling anyone. Promise."

"Thanks."

"Are you in love with her?" I ask.

"Jordan?" She considers. "I don't know. I was definitely infatuated for a while, but now I really don't know. I don't know what I feel or should feel." She hangs her head, so sad I almost reach out and hug her, telling her I understand, when a grade eight barges into the bathroom and Candyce departs without another word.

RESA'S HAND left a burning trail down Tristan's chest as his long fingers popped open the buttons of Tristan's shirt. Resa gazed at him, a seductive smile playing on his lips. "You're beautiful."

"So are you." Tristan reached a hand toward Resa and tugged him down into a kiss. Resa's hands glowed as they ignited every nerve ending beneath Tristan's skin. Tristan moaned and grabbed Resa's bottom lip with his teeth. Resa chuckled and continued his ministrations, his fingers meandering ever lower toward Tristan's zipper.

I hit save and take a deep breath. My face is burning, and my whole body feels hot. My own fingers wander down to the elastic band of my boxer shorts. In my mind, I'm Tristan staring up at Gabriel, and it's his hand slowly inching between my legs. The fantasy fizzles as I think about Gabriel and what he said about the nonexistent us. He's SMSed me twice since Sunday, both fairly bland messages that might as well have been about the weather, for all they conveyed about the state of our union.

Tuesday night, eight o'clock. Mom's at book club—dop and skinder night, Dad calls it—and it's time for my weekly fix of aliens and Liam St. Clare. Already in pajamas, I make myself some tea and grab a box of Romany Creams, preparing to settle in for an hour of entertainment. Dad's glued to the TV, remote clenched in his fist. Images of a distraught Hansie Cronje fill the screen, and my heart goes out to my dad.

I sit beside him and watch the minutes trickle past eight o'clock. Alien Resa has probably thwarted several government agencies by now. I don't say anything about changing the channel.

"That's it, Resa. It's all over." Dad stares at the screen as the footage replays. Hansie Cronje sacked. Hansie Cronje admits to match fixing. Hansie Cronje dishonored. I might not be the biggest cricket fan, but I can't help feeling upset for the Proteas and for our country. It hurts, watching an idol fall. I never knew the guy personally, and yet I can't help feeling a little betrayed and a lot disappointed.

I offer Dad a Romany Cream, and we crunch through chocolate, not caring about the crumbs.

Leaving Dad with the biscuits, I head back into the kitchen to make him coffee. He probably needs a Scotch.

For two hours, I sit in silent commiseration with my dad as team members, commentators, Ali Bacher, and every other sports authority take their turn speculating on Hansie's motives, on the future of SA cricket, and on the role others might've played in the debacle. I think this has officially been the worst week ever, and it's only Tuesday.

It's late by the time Mom gets in, and I hand over consoling Dad to her. I'd call Jordan, but Sheryl has refused to let me speak to her since Friday. Joining Riker on the duvet, I dial Gabriel instead.

GABRIEL

THE BURNS are healing, but I don't let them, using the edge of my nail to rip off the scabs. The pain is sobering, bringing clarity to my quagmire thoughts. I'm considering adding a new smiley to my burgeoning collection when my cellphone rings. Treasa. The last person I want to talk to or think about. She looks at me with stars in her eyes, and I don't want to be the one to snuff them out. She calls three times before I finally answer, just to end the incessant shrill.

"Sorry for calling so late," she whispers.

"I wasn't asleep."

"Did you watch tonight's episode?"

"I totally forgot." Too busy marinating in self-pity. I should've watched; it might have been distraction enough to save my skin. I'm an idiot. The burns are going to be a bitch under school pants tomorrow. I hop into the bathroom in search of Germolene and gauze.

"My dad was watching the news. You heard about Hansie getting sacked?"

"But I thought he wasn't involved?" I grit my teeth and smear my thigh with antiseptic cream.

"He admitted it to Ali Bacher, so now he's been fired, and the whole future of SA cricket hangs in the balance."

"He'll be banned from cricket for life." I'd be more upset if I wasn't feeling so drained. We all have to live with the consequences of our actions.

"That seems harsh," she says.

"Life is harsh." When a national hero falls from grace, there's no forgiveness, no second chance. And does he even deserve one? Do I?

"I think everyone's been really quick to judge, and it's not like I knew the guy personally. Anyway." She pauses for breath. "How are you doing? Did you enjoy time with your brother?"

"Sure." The lie is bitter on my tongue, and my leg stings as I wrap it up with a bandage.

"Thanks again for Sunday."

There's an awkward silence. I'm spent, with nothing left to give her, although I think she's looking for an answer to the dance question.

"I'll see you Thursday at choir, but I can't stay for the piano lesson. Got a huge math test on Friday." I could spare half an hour for her out of my study schedule, only I'd prefer to avoid her eyes this week.

"Okay." She sounds disappointed, and a second round of guilt needles my heart. I squeeze my leg over the bandage, pain robbing me of a breath for a minute as I consider my options. The sooner Treasa sees I'm not perfect, the better.

"Dirk's band is playing a gig this Friday at the skate park. Want to go?"

"Cool." There's excitement in her voice. "Just let me know the details and I'll check with my folks."

We finally hang up, and I limp back to my bedroom. I haven't worked on my sonata since last Thursday. Treasa's melody has plagued me since then, demanding its place on the stave. With a sigh, I pull out my notebook and start notating the music. Treasa hummed in a major key. This tune dreams of being in a minor, so I modulate and let the music turn melancholy. The music bleeds out of me for fifteen pages before I draw the final double-bar line. The second movement is complete.

TREASA

WEDNESDAY MORNING, they call my name over the intercom, telling me to go to the principal's office. I leave the classroom with everyone's eyes boring into my back. The walk down the corridor has never been so long and unnerving. Even vacant-stare Virgin Mary seems to have a diabolical glint in her eye for me today. This must be about Jordan.

My palms are slick with sweat, and my internal organs are playing Twister by the time I reach the office. The secretary ushers me in, and I perch on a brown leather armchair in front of Mrs. Owen's desk. She turns from her computer screen and levels me with her predatory stare.

"Did you write this note?" She nudges a scrap of paper across her desk. It's the one about Hannah's nipples. My throat constricts, and I think I may pass out. I nod, too afraid to lie.

"This sort of behavior is not tolerated at St. Bridget's." Her severe eyebrows meet in a crease above her aquiline nose. "Do you have anything to say for yourself?"

I swallow the prickly pear lump in my throat and open my mouth, explaining the feud between Jordan and Hannah, and that my note was an attempt to deflect Hannah's enmity. Mrs. Owen leans back in her chair and folds her arms. Mom will skin me alive if I get expelled.

"Treasa, given the circumstances surrounding the unfortunate event at the art exhibition, I am compelled to take disciplinary action."

Can this week get any worse?

"You'll be on litter duty for the next three weeks and will have detention this Friday."

"Okay." I can live with being the garbage lady during break, and detention doesn't bother me.

"Good. I assume this won't happen again."

"No, Mrs. Owen."

She nods and I think it's over, but she continues.

"Hannah and Jordan had their hearings this morning."

My jaw clenches with dread anticipation of the verdict.

"Given Jordan's disciplinary history and the nature of her artwork, the board decided it best if Jordan found a different high school."

"You're expelling her?" The world tilts on its axis.

"We're strongly suggesting she move to another school."

Expulsion. That's it. My life is over. I won't survive without Jordan. I don't want to be here without her. Maybe I can convince Mom and Dad to let me move schools too.

"You can't expel her." My voice quavers. "This was all my fault. If anyone should be expelled, it's me."

Mrs. Owen sighs and rolls a pen between her fingers. "Treasa, your note certainly didn't help, but Jordan's been flouting our rules for years. This is just the tip of the iceberg, really."

"Please don't expel her."

"The board's decision is final."

"And Hannah?" There's still a ray of hope. Maybe Hannah got kicked out too.

"Considering that this is her first serious offense, the board has granted her the right to return to school on Monday." Mrs. Owen almost sounds apologetic.

"What? Why? She started this whole thing!" Hysteria threatens my composure.

"Treasa!" Mrs. Owen slaps the desk with her palm. "You can return to class now."

Like an obedient dog, I leave the office and head back toward math, only I can't walk past that damn statue without the blood simmering in my veins. My jaw clenches, and my hands ball into fists. I want to smash it, to destroy it as completely as my day, my year, my life has been crushed. That's guaranteed to get me expelled.

If I'd never written that bloody note, none of this would've happened, and Jordan would still be right here with me. Mary smirks at me. I grab the statue's shoulders and tug. The thing is immutable, it won't budge a millimeter. I kick and punch it instead, screaming about the injustice of life.

"Treasa." A teacher places a hand on my shoulder, and I collapse in a hiccuping heap. I'm beyond the point of tears. I just want to disappear. Moments blur together. If I were an alien, now would be a good time for my temporal abilities to show up. I concentrate on turning back the minutes, turning back the years so I was never even born. It wasn't like my biological mother ever wanted me, anyway. She gave me away— maybe because she knew I was broken, destined to be a fuck-up.

Teachers yell at students to return to class, and Lethi and Sibo magically appear beside me, offering words of comfort and support. I need more than just words. They help me up and take me to the guidance counselor's office. They stay with me until Ms. Simmons appears with a cup of rooibos tea. Respect to Lethi and Sibo for not once asking me if I was okay. Maybe if I had a twin sister, I wouldn't need Jordan as much as I do.

"Her mom's on the way. Thank you, girls," Ms. Simmons says.

Sibo and Lethi each give me a hug before leaving me alone with the guidance counselor, who must've been a scarecrow in a previous life. I sip my tea, trying not to think about what'll happen when Mom gets here.

IT TAKES Mom half an hour to get to the school. Her face is as white as Christmas cake icing when she sees my shredded knuckles. I didn't even notice I'd hurt my hands, but that's what punching marble statues gets you. Ms. Simmons patched me up as best she could, dabbing Mercurochrome over the abrasions and plying me with more tea.

"Treasa, what happened?" Mom fusses over my fingers.

"I'm fine." I pull my crimson-stained hands away.

"You're quite clearly not fine. Now I want to know what happened here." Mom stands with her hands on her hips, glancing from me to Ms. Simmons. "Has this got something to do with Jordan?" She's livid.

"If we could step outside a moment." Ms. Simmons opens the door for her, and grudgingly, Mom follows. Even with the door closed and their lowered voices, I catch the gist of their conversation.

Jordan expelled. Me having a conniption fit. Me being troubled in general. Mom doesn't sound impressed. Poor Mom. She got a bum kid. She should've taken me back to the adoption agency before the warranty ran out.

There's a pair of scissors lying on Ms. Simmons desk. They're blunt-nosed kiddie scissors, but they'll do the trick. Surreptitiously, I turn the lock on the door. Mom and Ms. Simmons are too busy discussing me to hear the bolt slide home. I pick up the scissors and look at my wrists. No, I don't want to die, and if I did, I wouldn't do it that way, leaving a bloody mess for someone else to clean up. I don't want to die; I just don't want to be me.

Ms. Simmons has psychology diplomas framed on the wall. The glass provides a mirrorlike reflection, and I angle myself to get the best view of my face. Someone tries to open the door as I comb out my braid with my fingers. They knock, then bang on the wood, and I get to work on my hair, hacking away at brown curls. Mom's shouting now, demanding I unlock the door. I ignore her and keep chopping at my hair. They'll break it down eventually, and by the time they do, I won't be Treasa anymore.

GABRIEL

DIRK DROPS me off at my piano lesson five minutes early, promising to be back on time. I take a minute to air out my clothes so I don't smell like an ashtray walking into Ms. Hafford's home. She teaches from the comfort of her lounge, which is just fine because it means I get to play her baby grand each week.

"Mr. du Preez." She gives me a wide smile as she opens the door. The smell of talcum powder and mothballs wafts from her body. "Lesley McArthur dropped this off for you."

She hands me a letter of invitation before ambling into the lounge. It's an invitation to play at St. Bridget's autumn concert. At least this is an invitation I can accept.

"You've obviously made quite an impression there," Ms. Hafford says.

"The concert's in a week."

"Plenty of time to choose a piece." She settles her large posterior on the chair beside the piano. Ms. Hafford isn't fat exactly, more like the living definition of buxom.

"I could play Beethoven."

"Tsk." She's not impressed. "That's playing it safe. You should play Schumann. How's the memorization coming?"

"Slowly."

"What about the Liszt from last year? That's always a crowd-pleaser."

I shake my head. I'd really love to play a movement from my own sonata, even though that'll feel worse than getting up on stage naked. It would be baring my soul to the world for judgment, a soul that's more than a little tarnished.

The enormous grandfather clock chimes the hour behind her. Just one of the many relics left to her by her father when he died, apparently, cluttering her home that's otherwise oddly modern, replete with a koi pond in the atrium and bamboo growing in wavy glass vases.

"How's your sonata coming along?" Ms. Hafford folds her arms over her ballooning middle and leans back in her chair.

"I think it's done."

"Let me hear it."

"Right now?" I'm not ready. Not even at all.

She taps her foot in impatience. How such a large woman can have such tiny ankles is a mystery. I don't know how such small feet even hold up the rest of her.

"It's not perfect. Still a little rough."

"You've got a week to perfect it."

Reluctantly, I swivel around on the stool and leave the invitation on mieliepap-thick carpeting. This is the first time I've tried playing the whole sonata. The first movement is pretty polished, the third still needs some work on the triplets, but the second is a harmonic nightmare Ms. Hafford is going to hate. Whatever, this sonata isn't about her, and I don't need her approval.

I play the first movement and get a nod from Ms. Hafford.

"Could improve your fingering and ease up on the pedal, but not bad."

"You're not going to like the second movement."

"Try me, Gabriel."

So I play, indulging in every dissonant harmony while my right hand skitters up the register to play Treasa's melody. I don't wait this time before playing the third and final movement. Perhaps it would be more progressive, more modern to have a fourth or even fifth movement, but the harmony is strange enough without messing about with structure.

I play the final, triumphant chords, and turn to Ms. Hafford. She has her head back and her eyes closed. Did my music kill her?

"Ms. Hafford?" I ask tentatively. "You all right?"

"Fine, fine. Just recovering." She rolls her head forward to look at me. "How many Tristans did you use in that second movement?"

"Enough." I grin, and her coral pink lips part in a smile.

"Play that at the concert, and you'll definitely get their attention."

"Is it too much?"

Ms. Hafford cocks her head, her blonde bob brushing her right shoulder. "You wrote it, you tell me."

"I think it's okay."

"And I think you're holding back."

"I am?"

"Yes." She shoos me out of the way and wobbles onto the piano stool. "That section, that bit of melody in the right hand, bit of Pachelbel in the bass with harmony à la Wagner." Her fingers seek out the notes, and she plays back the passage almost as I wrote it. I wish I had perfect pitch like that.

"Here," she says, leaning into the chord. "Feel every note. You've poured your soul into this composition, now pour your heart into the playing." She makes the right-hand notes tenuto, and a lump forms in my throat as the harmony shifts mournfully in the bass. "Like that," she says and relocates from piano stool to chair, gesturing for me to sit down again. "Don't hold back, Gabriel. Just let go."

WHEN I get home, feeling a little violated after letting Ms. Hafford hear such an intimate composition I'm now planning on sharing with St. Bridget's, I highlight the date and time on the invitation from Mrs. McArthur before sticking it on the fridge. So hearing me play reminds my father of Mom. Why is that a bad thing? Couldn't it be a good thing too, like having a living reminder of who she was and how much she loved music? We never even talk about it, as if pretending she never existed will somehow take the pain away of losing her.

I'm not saying anything to my father. He'll see the newsletter; there's no way he can miss it. Whether he comes to the concert or not is up to him.

TREASA

MOM DRIVES me straight to the hairdresser, as if neatening my hacked-off curls will somehow fix what's broken inside me. I endure, ignoring the hairdresser's attempt at small talk. I keep my gaze down, avoiding the girl in the mirror.

"This'll come out of your pocket money, young lady." Mom pays with her credit card.

We drive home in silence, without even the radio to punctuate the tension hanging so thick between us you could cut it into slices and serve it on a plate.

Dad's in the kitchen, home early because Mom probably called him, unable to cope alone with her delinquent daughter. He says nothing when I walk in, just folds me into a hug, and I feel like a little kid.

"Everything will be okay," he whispers and kisses my hair.

"We need to talk." Mom folds her arms.

"Well, I'm sure you've got homework." Dad pinches my cheek and gives me a wink. Dragging my feet, I head to my bedroom and close the door behind me. I don't want to hear them fighting about me.

I put on Manson to drown out the sounds of parental feuding and finally approach my reflection. A slow smile lifts the corners of my lips. After the mess I made, they had to cut my hair super short, leaving tight knots of curls flat against my head. The hairdresser even had to shave the back of my neck, my hair is that short. I love it! Everything else has gone to hell, but at least the hair works. I don't look at all like Liam St. Clare, not even remotely like Gabriel, and that's okay, because I'm one step closer to being who I was meant to be.

Singing along to "Dissociative," I rummage through my cupboard for the band T-shirt I sometimes sleep in. So it's a Nirvana T-shirt with a huge cross-eyed smiley face on the front; at least it's black. I get to work with a pair of nail scissors, chopping out the sleeves. Leaving my school uniform on the floor in a crumpled heap, I pull on the T-shirt. The sides are too wide, showing my bra, and with boobs the size of Jupiter, there's really no fooling the world about my gender. Still, with the shorts I got in the boy's department and my close-cropped hair, I look a lot less girly.

It takes me a moment to realize the plaintive mewing isn't coming from my hi-fi. Riker paws at my door, and I let him in, catching a few words from Mom.

"… is unbelievable. I don't know what to do, what to think. Did you read it?" she asks.

"Give me a chance." There's a rustle of paper as Dad settles at the dining room table. Now I'm curious and slowly turn down the volume on my music so I can eavesdrop better.

"And they think this is indicative of gender… gender what?"

"Dysphoria. That's what that Ms. Simmons said, but I don't think she's got any kind of medical degree. Still." Mom huffs. "Every single creative writing essay she's ever written is about a boy."

"So, she likes boys." I can hear the shrug in Dad's voice.

"No, love. It's more than that. Do you remember—" Mom pauses and lowers her voice. I tiptoe down the corridor, staying out of sight.

"Do you remember," Mom continues. "As a child she was always a boy in every pretend game. It was always Aladdin, never Jasmine or any other princess. She's plain refused to wear dresses since she was five. And what about her birthday parties? Pirates, *Jungle Book*, where she had to be Mowgli. She never played with Barbies, never showed any interest in dolls."

"That isn't normal?" Dad sounds bewildered.

"No, it's not, for a girl."

"But her room's plastered with that boy, that kid from the alien show."

"I'm concerned. I don't think she's… straight," Mom says.

"It's the twenty-first century, Lissa. If we have a lesbian daughter, we just have to accept it," Dad says.

"You really think…." Mom's voice catches, and I roll my eyes. "It's not just that. Her behavior recently. The earring, her hair. Just look at what she did today."

"You want her to see someone?" Dad asks.

"I'd like to talk to her first. You get through to her better. I need you with me on this." Chairs brush against carpet, and I tiptoe back to my room before they catch me listening in.

Before I freak them out any further with displays of tomboyishness, I wiggle into a pastel T-shirt, sleeves intact, and pull on a pair of tracksuit pants.

A knock, followed by Mom's voice. "Resa, sweetheart. Can we talk to you?"

"Come on in." My mouth is dry.

Dad pulls out my desk chair, and Mom settles beside me, with only Riker between us. Mom nods at Dad to start, and he clears his throat.

"Want to tell us about what happened today?" he asks.

"Which part? The part where Jordan got expelled, where I caused a scene trying to smash the Virgin Mary, where I locked myself in Ms. Simmons's office, or the part where I chopped off my hair?"

"Treasa Rae, we are trying to help." Mom's already flustered. This is going to be a short conversation.

"Trying to help?" I glare at her. "Helping would be not hating my best friend. Helping would be not constantly trying to fix me."

"I just didn't want you to be embarrassed." Mom shuts her mouth, and Dad sighs.

"I wasn't embarrassed. You were. You can't handle having a daughter who doesn't wear sandals, let alone one with a buzz cut."

"Resa." Dad sounds exhausted. "Please, we're trying to understand."

"So am I!" I didn't mean to shout. Now that I have, I can't stop. I'm on my feet, hands in the air, and the words are pouring out of me like blistering-hot lava spewing from a volcano. "Do you know what it's like to live every day feeling trapped, feeling cheated by God and biology? Nobody asked me if I wanted this body." I grab at my boobs, wishing I could tear them right off. "Every day—" My voice cracks, and a new onslaught of tears threatens to wreck my complexion. "Every day, I wish I'd never been born, because then I wouldn't have to live this lie."

"And what lie is that?" Mom asks, her eyes wet.

"That I'm this!" I gesture to all of me. "When all I want is to be that." I point at a gigantic poster of Liam St. Clare, posed shirtless with his hands in his pockets and a smirk on his face.

"An alien?" Dad frowns.

"No, Dad," I say, and his expression changes to one of confusion as he looks to my mom for help. I take a deep breath and feel a weight lift off my shoulders as I say, "I want to be a boy."

GABRIEL

TREASA SENDS me an SMS just before midnight, telling me Jordan got expelled. I'm not surprised, considering her art and the damage she did to Hannah's face. Treasa and I spend an hour chatting via SMS until I run out of airtime. Although she won't be at school tomorrow for choir, she promises to see me at Dirk's gig. I'm both disappointed and relieved. I want to see her. Treasa makes life seem brighter, but I need to tell her the truth about me, and I'm grateful her absence from school will give me another day to prepare my confession.

Sleep eludes me. I lie awake listening to the insect chorus pouring through my open window over the distant grumble of thunder. Night slips toward morning, and I must've at least dozed off. My alarm clock blares at 6:30 a.m.

Half-asleep, I help myself to orange juice from the fridge. There's a glaring blank space between the fridge magnets. The invitation is gone. Perhaps my father took it. It's stupid, but I can't help the swell of hope filling my chest. It doesn't last long. I peel a banana and deposit the skin in the bin, dropping it on top of the paper already smeared with the remnants of coffee grounds and yogurt. It's the invitation.

Thanks, Dad—I get the message loud and fucking clear.

My father walks into the kitchen and picks up his car keys. "Let's go. Got an early meeting." He taps his watch. I could nod and grab my blazer and follow him to the car and say nothing, just waiting for that moment on the corner when I'll pop open the lock and hurl myself out onto the road. Instead, I reach into the bin and remove the crumpled invitation, scrunching it into a ball.

It's not much of a weapon; I lob it at him anyway, wishing it was an axe or a whirring chainsaw—something that would hurt him as much as seeing that piece of paper in the rubbish hurts me.

"*Ag, bliksem,*" my father swears as the paper makes contact with his pristine suit, splattering him in yogurt and coffee. "What the hell?" He's got a face like thunder, the vein at his temple throbbing as his forehead puckers in a scowl. The kitchen table is all that stands between me and a throttling.

"You could've just said no thanks." There's a crack in my voice, a fault line I'm pretty sure runs all the way through me, and it's about to split me open.

"Gabriel." He steps around the kitchen table, and I bolt for the back door. I evade his reaching fingers and slam the door in his face. I'm not afraid of my father hitting me—that I can handle—I'm afraid that this time I'll hit back. I run down the driveway and onto the street. My father bellows from the front door. All that matters is the distance I put between us with every step.

DIRK'S BAND is onstage, their final rehearsal before the gig tomorrow night. Dirk slaps his bass, barely audible over the frenetic drums and agro-punk lyrics being screamed by a guy in Doc Martens and a Sex Pistols T-shirt. For some reason, they let Dirk write the lyrics, even though he can't sing to save his skin. I don't know the other band members well. They're older, mostly from the technikon, with the exception of Nandi, who provides backup vocals and plays rhythm guitar. Seeing her all gothed out with her white eye makeup is surreal. She looks like a ghost in negative. Thank god Karla isn't here. I don't want to talk to her or share my bottle of Klippies.

The song comes to an ear-lambasting end, and so does the brandy. I am absolutely hammered. If-I-stand-up-I'll-puke hammered.

"Hey, man. You all right?" Dirk sits beside me on a graffiti-splashed picnic bench near the window. I take a deep breath through my mouth to ease the tides of queasiness, and the afternoon sun lances my eyes. The kids swishing up and down the ramps on their skateboards make me want to hurl all over again.

"He looks wasted." Nandi pries the empty bottle from my rigid fingers. "Best thing is to vomit. You'll feel better."

"I just need to sit." Talking takes Herculean effort, and my words slip sideways in my mouth.

"Come on, bru. Let's go." Dirk gets his arm under my shoulder and hauls me upright.

"Going to be sick."

"Just swallow for now." Dirk drags my drunk butt to the bathrooms. The miasma of stale urine and beer is too much, and I hurl. At least I manage to get most of it into the toilet and not on our shoes. I vomit until I'm pretty sure the only thing left to cough up is a kidney. Dirk says nothing as he hands me wad after wad of paper towel.

"Can I stay at your place tonight?" I ask between dry heaves.

"Of course." He pats me on the shoulder. "You want to talk about it?"

Shaking my head, I flush and haul myself to the basin to rinse my mouth. I splash water on my face and drag wet fingers through my hair.

"Want a Super C?" Dirk grins and holds out the roll of sweets to me.

"Thanks." I take three and start some serious sucking in an attempt to get rid of the sour taste on my tongue. "For everything."

"What are brothers for? I'll be out front when you're ready." Dirk knows me too well, knows I need a minute to put myself back together, only this time, I'm not sure I can.

TREASA

MOM LETS me stay home the rest of the week. I desperately want to speak to Jordan, but I'm terrified to pick up the phone. It's my fault she got expelled. Sorry just isn't going to cut it.

Sibo and Lethi call me Thursday afternoon while I'm curled up on my bed with Riker and Stephen Hawking.

"You have until the end of term to buy your ticket to the Charity Ball," Sibo says.

"Why so soon?" That's just a week away.

"The dance is right after we get back from holidays, Ree. You asked Gabriel yet?" Lethi says. Their voices sound distant. They must be on speakerphone.

"I don't know." All things considered, the dance seems trivial now. "I don't think I want to go anymore." If he'd said yes straight away, then I'd definitely be going and might even have let Mom persuade me to wear a dress. Not now, though.

"Because of Jordan?" Sibo asks.

"That and a million other things." I'm not sure the twins will understand if I start explaining that I want to be a boy and that the thought of donning a ball gown makes my skin crawl as if a thousand scarab beetles are burrowing through my flesh, and that I did ask Gabriel and he has yet to answer me one way or another.

"Just thought we'd let you know."

"Thanks." Although I don't think I'll be going, with or without Gabriel.

"Gabriel looked sad today," Lethi says, and my heart lurches.

"Why?"

"Like we'd go up and ask the dude."

"Fair enough. I'll call him." Will I? As if it's that easy.

"So are you two, like, actually dating?" There's a hint of excitement in Sibo's voice.

"I don't know what we are."

"Haw, Ree. It's not that complicated." Lethi sounds exasperated. It's more complicated than either of them can possibly fathom.

"I'll sort it out."

"Good idea," they say in unison.

We spend another ten minutes chatting about school, homework assignments, and choir pieces for the concert. When we finally hang up, I feel drained. Mom knocks on my door, and I try not to heave a sigh. More talking, more explaining, more feeling like crap.

"Resa, have you got a minute?" Mom has been walking on eggshells around me since my gender confession. I don't think she knows what to do about me. I wish someone did, because I certainly don't.

I nod and shift Riker out of the way so Mom can sit beside me on the bed. She studies my carpet for several excruciating moments before turning to me. I clutch my pillow to my chest: a shield and a source of comfort.

"I've been doing some reading about gender dysphoria. There's no clear cure—"

"You make it sound like I have a disease."

Mom meets my gaze briefly. "It's a disorder. A psychological one, and I think you should see someone."

"So they can convince me I want to be a girl?"

Mom chews on her bottom lip. "I think it would help."

"How?"

"From what I've read, I understand that this can be very confusing, frustrating, and traumatic. If a psychologist could help you come to terms with who you are, then I think it's worth a try."

I bristle at Mom's words. "Who I am and who I want to be are two separate things."

"I know, sweetheart, but that's what a psychologist will help you with."

"So you think going to a head doctor is going to make me want to be a girl?"

"You are a girl," Mom says, and I retreat into my continental pillow, dragging my knees to my chest.

"I don't want to be."

"This is the way you were made, Treasa. You can't change it."

"Yes, I can."

Mom looks startled, and her expression runs the gamut from surprise to incredulity. "No," she says, emphatic.

"I've been doing some reading too." Oh, the joys of the World Wide Web. "Hormone therapy, gender reassignment surgery. There's—"

"No!" Mom's long fingers ball into tight fists. "Absolutely out of the question. This is the way God made you. Sure, you want to be a boy now, but one day you'll want to get married and have kids and lead a normal life."

"Normal? Mom, I'm never going to be normal."

"Oh, Treasa, this is just ridiculous. You're being influenced by your friends and…." She strides to my desk, shoves my papers aside, and picks up the Marilyn Manson CD. "I mean, just look at this." She points to Manson's asexual crotch. "No wonder you're confused, with all this polluting your thoughts."

"Mom, I…."

"We'll get you help, my girl. But you're going to have to want to get better too. No more of this." She brandishes the CD. "No more aliens." She gestures to Liam St. Clare. "And no more friends with negative influences."

"You think the music I listen to and the TV shows I watch is what made me want to be a boy?"

Mom purses her lips.

"Ever since I was a kid, I've wanted to be a boy. I even tried to dress like one. Remember the fight we had at Woolworths that one time?" The memory snaps into focus, even though I've hardly thought about that day in years. "I wanted the dungarees in the boy's department. You bought me a skirt, and I threw a tantrum. How old was I? Four, five?"

"Three." Mom's shoulders sag. "I wish I'd picked this up sooner, recognized the symptoms." She clutches the CD. Any more force, and the plastic will crack.

"Symptoms? So you do think I'm sick."

"And it's my fault." Mom nods. "If I'd paid more attention, if I'd just understood...."

"Then what, Mom? You would've taken me back for a refund?"

Mom looks at me, and her gaze is a laser burning through the layers of my skin, paring me down to the bone.

"I'll get in touch with Ms. Simmons and see if we can find a specialist for you to see." She heads out of my bedroom, still in possession of the empty CD case.

I let her go, because no matter who she makes me see or how much they try to convince me I'm sick in the head, there are three things I know for certain:

I want to be a boy—I should've been a boy. God made a mistake.

I'm not going back to St. Bridget's, because I am never wearing a skirt ever again.

Gabriel—I will get to that gig tomorrow night, one way or another.

GABRIEL

"DOES YOUR dad know you're here?" Dirk's mom asks.

"Ja, he knows." There's nowhere else I'd be.

"You can stay for as long as you need to." She hands me a couple of clean shirts and a towel. "You need anything else?"

"No, thank you." It would've been wiser to pack a bag before running out of the house, but the definition of a rash decision is to not consider the practical ramifications of what you're doing. Now I'm stuck wearing Dirk's underwear and T-shirts until I can face going home again. His mom offered to go around for me, but that would just make things worse because she'd start asking questions, and my father would get defensive. Better I sneak in late at night or go and buy new clothes.

It's only been two days, and I'm already having withdrawals from piano. I got to play yesterday at St. Bridget's, though it's hardly ideal since I can't be there every day. If for nothing else, I'll need to go home at some point just for the piano.

Marlize and Dirk join me in the kitchen for a breakfast of Rice Krispies and burnt toast. "Gig starts at eight, but we're going earlier to set up, hey, roadie?" Dirk nudges me with his elbow.

"You need help with equipment?" Dirk's dad asks between mouthfuls of coffee.

"Ja, if you can. We need to move a ton of stuff."

"This is at that punk place, right?" Marlize chips in.

"Tony's Skatepark."

"Why Tony?" She sips the dregs of her cereal straight from the bowl despite her Mom's admonishing gaze.

"Like Tony Hawk," Dirk says, as if it should be obvious. "Also, the guy who owns the place is Tony."

"I'll be home by five. That okay?" Dirk's dad says.

"Perfect. Now I've got the roadies, all I need is groupies." Dirk beams and rubs his hands together. A red-hot blade cleaves through my ribs and twists in my chest. What I wouldn't give to have my mom and dad at a piano recital. I cross my legs, grating the rough cotton of my baggies against the fresh burns on my thigh.

TREASA SMSS me during the day, promising she'll be at the gig. I haven't spoken to her since Tuesday night. According to Lethi and Sibo, Treasa missed school because she hasn't been feeling well. I reckon it has more to do with Jordan's expulsion.

By 4:30 p.m, we're dressed and ready for the gig. Marlize painted our nails black and gelled my hair up into a mohawk. Dirk and I both got extra-dark eyeliner, despite my protests. The damn stuff makes my eyes water. Dirk dons a black wifebeater, to which he's safety-pinned red anarchy-A badges. He gives me one of the band's silkscreened T-shirts to wear, which makes me feel significantly more like a groupie than a roadie.

Two hours later, The Gatvols are set up and have done their sound check. I'm almost halfway through a bottle of *mampoer*, courtesy of the drummer. Nandi drifts toward me, wrapped in white lace. She's wearing white contacts, making her ever more wraithlike. Her whole vampire-bride look doesn't really reflect the angsty punk rock of the band.

"Karla's coming," she says by way of greeting and hands me a cigarette.

"I expected as much." The moonshine's made my words more sibilant than usual.

"Is that St. Bridget's girl coming too?"

"Should be." I light up and inhale toxic fumes that go straight to my head, buzzing unpleasantly behind my eyes. Or maybe I'm just drunk.

"I like the T-shirt." Nandi teases a thread in her white fishnets, widening a deliberate tear.

"Token groupie."

She smiles and might've said more, when the shrill announcement of an SMS interrupts our conversation.

"Treasa's here." I kill the cigarette, leaving the stompie on the concrete floor already littered with them. Tony's Skatepark isn't exactly a five-star establishment. Nandi relieves me of the mampoer, and I head outside.

It's getting dark; floodlights already illuminate the graffiti-smeared ramps as determined skaters cast crazy shadows with their moves. Marlize sits perched on a bench with her tween friends, their gaze riveted on a pair of boys in Ed Hardy T-shirts. I scan the parking lot but don't see Treasa. I double-check the message, not trusting my inebriated brain. She says she's here, waiting out front. Maybe she means around the other side.

"Hey, Gabriel." A figure waves to me as it emerges from the shadows beneath an itchy ball tree. It takes me a minute to recognize Treasa. She's shorn off her hair. It's soldier-boy short, the curls tight and clinging to her head. She's wearing baggy shorts, All Stars, and a sleeveless Nirvana T-shirt. The T-shirt is hardly flattering, somehow making her look flat-chested. She looks like a guy, in fact.... We're dressed almost exactly alike, down to the dark nail polish and raccoon-eye makeup. I blink, trying to clear my vision. The mampoer has addled my senses.

"It's me," she says as she steps closer into a reaching finger of floodlight. Nope, that's Treasa—not the alcohol making me hallucinate. My Celtic princess is gone, replaced by a boyish imitation brazenly wearing Treasa's smile. At least she hasn't plastered her face with foundation to conceal her freckles.

"Wow."

"I know, right?" A huge, Cheshire-cat grin spreads across her face as she pats her head.

"Why did you cut it?"

Her smile falters, and she kicks at a stone in the dust. "They expelled Jordan."

"I'm sorry."

"Not nearly as much as me."

I want to hug her. She looks so vulnerable, standing with her hands in her pockets. But I can't touch her, not until she knows the truth about who I am, which is the whole reason I downed the booze in the first place. No way I'll make it through that conversation without some Dutch courage.

"It wasn't your fault."

"So everyone keeps telling me," she says.

Guitars snarl as the band gets ready for their first set. The skaters abandon the ramps and stampede indoors.

"They starting already?" Treasa asks.

"In a bit." This is awkward. "Want to grab a Coke or something?" My mouth is too dry; the words feel like sandpaper on my tongue.

She nods and follows me to the bar. It's not really a bar, considering they don't serve alcohol. Karla's standing right in front of the stage, whistling and whooping. Best to avoid her and everyone else.

"Can we go outside for now?" I pass Treasa her Coke, the ice cubes tinkling. We settle at the top of one of the ramps, now deserted in favor of the music. My lips are numb from the alcohol. I'm definitely hammered.

"You ever skate?" she asks.

"Not so much skate as shred my knees and elbows." I'm more talkative when I've had a few.

"I've never tried. Always wanted to, but it was for boys only, according to my mom." There's a bitterness in her voice I don't understand. "I had roller skates, though."

"Like with four wheels?"

"Yeah, nothing as cool as rollerblades."

"You any good?" Images of Treasa in stripy socks at a roller derby like in the movies swim through my mind.

"Dismal." She sips her drink and pries away peeling paint from the concrete. "Listen, there's something I need to tell you."

"Me too." A vise tightens around my chest, and my guts twist into knots, making me want to heave. I should've stayed away from Treasa, far, far away so I wouldn't ever have to have this conversation and risk seeing her disappointment in me, her disdain, disgust, even. I never cared enough about Karla to worry what she thought about me, to even consider telling her the truth about my mom's death. Treasa is different. Treasa needs to know the truth if there's any chance of her ever liking me back as much as I like her. It's like; not love. Love is marriage and kids. This is kissing and fooling around and she's talking, but I've missed half the sentence.

"Sorry, what?" Maybe I shouldn't have drunk so much.

"I said—" She takes a deep breath. "This is so much harder than I thought." She turns to face me, and her blue eyes shimmer with tears. "I had a whole speech prepared."

"Well, you can take your time." I want to lie down. I just don't trust myself not to pass out.

"So you know how I told you I think I'm an alien."

I nod.

"I think I figured out why. It's because...." She hesitates and sets her glass down. Her hands are shaking. "I don't want you to hate me, but I need to tell you this."

"I won't hate you." There's nothing Treasa could've done that would be worse than what I have.

"I hate who I am," she says. "I hate this body, that I never got a say in any of it."

"There's nothing wrong with your body." I shuffle closer to her.

"Yes, there is. Something is very, very wrong."

Oh God, she's sick. Cancer, maybe even HIV from a blood transfusion or something. That's a sobering thought, slicing through the murk in my brain.

"How long?" I ask, working hard to keep my voice level.

"How long what?"

"How long have you got?"

She stares at me, blinking, before erupting into spine-wrenching laughter. "You think I'm dying? Oh, if only." Tears streak down her cheeks, leaving a dark trail of mascara in their wake.

"If only?"

"I'm not sick, Gabriel." She stops laughing and looks away. "I'm just in the wrong body."

"I don't understand." The cool air and cold Coke is helping my body recover from the mampoer assault. I may actually be completely sober by the time I get to tell her my story. Will I still have the balls to do it?

"It's called gender dysphoria." She stares up at the sky. A haze of orange obscures the stars, but the moon glows through the effluvium.

"And that means what?"

"It means I want to be a boy."

"So you can pee standing up?" I chuckle, and she takes my hand, staring at me. The sadness I glimpsed the first time I saw her is concentrated in the forget-me-not blue of her eyes.

"I should've been a boy."

"For real?" My thoughts are spinning like a gyroscope.

"Yes. My whole life, I've felt wrong, different, weird. Like there's this other me. Like I was never really myself. And it's taken me almost sixteen years to figure out why."

"And you reckon you want to be a boy?"

"Not just any boy." She squeezes my fingers. "A boy like you."

"Like me?" I pull away from her.

"You're perfect, Gabriel. Perfect face, perfect hair, perfect body."

Something inside me snaps, something tethering my sanity pops out of place, releasing the barrage of emotion I've managed to keep at bay for all these years.

"Perfect? You know nothing about me." I'm practically snarling. Treasa's mouth hangs open. "You think I'm perfect because I play piano well, because I'm some A-student and have a black belt in karate. Like any of that fucking matters."

"Of course it does," she whispers.

"I'm the antithesis of perfect."

"How can you say that?"

"You want to know why?" I'm shouting, my hands balled into fists. Treasa looks scared. Good. She should be; she should run from me before I do her any more damage. "I've got a brother who couldn't wait to get away from me, a father who can't stand my very existence, and a mother who wouldn't be dead if it weren't for me." I wipe at something wet on my jaw. A tear. Great, now I'm crying in front of her.

"Your mom died in an accident." Treasa wraps her arms around her knees, hugging them to her chest.

"No. That was a lie. Truth is, some bastard put a bullet through her head for her car keys."

"That's not your fault."

"It is, because I ran off to a party I shouldn't have been at. She wouldn't have been in the car, at that robot, if it wasn't for me."

"Gabriel." Treasa reaches for me, and her touch feels like a brand. I jerk away from her. "Please, it really wasn't your fault. It was just a horrible tragedy. No one blames you."

"They do. JP and my father. They both do, and you know what's so horribly fucking ironic?" Treasa says nothing, so I continue. "The reason my father doesn't want to listen to me play, the reason he smacks me around and why JP ran off to Maties, is because I look like her. I remind them of her. Isn't life just freaking fantastic?" God, I need a cigarette. Or maybe just my lighter.

"It doesn't change how I feel."

"Really? You still want to be a boy like me?" I get to my feet and start undoing my fly. "You want this face, and this hair and this body? Look!"

I pull down my shorts and yank up my boxers, revealing my inner thigh. Some of the freshest burns are still weeping, making it look extra gruesome. Treasa gasps and tears fill her eyes.

"If this is the boy you want to be, Treasa, then you are way more fucked-up than you thought." I wrench my shorts back up. Adrenaline courses through my veins, and I want to scream. The glass of Coke is still half-full as I lob it at the ramp with a yell. The smash and splinter is music to my ears.

A second glass hurtles past my ear as Treasa screams beside me. She twines her fingers through mine and squeezes my hand. I look down at her, at her too-short hair and smudged face. She reaches up and lays her palm flat against my cheek. The last person who ever touched me with such tenderness was Mom, but that was different. Treasa should be repulsed, she should hate me, and yet she voluntarily holds my hand; she chooses to touch me.

"I think I'm in love with you." The words are out before I can haul them back in and swallow them down into the black pit of denial where they belong.

Her lip trembles and fresh tears spill down her face. "I love you, Gabriel."

I lean down to kiss her, because if after knowing everything awful about me she can still love me, then maybe there is hope, and I just want to lose myself in her arms. She brings her elbows up to block my advance.

"I'm sorry." She bites her bottom lip. "I can't do this."

"We already have." Now I'm really confused.

"I know, but don't you get it? I want to be a boy." She takes a shuddering breath and presses up against me. "I want to be a boy, with you."

"I don't understand."

"When I think about being with you, I imagine us being together as two boys."

Her words are an acetylene torch, incinerating every feeling of desire and longing and hope. I extricate myself from her embrace and step away, keeping her at arm's length. Hurt creases her features, turning her face into a horror mask of angular shadows in the artificial light.

"I don't... I'm not gay... I'm...." None of this makes any sense. What the hell is she talking about, being a boy with me? She imagines me kissing her as a guy?

"I'm sorry...," she starts, and I hold up my hand to silence her. No words can fix this. Any of this. I can't be here. I can't see her without wanting to explode. My whole life lies in splinters, just like the glass at the bottom of the ramp. Head throbbing, heart aching, I slip down the concrete, leaving her calling after me as I melt into shadows, wishing I could just disappear for good.

TREASA

HE VANISHES into the darkness, and I'm left alone and empty on cold concrete between peeling swearwords and slogans of rebellion. Dirk's band thrashes, the vocalist screaming, the guitars growling. I'm craving silence, for all of it to just stop and go away.

Wrapping my arms around my legs, I draw my knees up to my chin. Mom was right. I shouldn't have come. I shouldn't have manipulated Dad into giving me a lift here. There are a lot of things I shouldn't have done, but I did. It's hard not to feel like the world would be better off without me right now.

I've blown it with Gabriel. Maybe I should've let him kiss me and do whatever else he wanted. Maybe if I'd never said anything, he'd still be sitting beside me. He said he thinks he's in love with me. I do love him, and he deserved to know the truth, although I'm not sure if being with me makes him gay, me straight, or both of us plain weird. Hiding the truth from him would've been worse, right? It would've been dishonest, and he deserves better than that, even if it means we're over before we even really started.

My heart cracks, then fractures, the pain bleeding out through my limbs right into my fingertips. No one will ever love me. Not now. Not like this. Not ever.

GABRIEL

I DOUBLE back through the parking lot and slip through a side door into the club area. Treasa's sitting where I left her and doesn't see me sneak inside. The band's going full throttle. Dirk's jumping up and down, slapping his bass as the lead singer practically has a seizure screaming into the microphone. Karla's bouncing up and down at the front, her hair whipping back and forth in time to the music.

Part of me knows this is wrong; a larger part of me doesn't give a shit. Alcohol, weed, sex—anything that'll make me feel numb for a while. The last is the easiest to get. I elbow my way through the writhing skank and grab Karla's hand. She spins around to face me, and her eyes light up. The song ends, and while the others whoop and cheer, I drag her toward the bathrooms.

We start kissing before I lock the bathroom door. She tastes of cherry Halls sweets, her hands already under my shirt. The bathroom stinks. I feel dirty even as I surrender and let this happen. I just don't care anymore. I can't. Caring hurts too much and inevitably leads to disappointment. It's easier not to care, not to feel anything beyond the base instincts of pain and pleasure.

"Didn't think you'd stay away." Karla grins up at me as her fingers open my fly.

IT'S A long walk home from the skate park through sleeping suburbs ensconced in darkness. Karla stayed for the second set; I needed to escape the noise and crush of bodies. Dirk'll be pissed with me for ditching him, but he'll get over it.

A dog barks from a distant backyard and sirens wail down the highway. I've never felt so alone. The shadows clinging to the trees and roadside foliage provide ample cover for would-be criminals. I scan the road ahead, almost wishing someone would finally jump out at me with a gun or a knife and end the fear I've had for five years.

AFTER AN hour of traipsing along twisting roads, I arrive, unscathed, at my house. I stink of toilet sex and cigarette smoke. All I want is to shower and go to bed. First, I have to get into my house. The lights are on in the kitchen and lounge, so my father's probably still awake. It's not even midnight yet. Stone-cold sober now, I shimmy up the wall using the bars of the gate for leverage. It gets tricky near the top, trying to avoid the razor wire on the wall and the bayonet-sharp points of the gate. With a grunt of effort, I launch myself over the spikes and land with a jarring thud on the driveway.

I don't have keys, so I'll have to knock. There's no getting through the burglar bars on my bedroom window.

My father answers as if he's been waiting by the door. We share a long, strained look before he steps back, gesturing for me to come in. Shit. I have a Mohawk, and I'm wearing not only nail polish, but eyeliner too. I'm surprised he didn't klap me on the spot.

I walk straight to the kitchen. The last thing I need tonight is my father smelling the mampoer on my breath as well. I never make it to the fridge and the palate-cleansing orange juice. My shoe box sits on the kitchen table, the letters I've written to Mom spread out in the open. The photos of her lie exposed as well. I turn to my father. His eyes are red-rimmed and not from booze. He's been crying.

"You went into my room?" I ask.

"I was vacuum cleaning."

"So you just went through my stuff?" Anger simmers in my veins.

"We need to talk," he says, monotone.

"This is private." I start gathering up the letters, shoving them back into the shoe box as my blood reaches boiling point. I feel violated, like I've been turned inside out and stuck under a microscope.

"Leave them." My father places his hand on top of the photos of Mom.

"These are mine. This is personal. You had no right!" My voice kicks up an octave. "These aren't yours. What the hell do you think you're doing?" I'm wound tighter than a piano string, and I don't have the steel reinforcing to stop me from breaking in two.

"Gabriel, please. Stop."

"Stop what? Stop hiding photos of Mom so you can destroy them like the others? Stop wearing nail polish?" I shove my fingers under his nose, goading him. "Stop playing piano? Stop looking like her? Stop breathing? What, Dad?"

For all his flab, my father can still move quickly when he wants to. Before I have time to react, he's got his arms around me. I squirm, trying to free myself before he starts hitting me. My hands ball into fists as I brace myself for inevitable impact. My father holds on tighter as I squirm, so I throw the first punch, aiming for his kidneys. He's large, and I can't quite get the angle right. He grunts and absorbs the blows I rain down on his sides. He isn't letting go, and he isn't hurting me—he's just standing there like a giant punching bag. I pause for a moment to catch my breath. My father starts shaking, his entire torso turning into a jiggling vibration as he cries and holds onto me even tighter.

I'm done. Broken. Finished. I lean into my father, the mohawk mashed under his chin. "I'm so sorry," he mumbles on repeat. "It wasn't your fault. None of this is your fault."

I can't breathe, crushed to his chest, and I couldn't care less. It's been five years since he hugged me.

"It's not your fault she's dead, Gabriel," he tells me through his tears, and I wrap my arms around him, hugging him back.

AM I AN ALIEN, TREASA TEST #07

HYPOTHESIS: Extraterrestrials can spontaneously regenerate after injury given enough resources, i.e. food and water.

GOAL: To prove that I can spontaneously regenerate after injury.

METHOD:

Inflict minor injury—paper cut (self-inflicted).

Eat a healthy meal and drink plenty of water.

Observe healing process.

Inflict major injury—broken heart (not exactly self-inflicted).

Eat a healthy meal, chocolate, and drink lots of rooibos tea.

Observe healing process.

RESULTS: Paper cut, while painful, seemed to heal within minutes. Skin showed no perforation two hours after initial injury. Broken heart shows no sign of healing yet despite it being days since initial injury was inflicted.

CONCLUSION: It is unclear how long a human being takes to heal a paper cut of this exact nature. Healing possibly within realm of human capabilities. Broken heart* may take longer to heal and may require more than Kit Kat and rooibos to fix.

*How long does it take a broken human heart to heal?

TREASA

SATURDAY AFTERNOON, Dad sits in front of the TV with a beer and biltong, watching an SABC special on Hansie Cronje. It's depressing. I can't watch a guy hailed as a national hero reduced to regrets and apologies.

Mom's baking. Again. We got pancakes for breakfast, cheese scones for second breakfast, and there's apple crumble coming for tea. I could help her, I should, but she'll ask about last night, and I don't want to lie. My heart is a chunk of rock. Part of me wants to call Gabriel and tell him it's okay that I poured my guts out to him and he just walked away, that I understand his confusion and anger. Another part of me wants to tell him he was a total jerk for leaving me there alone.

So he's not perfect. What is perfection, anyway? I never meant he was perfect in some grand ideal kind of way, just that he was perfect to me.

I retreat to my bedroom and switch out the Marilyn Manson CD for something that won't make me think of Gabriel. That doesn't leave much. Anything with lyrics is out, since no matter what heartbreaking situation the singer might be on about, it'll be about Gabriel to me. Beethoven and anything with piano is clearly out. Karl Jenkins and anything choir related is out. Resigned, I sit in silence and stare at my computer screen.

"I'M NOT gay," Resa said as he did up the buttons on his shirt. Tristan still lay in bed, the duvet pulled up to his chin. Resa was leaving again. He never stayed the night. Once he got what he wanted, he left.

"Doesn't having sex with boys by very definition make you gay?"

"You sound so human," Resa sneered. "Needing a label for everything. We are what we are."

"You just said what you're not."

Resa glared at Tristan as he pulled on his pants, slowly, deliberately making Tristan watch. Resa toyed with him, and Tristan let him.

"I'm not gay or straight or anything. I don't have to fit into a box."

"So what are we, then? Boyfriends, lovers, friends with benefits?"

Resa grinned and ran a hand through his tangled hair. "What does it matter?"

Tristan twisted the duvet in his fist, feeling so vulnerable, naked under the covers with Resa's lizard-green gaze focused on him.

"I love you. More than a fellow Kazarian, more than brothers. I love you, Resa."

Resa laughed, a deep belly rumble that made Tristan's blood freeze in his veins. "Of course you do." Resa smirked and opened his arms. "How could you not?"

"You might seem like the perfect guy, Resa. On the surface, at least. But I know your darkest secrets, and I still love you."

"I'm flattered." Resa shoved his arms into his jacket. "But that doesn't make you a romantic, Tristan. It makes you a fool."

Resa flung open the door and stepped into the cool of the night, leaving Tristan cowering under the covers. He was alone on a hostile planet billions of miles away from home, with no one but Resa to love him back.

THE PHONE rings, and I save the document, not sure if that scene is worth keeping. I glare at Liam St. Clare's impeccable face as I answer with a desultory hello.

"Hey, Ree. How you doing?"

For several long moments, I battle to breathe. Jordan was the last person I expected to call.

"Treasa, you there?"

"Yeah, I'm here."

"You drop the phone or something?" She sounds way too cavalier.

"Jordan, I don't even know where to begin."

"Save it. Honestly. I'm so over this whole St. Bridget's debacle. Between the parking lot skinder about my mom and comments about me being a slut, I'm actually kind of glad to be leaving it all behind."

"You are? All of it?"

She sighs. "I know you think you're to blame for all this, but you're really not."

"I wrote the note to Hannah."

"Ja, and that cow would've probably trashed my art anyway. I don't regret smacking her either. I only regret Gabriel stopping me before I got the chance to really pull some moves on her."

"Jordan." Again, I sound like my mother using that warning tone.

"What? They going to expel me again?"

I migrate from my desk to the bed and splay my fingers in Riker's fur. "Candyce told me."

"About?"

"The time she kissed you." Silence on the line. "Jordan?"

"Ja, I'm here. Just thinking. Would've been so much easier to just come out about everything at the time. Then none of this would've happened," she says.

"Candyce says she's lesbian."

"Good for her."

"Are you?"

Jordan takes another minute to answer. "I don't think so. I mean, kissing girls isn't weird to me, but I like kissing boys, and to be honest, while I don't mind kissing girls, it doesn't really turn me on like kissing boys does."

"Oh, okay."

"No offense, Ree."

"None taken." We sit in comfortable silence for a bit. Riker purrs, his whole body vibrating beneath my fingertips. That's how being around Gabriel makes me feel, like every atom in my body is quivering with energy.

"So what's up with you not being at school? I heard you cut your hair."

"There's something I need to talk to you about."

"I'm listening."

I should tell her face-to-face, but this way is easier. At least I won't have to see her face twist in disgust or confusion like Gabriel's did. The words come out in a stammering ramble as I struggle to explain everything that's happened the past few days and why.

"Gender dysphoria," Jordan says. "Dysphoria, it's a really beautiful word. Good name for a band too."

I smile despite the tears brimming in my eyes. I'm so sick of crying. All this *snot 'n' trane* doesn't change a damn thing anyway.

"So what do you think?" I ask.

"I think you should take this slow. You're not talking about piercing your ears or dying your hair here. You have to be 100 percent certain you want this."

"I know." My voice breaks a little. "Mom's taking me to see someone on Monday."

"You're not going back to school?"

"No, not until I've figured this all out. I'm done pretending I'm someone I'm not."

"I wish I'd been as brave as you back when Candyce kissed me. None of this would've happened if I'd just been honest, but it totally freaked me out. Initially. Now, I mean, like, whatever, right?" Jordan says.

"And what about Gabriel?"

"Give him time, Ree. You dropped one hell of a load on the guy. He's in shock."

I didn't tell Jordan what Gabriel confided in me about his mom. As for the fact that his dad hits him or that he burns himself—I can't even begin to process that information. My dad gets upset if he kills an earthworm. I can't imagine him ever being so enraged that he'd lift a finger, let alone a hand, to Mom or me. Dad is a placid lake. Mom is a tornado, but she bakes and keeps it under control. As for Gabriel hurting himself…. My stomach clenches as I think about the dark place he must be in to want to do that to himself.

"Hey, earth to Treasa." Jordan singsongs down the line.

"Sorry." Time to change the topic. "So what are you doing about school?"

"Urgh, it's a pain. Stormhof is the only place that'll take me immediately. St. Anne's and the Collegiate can only let me start next term."

"At least Stormhof is coed."

"Like I need more drama in my life," Jordan chuckles. "But maybe having boys in the class to balance out the bitchiness wouldn't be so bad."

"What about the NSA?"

"Nah, I love art, but I want to be an actuary, so what's the point of going to some fancy art school?"

"I miss you."

"I miss you too." Jordan's voice catches, betraying the tough-cookie guise she likes to wear.

"You still grounded?"

"For life, I reckon, but if you want to come hang out tomorrow, I'm sure I could twist my mom's arm."

I promise to check with my folks and hang up. My heart doesn't feel like a rock anymore, more like a gloopy mess that might actually reassemble itself into a working organ someday. One thing at a time. First, see the psychologist and deal with the fact that I was born the wrong gender.

GABRIEL

SEEING MY dad break down like that was profoundly disturbing. He's always been the unbreakable rugby oke, the guy who gets bloodied in the scrum and goes on to score a try. I never thought I'd see him cry, I didn't think he had tears in him.

We stayed up until 4:00 a.m., poring over pictures of Mom. He told me stories I haven't heard in years, some I've never heard, like the time he stole his dad's car to take her to the drive-in when they were teenagers and reversed into a speaker pole.

Sometime around 1:00 a.m., I caught a glimpse of the guy my mom must've fallen in love with, the big softy under the Kevlar exterior. There's a whole other side to my dad, not that having discovered he actually has a heart miraculously changes things between us. This is still the guy who tore up my university application forms and who refuses to listen to me play piano.

We both sleep late this morning and tumble into the kitchen in search of coffee just before noon. I slept through thirteen calls from Nathan and send him an apologetic SMS for missing the self-defense class. I wonder if Treasa went.

"*Vetkoek?*" Dad asks, already busy with a pan and oil.

"Dad, can I talk to you about something?"

His gaze flicks down to the nail polish I haven't managed to scrape off all my fingers.

"For the last flipping time, I'm not gay, all right?"

"Doesn't make wearing that crap okay." He brandishes the frying pan.

"Fine." I pick up a photo of Mom. The letters are packed up in the shoe box under my bed again. The photos, Dad wanted to leave out. He hasn't decided whether he can handle having them up again, but at least he's acknowledging Mom existed.

"You wanted to talk?" He squirts oil into the pan.

How do I broach the subject of Treasa with him? God, I wish Mom was here. "I met this girl," I start. "She goes to St. Bridget's."

That piques Dad's curiosity as he prepares the dough.

"She's a little strange."

"Stranger than that pierced girl you brought home?" He never liked Karla. I think he tolerated her only because he was relieved I hadn't brought "Karl" home.

"A little."

Dad's face creases, and he bites his tongue, concentrating on rounding the dough balls into similar shapes. The dough sizzles as it hits the oil, and the aroma of vetkoek fills the kitchen.

"Okay, strange how?" he asks.

"She…." I get up and go to the fridge, ransacking the shelves in search of apricot jam and cheddar. "She…." I can't have this conversation with the man who thinks my wearing nail varnish is indicative of my sexual preference.

"What? Ag, bliksem." Dad leaps back from the pan as the boiling oil hits his bare arm.

"She sings, soprano, like Mom." It's not what I wanted to say, but last night didn't suddenly make us best friends. Dad serves a dripping vetkoek onto a plate and passes it across the kitchen table to me.

"Nice girl?" he asks.

"I think so."

"You're young, Gabriel. Women are complicated." He turns back to the stove, having delivered his pearls of wisdom, which help not one bit. I demolish four vetkoek before hurtling out of the house and over to Dirk's.

DIRK SAYS nothing as we traipse to the koppie at the back of the park. He's pissed with me for bailing on him at the gig. I owe him an apology and an explanation.

We settle on the sun-warmed rocks, scattering lizards from our shadows. It's late afternoon, the sun dipping toward the horizon, streaking the gathering cumulus with purple and orange. A ruckus of red-billed hoopoes swoop into a nearby cypress, their raucous calls disturbing the tranquility of the park. Dirk winces and massages his temples.

"I'm sorry about last night," I say once the birds have calmed down. Dirk lights a cigarette and passes me the box.

"You going to tell me what happened?"

"Hooked up with Karla."

"*Jislaaik,* bru." He runs a hand through his hair and flicks ash at the ants scuttling across the stone. "Like, in the toilets?"

"Ja."

"That's *sif.*"

"I know."

"Wasn't Treasa at the gig?"

"Ja."

"So why'd you bonk Karla?"

I take a long, slow drag of the cigarette, savoring the burn and trying not to cough. "I think I'm in love with her."

"Karla?" Dirk's eyes widen, stark white against the remnants of eyeliner gunging up his lashes.

"No. Treasa." Despite what she told me, she's still Treasa, still the girl with the crystal voice and sad eyes who knows Rachmaninoff's hand span and can talk about Graham Hancock theories and inspire my compositions.

"Love can make a guy a bit deurmekaar, you know." Dirk slips into philosophical mode. It happens when he's hungover.

"Thing is, last night Treasa basically told me she's a boy trapped in a girl's body. A gay boy."

"What?" Dirk crushes his stompie into an anthill.

"I'm not sure I even understood. The mampoer and all."

"What exactly did she say?" Dirk squints into the sun.

"That she wants to be a boy... with me."

"That's messed up."

"Tell me about it."

"So you slept with Karla?"

"Basically."

Dirk whistles in dismay and shakes his head. "That's seriously messed up, man."

"I know." I finish the cigarette and flick away the stompie. "Now what the hell do I do about it?"

TREASA

FOR THE next few weeks, I'm going to be seeing a psychologist every Tuesday. Mom and Dad have to have private sessions with the therapist too, all for the grand purpose of trying to understand me, what I'm going through, and how best to deal with it. It, meaning my inability to accept being a girl and stop making life difficult for everyone else. Dad keeps asking why I can't be happy with being a tomboy. As if cutting my hair and not shaving my legs is enough.

My parents don't seem to understand, can't quite wrap their heads around the fact that anyone, let alone their daughter, would rail against nature and demand a do-over. They don't understand, but at least they're trying to. Mom actually helped me go through my closet. Anything floral, frilly, or skirt-shaped is destined for the jumble sale. Even though Mom did it with tears in her eyes, she never argued, not even when I tossed out the sandals I've hardly ever worn.

So, as per the head doctor's suggestion, I'm starting to dress more like a guy, and I've decided to keep my hair short. I've also stopped shaving my legs. Not shaving under my arms is just too weird, even though I know guys don't. There's been no mention yet of what it's going to take to make me a boy, physically.

Jordan helped me find a few websites. The info is sketchy, and most of it's about guys becoming girls. It's terrifying, really. As much as I want to be a boy, I wish I could spontaneously swap genders, just wake up as a guy tomorrow. Instead, I'm facing years of scalpel blades and hormone treatment with no guarantee of success, according to the Internet.

"You really want to be a guy and have inappropriate boners and scratch your ass and forget to shower?" Jordan asks, spread out on my bed in her brand-new Stormhof High uniform. It's the longest skirt I've ever seen her wear, the hem grazing her kneecaps.

"Is that all that being a boy is about?"

"No, there's the burping and farting and inability to match shirts and socks." Jordan grins. "Why not just be lesbian or bi, even?"

"Because it's not like that." I slam shut my math textbook. Mom has been diligently collecting my homework for me at the end of every day. Too bad she can't write my end-of-term tests for me too, although the school is being pretty accommodating and marking me absent instead of failing me. That's all thanks to my psychologist, who got me out of school for the rest of the term. Mom tried to get me to go back, but that's not even up for discussion. No way I'm wearing a skirt ever again or putting up with more taunting by Hannah and posse. No idea what I'm going to do about school next term. I have a month to figure that out.

"What is it about, then?" Jordan asks.

"I can't explain it."

"Try." Jordan sits up, giving me her full attention.

"It's like, as comfortable as you are being a girl, as normal and okay as it feels for you, it's the exact opposite of how it feels for me."

"But how do you know being a boy will make it okay? How do you know it isn't something else?"

"That's why the shrink says I have to live as a boy for like a year before even thinking about taking the next step."

Jordan chews on the end of her pen and nods. "Will you still be Ree?"

"It's usual to pick a new name."

"You could stay Resa." Jordan jerks her head toward the posters of Liam St. Clare.

"No. That's what my folks have always called me. It needs to be something different. Something unmistakably male."

Jordan taps her pen against her teeth in contemplation. "You could be a Todd or Chad?"

"How about something that doesn't make me sound like an Abercrombie and Fitch model?"

"Heathcliff? Edmund? Henry?"

"Something that doesn't make me sound Victorian."

"How about Frikkie?" She grins, and I chuck my textbook at her.

"I could go to Stormhof as a boy." And hang out with Gabriel every day.

"Not without a new name."

"True."

"And even then, you going to start playing rugby?" Jordan raises her eyebrows, and the reality of my situation crashes down around me like a meteor shower. No amount of wishing an X chromosome away is going to change who I am, what I am. I can pretend all I like with a haircut and boy's clothes. Underneath that, I'm still female. Which bathroom would I even use? One day at a time, that's what my psychologist said. One day, one thing at a time.

"How's Dirk?" I ask. Ever since she started at Stormhof, it's been Dirk this and Dirk that. She's clearly crushing, although she'd never admit it.

"He's actually sort of charming, in a dorky kind of way."

"You kissed him yet?"

"We barely know each other." She rolls her eyes, but her smile gives her away.

"And Gabriel?"

Her smile falters as she meets my gaze. "He doesn't talk much. He hangs out with us at break sometimes." She shrugs.

"And Karla?"

"Ja, she's around."

"Around Gabriel?"

"Not like that." She gives me a pointed look. "Gabriel doesn't just give her the cold shoulder, he gives her the entire Antarctic continent."

That makes me feel better. Gabriel said he thought he was in love with me. I guess thinking you feel a certain way isn't enough, though. He hasn't called or SMSed me since the gig. I haven't been at choir to see him, although Lethi and Sibo says he still goes as usual. Jordan and I haven't been back to the self-defense class either. Partly because of Jordan still being grounded, and partly me avoiding Gabriel.

"You should call him," Jordan says. "Talk to the guy."

"If he wanted to talk to me, he'd have called by now."

"Maybe, but you know what? If you want to be a boy so bad, why don't you grow a pair and pick up the phone?" She eyes the cellphone perched on my desk.

"I'm not sure."

"Boys should make the first move, right? So pretend you've got the balls you so desperately want and call him already." She throws her pen at me.

I stare at the phone, willing him to SMS me right this very minute. Of course, the universe does not comply.

"Later," I say.

Jordan rolls her eyes, mumbling, "Whatever," and I try to focus on algebra. The autumn concert is in three days. Gabriel will be there, accompanying the choir. Lethi and Sibo want me there, and I sort of promised them I'd go. Three more days. If we still haven't talked by then, then I'll suck it up and approach him in person, because that's the right and manly thing to do.

GABRIEL

MY BLAZER seems too small tonight, cutting into my armpits, a straightjacket across my shoulders. My tie feels like a noose. I loosen the top button and wiggle the knot lower before splashing cold water on my face in the staff bathroom at the back of the music block.

"You all right, bru?" Dirk knocks on the door. He insisted on staying to hear me play, and he insisted on bringing Jordan along to her alma mater. That alone made me nervous of performing my own composition. Then Jordan said Treasa will be here, and my hands won't stop shaking.

"Give me a minute," I say. Part of me hopes my dad will show up, but he SMSed saying he had a late meeting and wouldn't be home for dinner, without mentioning the concert. Not that I expect miracles. In the days since the shoe box incident, we've been on better speaking terms, and a few photos of Mom have found their way onto the fridge and into frames around the house. It'll take more than that to seal the Mariana Trench carved between us. It's not like he doesn't still see Mom every time he looks at me, even though I got a haircut.

"Mr. du Preez," Mrs. McArthur booms. She must be right outside the door. "We need you for warm-ups, please."

I take a deep breath and gaze at my reflection in the mirror, testing out the smile meant to reassure everyone. Looks real enough. Running my damp fingers through my hair, I follow her tie-dye train to the choir room and play the required chords as the girls sing vowel sounds.

Usually before a concert, I like to take time alone to visualize the piece, to play through the sheet music in my mind and ghost the notes across a tabletop. Tonight I won't have that luxury. Even my leg is starting to jump, my foot juddering on the pedal.

At seven on the dot, Mrs. McArthur ushers her choir onto the stage, and I take my place on the creaking piano stool at the Yamaha baby grand. The audience runs through a final round of coughs and splutters, of program rustling and seat shifting as the choir prepares. Mrs. McArthur gives me a smile and counts us in.

We open the concert with a stirring rendition of "Adiemus" before segueing into a sacred piece by Fauré. The Fauré relaxes me, the notes solid beneath my fingers, the music gentle and easy, free-flowing from the piano and from the throats of the choir. One voice is missing, though. There's a gap in the sopranos where Treasa's crystal vocals used to be. No one else will probably notice her absence. I do.

We wrap up with a pop classic by Cher, and the audience claps as the choir files off stage to take their designated seats. I scan the crowd. Dirk and Jordan are sitting together, a smudge of charcoal in the sea of St. Bridget's burgundy. I don't see Treasa, and I'm not sure if I'm relieved or disappointed.

Taking my place, I pick up the program that was left on my seat. I'm playing last. No pressure, then. All the other performers have the piece they're playing listed next to their name. Not me. I still don't know what to call my sonata. "Sonata in C Minor" is too bland, but Beethoven took all the good names: Appassionata, Pathétique, Tempest, Moonlight. How can I possibly compete with all that and not sound like I'm trying too hard?

It's so hot in the hall, even with the side doors open. The breeze is barely a trickle, and I'm soaked in sweat. The second-to-last player gets up with her clarinet and accompanist, and I swivel in my chair to scan the crowd. The spotlight on the performer plunges the audience into shadow, and I can't be sure if the figure at the back is Treasa or someone's brother.

I blow a cooling stream of air over my sweaty palms as the clarinetist jaunts through a jazzy number. The last piano chords reverberate, and the clarinetist bows, the audience claps, and now it's my turn.

I shrug out of my blazer and roll up my sleeves before approaching the piano. The spotlight blinds me as I squint at the expectant faces of my audience. I swallow, my mouth dry.

"Good evening, ladies and gentlemen. Tonight I'll be performing my own composition."

I hesitate as a figure steps through a side door. My father. I blink twice. I'm not hallucinating. It really is him. Dirk turns his head, following my gaze, and his eyes widen as a smile spreads across his face. He turns back to me and gives me a thumbs-up. My hands stop trembling, and I clear my throat.

"The piece I'm playing tonight is Sonata in C Minor, 'The Metamorphosis.'" I take a seat at the piano and close my eyes.

I play the opening chord, and my right hand introduces the first theme. This is for Mom, an ode to her memory. The first movement flows perfectly, each dynamic nuance measured and controlled by my fingers. A few people clap at the end, and I wait for them to settle before starting the second movement. This is for Treasa, the chaos and discord and the promise of a resolution. No one claps at the end of this movement. I crack my knuckles in the hush before starting the final part. The third movement is for me. I pour my heart into the piece, just like Ms. Hafford told me to. I let go, surrendering to the music.

TREASA

GABRIEL GETS up to play, and I applaud so hard my hands sting.

"Good evening, ladies and gentlemen. Tonight I'll be performing my own composition." His voice is shaky, betraying his nervousness. I wish I could go up to him, squeeze his hand, reassure him of his brilliance—not that he'd want me anywhere near him.

His gaze slides over the audience, lingering on a man standing near the doors. Could it be his father? Gabriel doesn't notice me sunk low in my seat beside my own dad. We arrived late to avoid the hordes and their questions. I'm not sure how we'll slip out again without being noticed, but being bombarded with questions about my hair and lack of school uniform tonight will be worth it if I get to hear Gabriel play the complete sonata.

"The piece I'm playing tonight is Sonata in C Minor, 'The Metamorphosis,'" he says. Metamorphosis. Could he have picked a more perfect name for the piece? Is he trying to tell me something? Of course not; he doesn't even know I'm here.

Gabriel starts to play, and I don't even try to stop the tears cascading down my cheeks. My dad takes my hand.

"Are you all right?" he whispers and hands me a crumpled tissue from his pocket.

"Never better." I smile through my tears, my gaze never leaving Gabriel.

The first movement ends gently, and a few people clap. He waits, closes his eyes, and begins the second movement. The melody in the right hand breaks my heart. It's my melody. Even in a minor key, I recognize the tune I hummed to him in the piano room. I never dreamed he'd actually use my little melody, and yet there it is in all its modulated glory, each note landing a hammer blow between my ribs. He pauses to crack his knuckles before diving into the third movement. His body judders as he plays the powerful chords, bombastic crashes that make me wince for the piano. Gabriel doesn't hold back, driving home the harmony with ever-increasing dynamics. His fingers are a blur across the keys, and as he comes to the final cadence, there's a high-pitched ping, and that soft smile I thought was only meant for me tweaks the corners of his lips.

Mrs. McArthur pales and peers at the piano, where a thin wire dangles out of the open lid.

"He broke a string," I whisper, my words lost in the thunderous applause as the audience gives Gabriel a standing ovation.

I've known him for almost three months, and I think I learned more about Gabriel in that eight-minute sonata than I ever did in all the time we've spent talking. Gabriel looks out at the audience, his face flushed as he takes another bow to continued applause. He searches through the crowd, and I think he might catch a glimpse of me, but his gaze settles once more on the man at the door.

The audience disperses, and my dad agrees to meet me in the car. I fight my way through the crowd to Jordan and Dirk.

"Did he snap a string?" Jordan asks.

"I think so. Did you see Mrs. McArthur's face?"

"That oke can play," Dirk says.

"Was that his dad at the door?" I ask.

"Ja, finally." Dirk smiles. "Maybe you should go rescue him. We'll wait in the car." He jerks his chin toward Gabriel where he's standing at the piano getting a telling off from Mrs. McArthur. A bunch of St. Bridget's girls are hovering like vultures, no doubt waiting to swoop in on Gabriel and fawn all over him. I push past them.

"Gabriel," I say when Mrs. McArthur has finished telling him to expect a bill for the string replacement. He turns, and a myriad of emotions play across his face.

"You're here."

"Wouldn't have missed it for the world." We stare at each other for a long moment before he runs a hand through his hair and steps past me to fetch his blazer from the back of his chair. "You broke a string."

"Never thought I would." The ghost of a smile flits across his face before his expression returns to serious.

"Was your dad here?"

"Apparently." He loops his blazer over his shoulder, looking just like he did on the day I first met him. "Could you give me a minute? Just want to find my father. Meet at the music block just now?"

"No problem."

Gabriel heads out the main doors while I seek the quiet around the back of the hall. I pace beneath the twisted boughs of a syringa tree, trying to figure out exactly what I want to say to him about everything. I SMS my dad, telling him I might be a while. He replies saying he's going to get pizza across the road, giving me at least half an hour.

"Sorry I kept you waiting." Gabriel lopes onto the patch of grass I'm wearing a track into.

"Did your dad enjoy the concert?"

"I think so." He seems more relaxed now that it's just us.

"Thank you," I say.

"For what?"

"For using that bit of melody in the second movement. That was the part I hummed, right?" Oh God, maybe I assumed too much. Gabriel smiles that secret smile, and my blood thrums in my veins.

"I should be the one thanking you. Never would've finished that sonata if it weren't for you."

"Really?"

"You make a great muse."

"Wow." Not at all what I expected him to say.

"I mean...." He swallows hard, and I think he may actually be blushing. "You're not wearing your uniform?" He sits down on the nearby bench, and I join him, leaving a few centimeters of air between our thighs.

"Don't think I'm going back to St. Bridget's."

"Not this term, or not ever?" He studies the grass at his feet.

"It's an all-girls' school."

"So no grade ten dance, then?"

"I guess not."

He nods and leans back, looking a little relieved. For a moment, there's just the rustle of the leaves above us and the chorus of crickets in the flowerbeds punctuating the silence between us. Then Gabriel clears his throat.

"Before I met you, I didn't think life was worth living. It was gray and dull, and every day was the same. You changed things. I can't even begin to understand what I feel for you, but I do." He reaches a long finger toward my face, his fingertip grazing my temple as he smooths back a curl. I can barely breathe, let alone form coherent speech.

"I don't understand why you cut your hair or why you want to be a boy, but I do get wanting to be who you truly are and not the person others think you should be." He takes my hand, and his touch sends a jolt of lightning up my arm. I want so badly to kiss him right now. I bite my bottom lip so hard it hurts.

"I'm sorry," he says. "I'm sorry I ran away the other night. I could give you a dozen excuses, but I won't. It was wrong, I should've stayed."

"It's okay." I find my voice. "I kind of laid a lot on you."

"I meant what I said."

"Which part?" My pulse throbs with the intensity of a newborn star.

"That I'm falling for you, only...." He drops my hand and looks away. Now my heart feels like a black hole. "What you said about wanting to be a boy with me. That—" He wrings his hands. "That creeped me out. I have no idea what to say to that."

"This is creeping me out too, you know. It's a lot to deal with, to live each day in a body you hate." I draw my knees up to my chest.

"So you're serious about wanting to be a boy?"

"Deadly."

"Is there a twelve-step program for this sort of thing?" He meets my gaze and must register the confusion on my face. "It creeps me out, but that doesn't mean I don't care or don't want to know. If you tell me more, maybe I'll be able to understand." His expression is so earnest; I'm just not sure I can trust it.

"I thought this was the part where you say, 'You're a freak, and I never want to see you again.'"

"You're a total freak," he says with a grin. Damn, that smile makes me melt, even when he's technically insulting me. "And so am I, remember." His gaze drops to his leg. I'd forgotten all about the weeping wounds burned into his skin. I lay a gentle hand on his knee. Any higher would be too close to his crotch, and that would make things super weird.

"So you're not sprinting for the hills? You don't mind being my friend?"

His eyebrows knit together above his nose. "Hardly. I think I would've liked to be more than just friends, but if it's a friend you need, then I can be that too."

This boy constantly takes my breath away. He is perfect, even if he doesn't know it. "There aren't formal steps, exactly, but there is something I'd like you to do," I say.

"Whatever you need, Treasa." He takes my hand again, an anchor in the storm to come.

"I need a new name."

"And Resa won't do?" he teases.

"No, but I think I know a name that'll be a perfect fit."

"I'll call you whatever you want me to." He sidles closer to me on the bench, his eyes peering into mine with a soul-blazing intensity.

A smile spreads across my face, and for the first time I feel like me, the real me. Not an alien, not some nerdy loser girl or brace-faced freak. With a new name, I can leave that other me behind and be reborn.

"Tristan," I say and lean into Gabriel's embrace. "Call me Tristan."

SUZANNE VAN ROOYEN grew up in South Africa, but currently lives in Finland where she finds the cold, dark forests nothing if not inspiring. Although she has a Master's degree in music, Suzanne prefers writing strange tales about quirky characters. When not writing, she teaches dance and music to middle schoolers, and manages publicity for Entranced Publishing. When not doing any of that, you'll find her entertaining her shiba inu Lego, attempting to play guitar, or baking peanut-butter cookies. Suzanne is represented by Jordy Albert of the Booker Albert Agency.

Connect with her online here:

http://suzannevanrooyen.com
https://www.facebook.com/pages/Suzanne-van-Rooyen/304965232847874
https://twitter.com/Suzanne_Writer
https://www.goodreads.com/author/show/5306442.Suzanne_van_Rooyen
E-mail: suzanne@suzannevanrooyen.com

Harmony Ink

CPSIA information can be obtained at www.ICGtesting.com
Printed in the USA
BVOW04s0353050514

352491BV00012B/200/P